"Why didn't you tell me about my son?" Quinn demanded.

"I didn't want you to know," Carrie said, as if it were the most obvious thing in the world.

"You didn't want me to know?"

"Put yourself in my place, Quinn," Carrie said. "I was eighteen years old, in love and convinced that the boy I loved was trying to help my brother out of whatever trouble he was in. And overnight I lost my brother and discovered who you really were. By the time I found out I was pregnant, you were long gone. What would have been the use of trying to find you at that point?"

"You should have told me." Quinn ground out the words. "I would have come back."

Dear Reader,

Many of you love the miniseries that we do in Intimate Moments, and this month we've got three of them for you. First up is *Duncan's Lady*, by Emilie Richards. Duncan is the first of "The Men of Midnight," and his story will leave you hungering to meet the other two. Another first is *A Man Without Love*, one of the "Wounded Warriors" created by Beverly Bird. Beverly was one of the line's debut authors, and we're thrilled to have her back. Then there's a goodbye, because in *A Man Like Smith*, bestselling author Marilyn Pappano has come to the end of her "Southern Knights" trilogy. But what a fantastic farewell—and, of course, Marilyn herself will be back soon!

You won't want to miss the month's other offerings, either. In *His Best Friend's Wife*, Catherine Palmer has created a level of emotion and tension that will have you turning pages as fast as you can. In *Dillon's Reckoning*, award-winner Dee Holmes sends her hero and heroine on the trail of a missing baby, while Cathryn Clare's *Gunslinger's Child* features one of romance's most popular storylines, the "secret baby" plot.

Enjoy them all—and come back next month for more top-notch romantic reading…only from Silhouette Intimate Moments.

Yours,
Leslie Wainger
Senior Editor and Editorial Coordinator

Please address questions and book requests to:
Silhouette Reader Service
U.S.: 3010 Walden Ave., P.O. Box 1325, Buffalo, NY 14269
Canadian: P.O. Box 609, Fort Erie, Ont. L2A 5X3

GUNSLINGER'S CHILD

CATHRYN CLARE

Silhouette®
INTIMATE™ MOMENTS®
Published by Silhouette Books
America's Publisher of Contemporary Romance

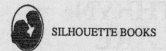

SILHOUETTE BOOKS

ISBN 0-373-07629-0

GUNSLINGER'S CHILD

This edition published by arrangement with Harlequin Enterprises B.V.

® and TM are trademarks of Harlequin Enterprises B.V., used under
license. Trademarks indicated with ® are registered in the United States
Patent and Trademark Office, the Canadian Trade Marks Office and in
other countries.

Printed in U.S.A.

Books by Cathryn Clare

Silhouette Intimate Moments

Chasing Destiny #503
Sun and Shadow #558
The Angel and the Renegade #599
Gunslinger's Child #629

Silhouette Desire

To the Highest Bidder #399
Blind Justice #508
Lock, Stock and Barrel #550
Five by Ten #591
The Midas Touch #663
Hot Stuff #688

CATHRYN CLARE

is a transplanted Canadian who followed true love south of the border when she married an American ten years ago. She says, "I was one of those annoying children who always knew exactly what they were going to be when they grew up." And she has proved herself right with a full-time career as a writer since 1987.

"Being a writer has its hazards. So many things that I see—a car at the side of the road, two people having an argument, a hat someone left in a restaurant—make me want to sit down and finish the stories suggested to me. It can be very hard to concentrate on real life sometimes! But the good part of being a writer is that every story, no matter how it starts out, can be a way to show the incredible power that love has in our lives."

To my editor Anne Canadeo,
with thanks for her sharp eye
and many good suggestions

Chapter 1

Quinn McAllister took off his helmet and frowned. At first he'd thought his ears were ringing from the sudden silence after he'd shut the motorcycle off. The hushed quiet of Stockbridge, Illinois, could be a shock to anyone used to the noise of a city.

But the ringing got louder, and after a moment he figured out that the sound was coming from the old St. John house. An alarm, he thought. A smoke detector maybe, or a burglar alarm.

He had planned to take this slowly, maybe asking the kid raking leaves next door whether old Doc St. John still lived in the place, maybe just waiting until he caught a glimpse of somebody entering or leaving. But the alarm worried him. Nobody seemed to be responding to it.

And then he saw smoke, curling up in front of a window in the kitchen. That was enough to get him off his bike and up the front walk, wincing a little as he tried too fast to stretch out the kinks from the three-hour drive down from Chicago.

The front door was still painted deep green, trimmed with white. In spite of the shrill alarm bell inside the house, Quinn paused for a moment, shocked at how utterly familiar this was. He knew exactly how the heavy brass door knocker would feel in his hand, solid and cool and imposing. As if it were testing anyone who came calling here, Quinn had always thought. *Are you worthy to be associating with one of Stockbridge's best families?*

Old Dr. St. John had considered Quinn an acceptable visitor ten years ago. So had David St. John and his sister, Carrie. They had all been very wrong.

"Come on, answer the door, damn it." Quinn lifted the knocker again, and brought it down harder against the door. He could hear voices inside the house. Kids' voices, he thought, as distant high-pitched laughter mixed with the insistent ringing of the alarm.

How likely was it that Carrie still lived here, with a family of her own? Quinn's stomach clenched at the thought, and the familiar ache in his left side caught at him. *You knew it was possible,* he reminded himself. *You could be about to run into her husband, her children. You knew it could happen.*

Well, no matter who lived here now, they didn't seem to realize that they had a fire in their kitchen. Quinn abandoned the front door, and sprinted around to the annex where the kitchen was. He found the back porch door unlocked, just as it had always been.

The kitchen was full of smoke, roiling up from the stove in the corner. "Damn!" Quinn muttered, as he propped the door open and set his helmet down on the counter. The bitterness of the atmosphere clutched at his throat, and he coughed. Coughing was one of the things that hurt his side the worst, and he gritted his teeth against the sharp pain as he headed into the room, waving his arms to clear the smoke and moving quickly toward the stove.

The moment before he got there, he heard her.

"Just turn it off," Carrie St. John was calling, clearly, from another room. "And open a window. I'll be there in a minute."

Quinn stopped dead. Was she calling to him? Her tone was matter-of-fact, unworried. And it still had that slight huskiness that was as smoky as the air he was breathing and sexier than anything he'd ever been able to imagine. He tried to move, to shut off the stove as he'd set out to do. But the shock of hearing Carrie, of suddenly knowing he was so close to her, kept him rooted where he stood.

Until the sound of approaching footsteps got him moving. He took in a deep breath, coughed again, and clamped an elbow against the sharp pain in his side as he straightened up, bracing himself for the sight of Carrie St. John coming toward him out of the smoke.

The figure hurrying into the kitchen was the right size, compact and slender, but it wasn't Carrie. It was a teenager, dressed in a baggy shirt and jeans. She stood on tiptoe to shut off the ceiling alarm, then turned toward the stove. At the sight of Quinn, she gasped.

"It's all right," he said quickly. "I heard the alarm and came to see what was burning."

The girl put a hand to her chest. "You scared me," she said, and added, "Are you a parent?"

Quinn couldn't imagine what the question meant. "A parent?" he repeated. "No, I'm—" What the hell was he, anyway? If he said *I'm a ghost out of the past,* the girl would just look at him as if he were nuts. Maybe he was, coming back here after all this time.

He closed his eyes. A year ago, lying in a Chicago hospital room and realizing just how close he'd come to dying, this had all seemed very simple. He needed to come back to Stockbridge. He needed to find out what he could about David St. John's death. And he needed—more desperately than he'd admitted to himself until a teenager's bullet had nearly ended his own life—to see Carrie again.

"I came to see Carrie," he said finally. The girl nodded, accepting the explanation as she moved to turn off the stove and get a window open.

"She's almost done," she said. "Don't worry about the smoke. She does this every week or so. You'd think she'd give in and stop trying to cook, but—well, you know Carrie. She always thinks things are going to work *next* time. This'll clear in a minute."

And then the girl was gone, leaving Quinn alone in the kitchen, rocked by his own memories of sitting here with David St. John, watching Carrie make and then burn an entire batch of peanut butter cookies. His throat ached from more than just smoke as he remembered how amused she'd been at her own ineptitude in the kitchen, and the way her glossy brown hair had moved when she'd tilted her head back to laugh.

"Apparently I'm the first person in the history of Stockbridge High to be flunking Home Ec," she'd said. "Mrs. Pearson says the janitors have a bet about how many more things I can set on fire between now and the end of the year."

Quinn felt quite sure she had attempted—and incinerated—more batches of cookies since then, and had still remained optimistic that one of these days she would catch on to the secret of how to get it right. That hopefulness of hers, that eagerness to reach out for the next time, was one of the things he'd loved most about her.

And now he'd come back to remind her of the time in her life when things had gone most disastrously wrong. What right did he have, really, to disrupt the happy present that Carrie had obviously created for herself?

"No right at all," he muttered out loud. "Just these questions inside me that won't let me alone."

He took a chair at the table and watched the smoke in the kitchen slowly clearing. There was a mirror over the sink, and he could see his face in it. *You look like you came to demand the family silver, McAllister,* he told himself. *Lighten up, or she's not likely to give you the time of day.*

Quinn took in a big lungful of air, concentrating on the impossible task of "lightening up" in this house where his most painful and most exhilarating memories were waiting for him around every corner. His breathing was almost back to normal when he heard Carrie again.

There were two sets of footsteps coming across the big front foyer, and two voices echoing in the tall open space. One of them was a child's. "If it burned, then we *have* to have pizza, right?" Quinn could hear laughter under the cajoling words, as though this was a familiar family joke.

"Not necessarily. We could just make a big salad," Carrie teased.

"*Mom...*" came the reply.

"Hey, at least there's no danger of overcooking it."

"But it's Friday night."

"So?"

"We can't have salad on Friday night. It's *boring.*"

Carrie laughed then, and Quinn felt the warmth of the sound spread right through him. She still sounded as though the world was a good place and she was glad to be in it. Was it possible, after the tragedy she'd lived through, that she had kept hold of the simple pleasures her life had to offer her?

He wanted to believe it was true. He *needed* to believe it, needed to know that promises weren't always broken, that some dreams could come true. The music of Carrie's laughter had always given him a kind of hope he hadn't quite known how to handle. It had offered him a glimpse of something he didn't fully understand but had clung on to during some of his darkest moments.

All of that was still here, in the throaty sound of Carrie's laughter. "You're right," she was saying now. "Salad is kind of boring for Friday night. Why don't we call Susannah and see what she and the girls are doing? Maybe we could all go to The Kettle and have spaghetti.''

"All *right*."

The voice was a boy's, Quinn thought. The kid came into the kitchen first, enthusiastically bounding into the room. He was small boned but sturdy, like his mother, and he had Carrie's brown eyes. His hair was lighter, almost a tawny blond, and his jawline was longer, more pronounced than Carrie's. But their grin was the same. Quinn's heart started to beat faster at the boy's version of that wide, all-embracing smile he remembered so well.

Carrie was a few steps behind her son. She was laughing again. "Someday, kiddo, you're going to understand why I get so tired trying to keep up with you on Friday nights," she was saying. "After a week of looking after little people who never slow down—"

The boy had launched himself almost as far as the kitchen table, and Carrie was at the doorway. They saw Quinn at the same moment.

"Hey," the kid said. "Who're you?"

For a long moment Quinn could almost feel the silence in the room around them. He watched the smile leave Carrie's face, and saw her reach for the door frame as if she needed its support. He shifted slightly in his chair, bracing himself to meet whatever her response might be.

At first, he couldn't tell what she was feeling. She was looking at him as if she weren't quite sure he was real.

"Quinn?"

His name came out as a question, a whisper. Something loosened itself in Quinn at the sound of it, something he'd worked very hard to keep tied up and under control. He found himself breathing faster as he looked into Carrie's eyes. It was an effort to keep from saying what was running through his mind. *I needed to come back here. I needed to hear you say my name again.*

Instead, he said slowly, "Hello, Carrie," and nodded at her son. "Hi."

The boy nodded back. Carrie didn't move. She was wearing an outfit that made her look almost as young as the teenaged girl who'd been in the kitchen earlier—an oversize blue sweater over black leggings and a pair of sneakers. She looked as slender, as vibrant as she'd been at eighteen.

Quinn thought he'd remembered every detail of that small, strong body. But he hadn't.

He'd forgotten the way her wide, generous mouth turned down at one corner when she was thinking hard.

Even in his wildest imagination, aching for Carrie in the dark nights when he couldn't stop thinking about her, he hadn't been able to picture how long the dark sweep of her eyelashes actually was, fringing those unforgettable brown eyes.

He hadn't pictured the faint lines of laughter and pain at the corners of her eyes and mouth, either, because those hadn't been there ten years ago. On the surface, Carrie St. John's youthful radiance hadn't changed. But she knew things now that she hadn't known at eighteen. Quinn could see the proof of it in her face.

She finally spoke. And when she did, there was no mistaking her reaction to the sight of her brother's one-time friend, her one-time lover.

She was afraid.

Quinn didn't understand it, but it was impossible to miss the fear that was making her voice tremble as she said, "Who let you in?"

He nodded at the back door. "I saw the smoke and heard the alarm," he said. "I knocked, but no one answered."

"We don't—use the front door anymore."

She spoke as if her thoughts were somewhere else. Quinn frowned, and was about to speak when Carrie turned to her son. "Davey," she said, "I want you to go and wash up. I'll call Susannah and see about dinner."

Davey. Of course she would have named her son after the brother she'd lost. He wondered how old the boy was. Eight, maybe? He didn't trust his own guesses about kids' ages anymore. Too many of the young boys he met nowadays were packing deadly weapons. It tended to make them look a lot older than they really were.

There was something familiar in the way Davey was setting his jaw now, getting ready to argue with his mother about the necessity of soap and water. That wasn't Carrie's expression, Quinn thought. Was it possible Davey's father was someone he'd known when he'd been here before? Some high school classmate, perhaps?

"How come I have to wash up?" The boy looked from Carrie's face to Quinn's, obviously picking up on the fact that Quinn wasn't just a casual caller.

Carrie walked to where her son stood and bent over to his level with her hands on his shoulders. The easy, motherly gesture made Quinn ache unexpectedly inside. *You knew she might have a family,* he reminded himself yet again. *She always said she wanted a lot of kids.*

"You have to wash up," she was saying, "because I'm asking you to." There was a quiet force in her words, clearly conveying the message that this wasn't something she wanted to argue about. Quinn wondered how the hell she managed to do that and still sound so gentle.

"I want you to get changed, too," she was going on. "Those pants are overdue for a trip to the washing machine."

"Mom..."

The protest was halfhearted. Carrie cut it off by planting a quick kiss on Davey's forehead and then giving him a little push back out into the foyer. The boy hesitated, unsure about the undercurrents flowing between his mother and this tall stranger in the blue bomber jacket.

Then he took off toward the main staircase. His exuberant footsteps echoed in the big open space.

Quinn waited until the sound had faded. "Either your father's not still around or he's revised his policy on running in the house," he said.

"My father died several years ago." Her tone was matter-of-fact, but he could still hear that thread of anxiety running through it. "Quinn, whatever you're doing here..."

She was trying to get rid of him, he realized. There had always been the possibility that she would refuse even to talk to him, refuse to listen to his reasons for coming back.

He couldn't exactly blame her for that. But he wasn't just going to get up and go, either. For Quinn McAllister, the road back to this place had been a long and rocky one. He wasn't leaving Stockbridge again until he'd done what he could to make amends for his mistakes of ten years before.

"That's a nice-looking kid," he said, cutting in on top of Carrie's words.

"Thank you." Her voice sounded stiff, as if he'd approached forbidden territory.

Quinn went ahead anyway. "Where's his father?" he asked.

"I—we're not together anymore."

"Divorced?"

"Separated." She said the word quickly. It was clearly something she didn't want to go into.

So life hadn't lived up to all its promises for Carrie St. John, after all. And yet she was still able to summon up that lighthearted laughter she'd been sharing with her son in the moments before they'd seen Quinn. Where did it come from, he wondered, that ability to keep hold of love, to keep believing in a better tomorrow?

"Only one child?"

"Yes. Quinn, you've got to go. Coming here was a mistake."

"How do you know that, when I haven't said why I'm here?"

Something very much like panic came into her brown eyes. Quinn was speaking quietly, but with all the sincerity he could muster. The effort of doing that, of sounding calm when what he really wanted to do was stride across the kitchen and take Carrie St. John into his arms, made his voice shake a little. Carrie seemed to notice it, and to know what it meant.

She looked away from him and he had the feeling she was searching for escape routes. She didn't seem to find any. Her eyes, when they met his again, were anguished.

"I don't care why you came," she said. "I just want you to leave."

"Not until you've at least heard what I have to say."

"Oh, God, Quinn . . ."

She shook her head. He recognized the frustration in it, and remembered the gesture from all the times she'd confided in him about her brother, and how worried and frightened she was for David.

"Carrie?" He got to his feet slowly, telling himself that he was crazy even to be thinking about moving closer to her. "What is it that's scaring you? Your son's already seen me, and if you don't have a husband who's going to come home and find me here—"

His mind jumped ahead while he was speaking. Carrie was separated from her husband, but what if there was someone else in her life? Was that what she was afraid of? A confrontation between a long-ago flame and a current lover?

It didn't fit with what he knew about Carrie St. John, unless she'd changed more than he had thought. The Carrie he'd loved had faced life squarely, refusing to run when things got difficult. But ten years was a long time. And she'd had some good reasons to learn to be suspicious.

"Is that what it is?" He tried hard to keep his voice neutral, but a defiant edge got into it anyway. *I know I have no right to feel this way about you,* he wanted to say. *I never did have any right. It's just something I can't seem to do anything about.*

Carrie shook her head again. He didn't think she was answering his question so much as cutting off the conversation. She seemed to have come to some kind of decision, judging from the new firmness in her expression.

"Stay right there," she told him. She was using the same no-nonsense tone she'd used with Davey a few minutes ago. "I have to make some arrangements. And then I'll listen to you, if that's what it takes to get you to leave." That deep-seated fear came through again, in her voice and her eyes, as she added, "But then you'll have to go, Quinn. You just have to."

She stepped out of the room quickly. Quinn sat down again, listening to the light sound of her sneakers against the polished wood floor of the foyer as she headed for the other wing of the house. A few seconds later he heard her voice, speaking quietly. She was calling someone on the phone, he thought.

He felt as though he'd just finished a marathon, and he realized for the first time what an effort it had been keeping himself under control while facing Carrie.

You knew it would be hard. Quinn's short laugh grated in the quiet of the kitchen. *Yeah,* he thought, *and I knew I shouldn't fall in love with her the first time, too. Didn't stop me, though, did it?*

He started to clasp his hands behind his head. It was a gesture he'd always made when he wanted to look confident and didn't feel that way. Halfway there, though, the pain in his side caught at him, and he stopped. He was lowering one elbow to the kitchen table again when he saw

Davey St. John's young face peering at him from the doorway.

"Are you going out to dinner with us?"

The question was tentative, but not unfriendly. Quinn liked the look of the boy's face. There was something in it that made him think Davey was a kid who thought about things, all sorts of things.

When was the last time he'd had a conversation with a boy this young without wondering what the boy's older buddies were up to behind his back? He'd gotten so that he assumed all kids were mixed up in business that was too old and too dangerous for them, that all kids were at some kind of risk.

This kid wasn't any of those things. He seemed perfectly happy to chat with a stranger, while obviously bearing in mind that his mother hadn't put her seal of approval on the man yet. Quinn leaned forward, and looked into eyes that were an exact mirror of Carrie's.

"I don't think so," he said. "Your mother and I have some things to chat about."

"What things?"

"Nothing much." *Love. Murder. Betrayal. The little stuff.* "We used to know each other, a long time ago. I probably should have called before I dropped by. I think she was kind of surprised to see me."

"Yeah." The little gleam in the boy's eyes told Quinn he recognized a major understatement when he heard one. "Is that your motorcycle outside?"

"Yeah."

"Can I have a ride on it?"

"I don't know. It depends on what your mother says about that." *Not in a million years* was Quinn's best guess.

"Okay." Davey's gaze traveled to the helmet, still sitting on the counter. "Can I try your helmet on?"

"Sure." Quinn handed it over. "It's going to be a little too big for you."

"That's okay." Davey settled the black helmet on his head and grinned happily at Quinn. Quinn didn't know which hurt more, the innocence of the boy's responses, or the fact that his smile was identical to Carrie's.

"Cool," Davey said. "It sounds like I'm in outer space." He experimented with a couple of noises, laughing when they resonated inside the oversize helmet.

"So it's just you and your mom who live here, huh?" Quinn already knew the answer, but he wanted to keep this unexpectedly pleasurable moment going if he could. It was like breathing fresh air just to be with a kid who wasn't packing a gun or an attitude or a grudge about the whole world.

"Yeah." Davey half turned his head inside the helmet and laughed again.

"How long have your mom and dad been separated?" It was a question he would have asked any kid, he told himself. It was bound to be a big deal in the boy's world, and something any old acquaintance of his mother might ask about. Quinn wished he didn't feel so bad about asking Davey questions that Carrie had clearly not wanted to answer for herself.

Davey turned to face him again. His brown eyes looked puzzled now. *Where* had Quinn seen that long, stubborn jawline before? The slant of it was maddeningly familiar.

"I don't have a dad," Davey said.

Quinn searched his mind for a reply and couldn't come up with one. After a moment, Davey went on. "My dad lived in Stockbridge a long time ago, but he had to leave, and he couldn't come back. That's why there's just my mom and me."

The words had the ring of something the boy had repeated many times, something he'd been taught, something he didn't completely understand but was willing to pass on as the truth. For a moment Quinn puzzled over it, with the feeling that he wasn't catching everything that was going on here.

"Do you...know his name?" The words came out slowly.

Davey shook his head, and seemed to find the helmet too heavy. He reached up and took it off, handing it back to Quinn.

For a moment they both held on to it, Quinn's big hands nearly meeting Davey's small ones. As he looked down at the shiny black surface, and the little fingertips that were almost touching his own, something under the foundation of Quinn's world began to rock, slowly at first, and then with growing force.

"Davey?" He said the boy's name quietly, but some of what he was suddenly feeling must have gotten into his voice, because Davey's gaze came up quickly to meet Quinn's. "How old are you?"

He knew the answer before the boy spoke. It was there in Davey's tawny hair, in the line of his jawbone, in the stubborn way he'd set his chin when he'd been getting ready to argue with his mother.

"Nine and a half. I'll be ten in three more months."

Quinn got to his feet awkwardly, almost blindly. Somewhere inside him a voice was urging him to run, to get the hell out of there, to get back on his motorcycle and just drive. He needed air, he thought. Cold air, to clear his brain. What Davey St. John had just said had thrown Quinn's whole world into confusion, and he didn't know where to turn for something solid to hang on to.

He wasn't aware that he'd kicked over his chair until he heard it hit the floor. Davey was looking up at him with big, startled eyes.

He wanted to reassure the boy, yet couldn't do it. He knew he must look wild, grabbing hold of his helmet and looking around the kitchen as if he were trapped here and desperately searching for escape routes.

Carrie had looked exactly this way just a few minutes ago, he remembered. She had seen the same thing—ghosts out of the past, surrounding this house again after all these years.

Quinn looked back down at the boy, at Carrie's son. *His* son. His mind still refused to absorb what he knew had to be true.

Davey was no ghost, but a flesh-and-blood legacy of the all-too-brief time that Carrie and Quinn had loved each other. And that changed everything.

"Susannah's on her way, honey." Quinn jumped at the sound of Carrie's voice. He hadn't heard her coming, hadn't been aware of anything outside his own roiling thoughts and the curious stare of the boy in front of him. *My son... Dear God...* "Grab your jacket, okay?"

She stepped into the kitchen wearing an expression that told him she was determined to keep calm about this sudden disturbance in her life. One look at him shot that all to hell.

Chapter 2

Carrie allowed herself a quick sigh of relief as she watched Susannah's car pulling up the driveway. Susannah was a good friend, and familiar enough with Carrie's past that she'd known immediately what Quinn's sudden reappearance meant. Within minutes of Carrie's phone call, Susannah was here to help by taking Davey out to dinner.

"And if you want me to stick around, I'll be more than happy to," she said quietly through the rolled-down window, as Davey climbed into the back seat with her own two children.

"Thanks, Susannah, but I can manage."

"Are you sure? From what I remember about Quinn McAllister—"

"I'm sure, Susannah."

"You don't *look* sure."

Carrie shook her head. "I always knew this was a possibility. I won't deny it's a shock, but believe me, I've spent enough time rehearsing what I would say if he ever came back."

"You always said you figured someone would have killed him by now."

"I know. That was always a possibility, too." Carrie winced at the way her feelings twisted inside her at the thought of Quinn dying. How many times had she thought *I hope he's dead* and then realized it hurt too much even to consider it?

She was really frightened now. Not just by the chance that Davey might find out who Quinn was, or the idea that Quinn had come back into her life again. What scared her most was that in spite of all the good reasons why she shouldn't, she still felt so vulnerable to the hunger she had seen in his bright, blue eyes.

She felt a lot of emotions for Quinn McAllister. Bitterness and resentment and anger were among them. But so was longing. She'd never been able to weed that out of her other feelings for him, and that made him doubly dangerous to her now.

"I'll be all right." She gave her friend's shoulder a quick squeeze, responding to the concern she could see in Susannah's face. "Just give me an hour, and I'll make him understand."

"I hope you're right..."

Susannah had been in Carrie's senior class in high school. She, too, had known Quinn when he'd been posing as a foster son to Stockbridge's chief of police. She'd been as taken in as anyone by his act, and as shocked as anyone by the revelation that he was actually a special agent for the FBI, working undercover. He was chosen for this assignment because his youthful good looks let him pass easily for younger than his twenty-two years.

Susannah had left Stockbridge, married, and returned home divorced with two small children to raise. She knew all about small-town gossip, too, as Carrie did. It had made the two women particularly good friends these past few years.

Part of Carrie wanted to cling to the support Susannah was offering now. But she made herself wave a determined goodbye as the car pulled back down the driveway. Confronting Quinn was something she knew she had to do on her own. She took in a deep breath and walked back into the house, hurrying through the few late autumn leaves that had piled up along the path.

He wasn't in the kitchen anymore. Carrie pulled the door shut behind her, and called his name.

"Quinn?"

It felt so strange to say it out loud, to know that he was here in her house. She paused for a moment, and tried to slow her beating heart down a little before calling a second time.

"Quinn?"

Was he in the house, after all? For a moment she felt a wave of panic roll over her. Had he disappeared again? Was he going to walk into her life and then out of it without a backward glance, the way he'd done before?

She'd managed to get on with her life by not thinking too much about the dark days right after Quinn had left the first time. But now it all rose up to meet her—her anguish over her brother's death, and the panic after she found out she was pregnant, all laced with the knowledge that the *boy* she'd thought she loved had been lying to her all along.

She closed her eyes against that black wave of memory, and opened them to find that she'd pressed one hand tightly against her belly without realizing it.

The gesture shocked her. How many times had she done that, in the months of her pregnancy? Whenever she had felt herself getting caught up in her own fear and grief, she had held her hand hard over the baby growing inside her, telling herself that *one* good thing, at least, could still come out of everything that had gone wrong.

"Oh, God." She took in a shaky breath, and stood up straighter. *You're going to have to get a grip, if you're going to get through this in one piece.*

And then she heard Quinn's rough voice, calling to her out of the shadows of the big front foyer. "I'm in here," he said. He didn't sound any more in control of himself than she was, and she decided to take that as a good sign.

Until she saw him. He was leaning over the billiard table that stood at the back of the foyer, near the doors out to the backyard. It was dim in the open space, but there was enough light coming in from the yard to show her Quinn's face as he looked down at the table where he'd spent so many hours hanging around with David.

He was leaning on one hand, his big shoulders hunched over slightly. The other hand was gripping the edge of the table, hard.

He looked as though he'd started walking across the foyer and had been drawn to this spot almost against his will. He looked marooned there, she thought. He looked lost, and not sure what to do about it.

He looked lonely.

Oh, God. She said the words silently this time. It was the buried loneliness she thought she'd seen at the heart of Quinn McAllister that had gotten her into such deep trouble the last time.

She'd never decided whether the silent hunger she sensed in him was genuine or not. But she did know that she couldn't possibly afford to let it affect her now.

She had stopped short at the sight of his strong back bowed over the billiard table. Now she forced herself to move again, heading for the small lamp that stood on a side table against the wall. A couple of wing chairs and an area rug almost made a room out of this part of the immense foyer, and with the soft light on there was a sense of refuge, of homeyness.

There was none of that in Quinn McAllister's eyes. He turned slowly, straightening his shoulders as though he were carrying something heavy. And when he spoke, his voice was thick with an anger that startled Carrie.

"Why the *hell* didn't you tell me?"

Wait a minute, her brain protested. *She* was the one with a right to be angry, not Quinn. But his eyes were registering blue fury now, pure and unmistakable.

"I didn't want you to know." She said it as if it were the most obvious thing in the world. And to her, it was.

"It's true, then." It wasn't a question. The words were heavy, pulled from deep inside him, it seemed.

"That Davey is your son—yours and mine? Yes. It's true."

"And you didn't want me to know."

"Of course I didn't."

"Damn it, Carrie—" He cut himself off. He looked as if there were too many things he wanted to say, and they were threatening to choke him.

Carrie seized the moment for herself. "Put yourself in my place, Quinn," she said. "I was eighteen years old, in love, and convinced that the boy I loved was trying to help my brother out of whatever trouble he was in. And then overnight I lost my brother, and discovered who you really were. By the time I found out I was pregnant, you were long gone. What would have been the use of trying to find you at that point?"

"I would have come back." He ground the words out. "You should have told me."

"I didn't *want* you back." She saw him flinch at the simple statement. "You would have come back to a whole lot of people who hated you for what you did, for how you lied to us. And I had more reason to hate you than anybody else."

He turned slightly away from her, facing the French doors that led outside. He had changed so much, and so little. His hair was darker now, without those blond highlights that the sun had burnished into it the spring of her senior year. And he wore it shorter, above his ears. She remembered teasing him about how wild it had once looked, telling him the long-haired-outsider thing was passé, offering to trim it for him and being astonished when he took her up on it.

She remembered the feel of it between her fingers, heavy and smooth, like corn silk warmed by the late summer sun.

The navy blue jacket he was wearing might almost be the same one he'd worn ten years ago. It looked threadbare enough to qualify. His sneakers were well worn, too, and so were his jeans. The way they rode his lean hips made Carrie's whole body pulse with remembered longings, remembered pleasure.

His face was as familiar as if she'd been seeing it every day, instead of having had her last glimpse of it ten years ago in the front seat of a police cruiser heading away from the scene of her brother's murder. Those blue eyes, piercing, missing nothing. His full mouth, serious, stubborn. Making her think that whatever he said, in that quiet, loner's way of his, it would be the truth.

Carrie's eyes lingered on the long, determined length of his jaw, that masculine line she'd once traced with her fingertips just before Quinn had merged his mouth with hers. She saw that obstinate jawline every day of her life, whenever she looked at her son. Seeing the prototype now made her ache from one end of her body to the other.

Some of that ache found its way into her voice as she said, "It would have been a mistake for you to come back. It's a mistake for you to be here now. Surely you can see that."

He took a slow breath, and turned to look at her again. It was his eyes that had changed most, she thought. They looked wary, as if Quinn had seen things in the last ten years that had hurt him badly, things he was holding inside. And they looked tired.

And at the moment, they were still angry. "What I can see," he said, "is a child who looks half like me and half like you. And that child, if nothing else, gives me the right to be here."

"Gives you the *right?*" Carrie had been dangerously close to letting herself be softened by the buried pain in Quinn's blue eyes. Now, though, she snapped to attention again, alerted by a defensiveness about her son that went as deep as any feelings she'd ever had.

"You have no rights to Davey," she said pointedly. "If I'd known who you really were, I never would have fallen in love with you. I certainly wouldn't have slept with you. As far as I'm concerned, your connection with my son began and ended that single night we made love."

"I see." Quinn stepped away from the edge of the billiard table, and strode into the darkness of the foyer, then turned and came back. The flickering lights in his blue eyes made Carrie think his anger was still growing. She fought against her increasing sense of alarm at the idea of his dangerous presence here in her house, in her life, in her son's life.

"So you went with the old you-have-no-father line, right?" The words sounded harsh.

"I've always told him as much of the truth as I thought he could handle at whatever age he was. He knows his father was someone I loved once, who had to leave Stockbridge suddenly and couldn't come back. And it's true. You know it is, Quinn."

"*Damn* it!" He was almost back to the billiard table now, and he reached out an open hand and slammed it against the heavy rim. The slap of flesh against wood echoed in the shadowy hallway, mixed with Quinn's expletive.

He swore again, tilting his body sideways for some reason. He looked as if something hurt him, and she caught herself nearly asking what it was. Then she bit back the words. She refused to give in to any lingering concern Quinn McAllister still inspired in her.

When he looked back at her, his eyes were blue-black, his rage almost palpable now. "I won't let you do this, Carrie," he said.

"Do what?" She was almost afraid to ask the question, but she had to know exactly what he meant.

"I won't let you cut me off like this."

Her quick protective reflex kicked in again. "You cut yourself off," she pointed out. "By lying to us, by lying to *me*. By standing by and letting David die. You are not welcome here, Quinn McAllister."

She was astonished at how hard it was to say the words. They were part of the scene she'd practiced so many times in her mind, part of her final kiss-off to the man who had wounded her and her family so deeply.

But delivering the line in her imagination was very different from saying it to Quinn McAllister's face. She saw his eyes narrow quickly at the blunt words, and watched him square his big shoulders inside the navy jacket, as if he'd just taken a body blow and was refusing to admit he was hurt.

"I don't care if I'm welcome or not." He said the words quietly, and Carrie could hear echoes of his own younger self, saying *I don't mind if I don't fit in.* "And I don't care if you believe this or not, Carrie, but your brother was my friend. One of the closest friends I've ever had. And you..."

He paused. "I lied to you about who I was, but I never lied about what I felt for you. Never."

He was glaring at her now. The ferocity of his eyes was making Carrie's pulse pound in her throat. His voice had gotten quieter, but the intensity of his anger still vibrated in it. "And," he said, pointedly, "that boy is my son. That changes everything."

"No." She said the word instinctively, protesting the defiance she could see in his eyes. "You can't do this to us."

"Do what?" His short laugh was bitter and unamused. "I haven't got the first idea what I'm going to do, Carrie. My whole world just split apart and I'm still trying to figure out where the hell everything is. I don't know what I'm going to do, but I do know I'm not leaving Stockbridge until I've done it."

Staying in Stockbridge was what she had been talking about. It was impossible, and he seemed to be contemplating it.

"Please, Quinn." She was surprised at how imploring her own voice sounded. "It was all based on lies. None of it was real. You can't make it real, not after all this time."

"Not *real?*"

That bitter sound tinged his voice again, and he turned abruptly so he was looking right at her. Carrie realized suddenly how close they were standing. Her heart seemed to jam itself up into her throat.

"By God, Carrie. Don't *ever* try to tell me what we shared wasn't real."

His voice shook as he said the words, and Carrie thought she heard more than just anger in it. She didn't have time to sort out the emotions that bolted through her at the sound. Before she could move or react, Quinn had taken a long step forward and erased the gap between them.

He pulled her toward him almost roughly. And then his arms surrounded her, exactly the way she remembered them, strong and sinewy, closing around her slowly at first, and then with gathering strength, as if he'd been resisting this and he suddenly couldn't resist it any longer.

"Quinn—"

She tried to tell him to stop, but the words refused to form on her lips. She was too startled by the nearness of him, by the familiarity of his full, determined mouth and the thousand unspoken feelings in the depths of those troubled blue eyes. In the moment before he lowered his head to kiss her, she suddenly felt adrift in time, not sure if this was really happening or if she was just letting old memories overwhelm her.

She'd worked so hard to forget how it felt to be this close to Quinn McAllister. But as his mouth touched hers, the remembered taste of him flooded her senses. And the faint masculine scent of his skin wrapped itself around her, earthy, arousing.

The line between past and present blurred even more. She knew she should be resisting this, but it was getting harder to remember why. Did she hate this man, or love him? As he kissed her, she couldn't be sure.

He was deliberately conjuring up these memories, she thought, covering her mouth so intimately with his, swirling his tongue alongside her own, pulling her against him so she could feel the male strength of his body. Behind her closed eyelids she was overwhelmed with images she'd tried to banish—Quinn's long, lean torso; the hard, rounded slope of his shoulders; his hands, big and gentle and reverent, against her skin....

Carrie felt herself moan. Tried to pull the sound back before it could betray what she was feeling. Couldn't catch it in time.

The sound seemed to electrify Quinn. He dove deeper, claiming her mouth as if he were a triumphant lover returning home after being away too long. His hands were knowing, possessive, hungry. She felt his palms outlining her under her blue sweater, circling her waist, surrounding every curve and hollow of her body with an intimacy that devastated what was left of her self-control.

I missed you.

The words swept into her mind with a force that shocked her.

I've missed you, Quinn.

She hadn't known that thought was there, lurking somewhere in the depths of her unconscious. It was so powerful, so clear, that for the moment she didn't have the willpower to resist it. Quinn had come back—he was holding her in his arms, kissing her as though he had never stopped, as though the intervening years hadn't happened. And she had missed him. That was all she could think of. Right now.

She raised herself on her toes, moving closer into his embrace, gliding her arms around his waist, feeling his hard, flat belly against her. It *was* the same jacket he had had ten years ago, she was sure of it. The slight rustle of the well-worn fabric as she nestled inside it was like a lover's whisper, familiar and tantalizing all at the same time.

She wanted to hold him close, to recapture that single moment they had once shared and then lost. She could feel the hard strength of his chest as she moved her hands upward, exploring him with fingers that were daring and gentle. She was reaching—crazily—for her own long-ago hopes and dreams. The feeling that she could magically step back into the past made her bold as she slid her palms over the powerful body she remembered so well.

And then Quinn went suddenly still.

At first she thought it was the unexpected intimacy of her touch that had startled him. But the way his ribcage had gone rigid under her hands told her that something else was happening.

Something was wrong. Quinn had lifted his mouth from hers, and she could feel him holding his breath after the one quick gasp that had alerted her.

"Quinn?"

He shook his head, and stepped away from her. He was moving tightly, the way he had after he'd slammed his hand against the rim of the billiard table, and once again Carrie found herself wondering if he was all right.

He was moving farther away, leaning on the back of one of the wing chairs with his left elbow clamped tightly to his side. His eyes were closed, and in the dim light Carrie could see lines she hadn't noticed in his face before, furrows that seemed to have been cut there by whatever intense and private pain he was wrestling with now.

She was feeling a different kind of pain of her own, as she realized how far she had let herself be carried by the dangerous passion she still felt for this man. She hadn't known those feelings were still there, or that they were so strong. She *did* know, now that she was no longer in his arms, that giving in to them again would be absolutely the worst thing she could do.

Even that realization wasn't enough to hold back the concern that welled up in her as she watched him. He was holding everything inside, the way he'd always done, she thought.

"Quinn, what's wrong?"

Quinn heard a note of exasperation in her voice, as though she didn't really want to ask the question. He shook his head again, waiting for the knife-edge of pain inside him to subside enough to let him speak.

"What happened? Are you hurt?"

"I don't want to talk about it." His voice was hoarse. Getting the words out didn't do anything to dull the pain.

He heard her quick sigh, and clenched his teeth against the bolt of memory that rocked through him, making his side hurt even more. He'd heard that sigh before, each and every time he'd insisted he preferred being a loner, that he didn't need companionship, that he was fine on his own.

Once, and only once, he had let himself be persuaded to drop his guard, to let someone into his solitary life. Once, briefly, he had felt the power that love had to rearrange everything he'd thought was settled and absolute.

The problem with love was that once you let it in, you couldn't tell what it might do. Quinn had learned that the hard way, after his one experience of love had rearranged not only his own young life, but Carrie's as well, suddenly, tragically.

Since then he'd gone back to his own way of doing things, the solitary way he knew and trusted. He needed to do that right now.

And he needed to have his head read, too, he thought. What had possessed him to kiss Carrie St. John, to touch her, to hold her close, when everything between them was so uncertain? He'd been furiously angry with her just minutes ago, but now even that had gotten swept into a churning sea of emotions that he knew he was going to have a hell of a time sorting out.

He forced his eyes open. The nearly healed gunshot wound still tugged at him, and he couldn't hold back a low growl as he made himself stand up straight and look at Carrie again.

"I'm staying at the hotel." He didn't have to tell her which one; the Courtyard Hotel was still Stockbridge's one and only place for visitors to stay. "I'm going back there now. I have to think about... all this."

He knew he sounded harsh, but his side still hurt too much for subtlety, and his thoughts were badly mixed up. He saw Carrie frowning at him. Her eyes were troubled.

"How long are you staying?" she asked.

"I don't know." He started to button up his jacket, feeling somehow as though he were buckling on a suit of armor.

"Quinn?"

He could hear indecision, and challenge, and even some of the astonishing passion of a few moments ago, all rolled into the simple sound of his name.

"Why did you come back?" She seemed half afraid to ask it, or to know the answer.

The funny thing was that Quinn wasn't sure what to tell her. He'd been so sure of himself just an hour ago, when he'd gotten off his motorcycle in front of the house. An hour ago, he would have said "I've come to answer the questions about David's death that have been bothering me for the last ten years." He had an indefinite leave of absence from his job, and he'd planned on staying here as long as it took to lay some of the uneasy ghosts in his own past to rest.

But now everything was different.

He had a son. *They* had a son.

Davey. He said the boy's name silently, still shaken by the idea of it. *I have a child....*

He hadn't begun to come to terms with that yet. Reverting to Plan A was the only thing he could think of to do at the moment.

"I came because I wanted to know who killed David," he said. "I got tired of wondering about it."

"No..." Her protest was quiet, but immediate. He could see her getting ready to argue with him, and he cut her off quickly.

"Now I don't know *what* the hell I'm doing here." He did up the last button on his jacket, and ran a hand restlessly through his hair. "I *do* know I'm not going to be able to sort it out if I'm standing this close to you."

Her lips parted slightly at his words, as if she were taken aback by his desperate honesty. It was sweet torment just to look at her, at the startled loveliness of her face in the soft light, and the slender body he remembered with such intimacy.

He was only proving the truth of his own words. He needed to get out of here, and to figure this out on his own. He turned and started across the foyer toward the kitchen, surprised to notice that it had become completely dark outside while they had been standing here.

Carrie didn't follow him. When he reached the kitchen
door and looked back at her, she was still standing next to
the billiard table. She had one hand pressed against her
lips, as though she were stopping words or tears or both.
The sight of her made Quinn's whole body ache.

He paused at the door, and almost said *I'll call you.* But
the words sounded too impersonal, too businesslike. And
besides, that was exactly what he'd said to her ten years
ago, after the first time they'd kissed and Quinn had realized how far he was stepping outside the very strict rules his
profession had laid down for his conduct on a case.

Ten years ago he'd made a lot of mistakes. It was important now—even more important than he'd known—to
get it right this time. Quinn growled a curt goodbye as he
grabbed his helmet and stepped outside. The cool November air met him like a very welcome slap in the face.

Chapter 3

Leo LaPlante gave a long, slow whistle. "I can't say I think it's the wisest thing to do, Quinn," he said.

Quinn declined the chief's offer of more coffee, putting a hand over his mug. "Doesn't it bother you to know that David St. John's killer is still walking around somewhere?" he asked bluntly.

Leo set the coffeepot back on the stove, and sat down at his kitchen table again. He was a heavyset man with rapidly thinning red hair and a shrewd expression. He was in his early sixties—a year away from retirement, he'd told Quinn—and after his first astonishment at the surprise visitor on his doorstep this Saturday morning, he'd welcomed Quinn like the former foster father he had once pretended to be.

That didn't mean he was offering any encouragement about Quinn's plan. "Of course it bothers me that we could never close the case on David's murder," he said. "But I thought at the time—and I still think now—that the chances of finding out exactly which mob hit man pulled the trigger are approximately nil.''

"I don't think it was a mob killing.''

Leo laughed out loud. "Oh, come on, Quinn.''

"I'm serious, Leo.'' Quinn adjusted his long legs under Leo's table. It was almost as unsettling to be back in this house as it had been to be at Carrie's. Leo LaPlante's home had always felt too small to Quinn. The chief liked clutter and had a fondness for oversize furniture. Quinn's big frame had only barely fit into the place in the four months he'd lived here.

"I may have made some mistakes on that case,'' he said now, "but I had done my homework on the mob family we knew was running drugs through Stockbridge. I knew their style, who their shooters were, how they operated when somebody started talking to the authorities. Nothing about David's death fit those patterns.''

"What are you saying, Quinn?''

"That someone local shot David. I think it was someone from Stockbridge, not some hired gun from the city.''

There was a long silence in the small kitchen. Quinn could hear the ticking of the clock on the wall, and the occasional car going by, someone probably on the way to do the Saturday morning shopping. Things didn't change much in Stockbridge, Illinois, he'd already noticed. And that meant that whoever had killed David could very well still be here, prospering, perhaps doing the grocery shopping along with everybody else on this crisp November morning.

"This was the first case I ever handled on my own, Leo,'' he said. "I made some bad errors in judgement. I'd like to correct that, or as much of it as I can.''

"Why now, after all this time?''

Quinn shrugged, and felt the slight tug in his side, reminding him of the bullet that had nearly ended his life and made him start thinking about all of this again. He didn't really want to get into all the details with Leo La-Plante. "Call it an early midlife crisis," he said.

Leo chuckled. "You're what—thirty years old?"

"Thirty-two."

The older man's chuckle faded, and he shook his head. "I'd forgotten it's been ten years," he said. "Of course, it should be easy enough to remember, with young Davey—" He cut himself off abruptly.

Quinn finished the sentence for him. "With young Davey turning ten next February," he said. "It's all right, Leo. I've been to see them. I know about the boy."

He had wrestled with himself half the night to get to the point where he could say those words almost casually. The thought of Davey still opened up a chasm inside Quinn that scared the hell out of him, but he wasn't about to let the rest of the world know that.

He was glad the subject had come up on its own, because there were things he needed to know, things Leo would be able to tell him. "I suppose everybody in town knows I'm Davey's father," he said.

"Hardly anybody knows for certain. Hell, *I* didn't know for certain, until just this minute. But we all figured it had to be you. Carrie was a popular girl in high school, but she never had any really serious boyfriends until you came along."

Until I came along pretending to be something I wasn't. Quinn's gut clenched, and the sharp pain stabbed at his side again. *Get on with it, McAllister,* he told himself grimly. *There are still things you have to find out.*

"How did she handle things, after I'd gone?" he asked.

Leo LaPlante shrugged. "Better than you might have thought," he said. "For an eighteen-year-old girl in her situation, she was pretty self-sufficient. Which was good, given what happened to her father."

"What happened to her father?" Quinn's voice was sharper than he'd intended.

Leo seemed to have picked up on the agitation under Quinn's quiet words. "Quinn, are you really sure you want to get into—"

Quinn cut him off. "What happened to Carrie's father?" he demanded.

"The old doctor had a stroke right after David's death. At first they thought it was nothing serious, but he just didn't seem to bounce back from it. He ended up selling his practice not long after that and retiring. It wasn't that he was exactly sick or anything. He just wasn't really well, either."

Quinn closed his eyes and pictured Carrie and David's father—white-haired, rigid, formal and always a little distant, even with the twin son and daughter who were his only family in the world. Yes, he could easily imagine old Dr. St. John breaking under the strain of David's death. He opened his eyes again and glared at his former colleague.

"So, Carrie was completely on her own." Quinn ground the words out. He'd hated himself for walking out of here ten years ago, even though he'd known it was the only thing to do. But he was even less pleased with himself now, learning what Carrie had gone through. She'd survived on her own—survived and triumphed, if her loving relationship with her young son was any indication. No wonder she'd looked so appalled when Quinn had turned up yesterday.

"She was completely on her own," Leo was echoing. "And I have to say I admired her, although she would never have let me tell her that."

"Why not?"

"She blamed me, to a certain extent, because I had known all along who you really were. She's still bitter about that, I think."

"I can't say I blame her."

"No." The police chief looked down into his cooling coffee and shook his head. "No, she didn't have an easy time. But she refused to let people pity her. I give her points for that."

Hell, it was getting too damn difficult to keep a lid on his feelings. Quinn untangled his legs from under the table and got up, wishing there was more room to pace in Leo's small house. He remembered wishing exactly the same thing ten years ago, when it had first occurred to him that he was letting his feelings for David and Carrie get in the way of his professional reasons for being in Stockbridge.

"My being here isn't exactly going to make her life easier, is it?" he said roughly.

Leo shrugged again. "Might be the understatement of the year," he said.

"I'd forgotten about small-town gossip."

Carrie hadn't, Quinn was sure. For the first time he considered walking out of here, right now, with no explanations to anyone, simply fading back into his real life and admitting that Carrie had been right when she'd insisted it had been a mistake for him to have come back at all.

But then there was Davey...

He had a son here. A child with his own stubborn expression and Carrie's warm brown eyes. How the hell could he walk away from that?

He owed that boy something, although he wasn't sure what. And he owed Carrie the real explanation of her brother's death. He couldn't imagine leaving Stockbridge again without taking care of that.

He forced his mind away from the image of Davey's face, and Carrie's, and back to the matter at hand. "Well, like it or not, Leo, I'm going to dig up what I can about David's murder," he said. "Can I count on your help, or not?"

Leo sighed, and got out of his chair. He emptied his now-cool coffee into the sink, and turned to face Quinn.

We've all gotten older, Quinn thought suddenly. Leo's heavyset face, like Quinn's own, was showing some signs of wear and tear.

"I still don't think it's wise," the chief said slowly. "But I know that look on your face, Quinn. You're going to do this whether anybody else approves or not. In which case, I'd rather be helping you than trying to stand in your way. What is it you need to know?"

The Courtyard Hotel was on the edge of town, not far from the one major road that connected Stockbridge to the rest of the world. Quinn's room was on the highway side, and even late into the night he could hear the trucks rolling by. The faraway sound of their wheels humming in the night was a perfect accompaniment to his mood.

He'd been tossing restlessly on the bed for what felt like hours when the phone rang. He wasn't sure if he'd been waking or sleeping. Either way, thoughts of Carrie and of their son kept hammering at him, demanding answers and responses he didn't trust himself to give.

The ringing continued. Quinn jerked to a sitting position, heart pounding, his thoughts confused. His right hand had reached instinctively for the gun he'd put into the drawer of the bedside table before he'd figured out that the noise wasn't a threat.

At least, it wasn't a direct one. As soon as he heard the sound of Carrie's voice on the other end of the line, he knew that something had gone wrong.

"Quinn." She was speaking abruptly, decisively.

"Carrie? What is it?"

"I was calling to ask you the same thing."

Quinn tried to get his wits together as he groped for the clock radio next to the bed and blinked at the glowing red numbers. Finally his eyes focused enough to read four a.m.

"What the hell—"

Carrie's voice got a little crisper. In spite of his confusion Quinn recognized the tone that meant *We're not going to argue about this.* "I don't care what time it is, Quinn, or whether you were asleep. Davey and I were asleep, too, until somebody started heaving rocks through our windows. I'd appreciate it if you could get yourself over here right now and tell me what's going on."

Quinn swore into the phone, but Carrie had already hung up. It took all of two minutes to get into his jeans and jacket, and another thirty seconds to hang the Do Not Disturb sign on his doorknob and add the extra precaution of a little strip of paper tucked in the frame as he closed the door. If he'd managed to stir something up this quickly, he wanted to make damn sure his room wasn't visited while he was out.

The St. John house was blazing with light as Quinn careened up the driveway on his motorcycle. He pulled in next to a police car, and hurried toward the front door.

The house had three sections: the central three-story brick structure, with its white columns and imposing front entranceway; the small annex where the kitchen and dining room were; and a side wing that held a large family room with three bedrooms upstairs.

Quinn could see people moving around in the side wing now. When he had changed course and headed in that direction, he saw that all the windows on the ground floor had been shattered, leaving jagged holes and fluttering curtains open to the November night.

"Ah, hell," he muttered, as he sprinted to the side entrance.

Inside, he found two uniformed cops and an elderly man who was busy cutting up plastic sheeting and tape. One of the cops looked familiar, a big, brawny guy with a massive chest and a combative expression. Quinn couldn't place him until he saw the name on the man's badge, Delaine.

He remembered that Nelson Delaine belonged to one of the groups of boys he'd been keeping an eye on when they'd all been in their senior year at Stockbridge High School. Nelson had been the bully of the bunch, always looking to stick his burly chest into somebody's face.

So he had turned policeman. Quinn found that interesting. Personally, he hadn't seen a lot of career prospects for Nelson Delaine beyond working as a bouncer in a small-town bar somewhere.

The other cop was younger, female, and unfamiliar-looking. Quinn's thoughts were interrupted by Nelson Delaine.

"Well," Delaine said. There was an unpleasant satisfaction in his voice. "If it isn't Quinn McAllister, the boy wonder of the FBI. Imagine seeing you back in these parts."

He didn't seem surprised to see Quinn. Carrie must have broken the news about Quinn's return, or maybe Delaine had heard about it from Leo LaPlante. In either case, Delaine didn't seem to see it as an occasion for much rejoicing.

"Kind of a funny coincidence that you show up and then Carrie gets her windows busted, wouldn't you say, McAllister?"

For the first time Quinn noticed that the place was set up as some kind of nursery. There were toys in big colored bins all around the edge of the room, and the curtains that were flapping slowly in the predawn breeze had bright clowns and balloons on them. Stacked at one end of the large space he could see a pile of carpet scraps, and there were kids' drawings pinned all over the walls.

All of this couldn't be for the use of one nine-year-old boy, he thought. He remembered the sound of children's laughter yesterday afternoon, and the presence of the teenaged girl who had asked Quinn whether he was a parent. Carrie must run some kind of preschool, he thought, or maybe a day care center. It looked as though she had found a way, after all, to surround herself with a lot of kids, as she'd always said she wanted to do.

That made it even harder to look at the damage someone had inflicted on this cheery, comfortable room. And even harder to listen to Nelson Delaine's snide hints that Quinn had been involved.

"Are you saying you think I did this?" Quinn had never had much patience for beating around the bush.

Delaine held out a crumpled sheet of paper. "Not necessarily," he said, "but you've got something to do with it, according to this."

Quinn frowned, and took the page Delaine held out to him. The letters seemed to have been traced onto it, using the kind of plastic template you could buy in any stationery store. The message was starkly simple, and very much to the point.

TELL QUINN MCALLISTER THAT MORE BAD THINGS WILL HAPPEN IF HE STAYS IN STOCKBRIDGE.

Bad things. Quinn almost laughed at the childish sound of the phrase, except that the evidence of its truth was all around him. The floor of Carrie's playroom was covered in broken glass, and he could see fist-size rocks strewn here and there.

He glanced at the note again, then handed it back to Nelson Delaine. "Was it tied around a rock?" he asked.

Delaine nodded. "We do things the old-fashioned way here," he said. "So sue us."

Quinn wasn't interested in Delaine's digs. His deepest concern—the one that had hit him the instant he'd heard her voice on the phone—was Carrie.

"Where's Carrie?" he demanded. "And Davey? Are they all right?"

The younger police officer answered him. "She's putting him to bed in the main part of the house," she said. "They usually sleep up above this room, but that didn't seem like such a great idea after this."

She went back to helping the older man cut off lengths of duct tape, and Quinn cursed softly, scuffing the sole of his sneaker in the broken glass under his feet.

"We'll want a statement."

It took him a moment to realize that Nelson Delaine was speaking to him. "A statement?" Quinn frowned. "I don't know any more than you do at this point."

"Sure you do. You know why you're here, and who you might have talked to that might have done this."

"I've talked all this over with Leo LaPlante. He knows what I'm doing here."

"Hey, McAllister." Delaine stuck his face a little closer to Quinn's, and Quinn felt some of his old dislike for this one-time schoolyard bully coming to the surface again. "Just because Leo always liked you doesn't mean everybody did, you know? Me, for example. I always thought it was a rotten thing you did to the St. John family."

Quinn glared back, and hoped Delaine couldn't see that the comment had scored a direct hit in a place where Quinn was all too vulnerable.

"So, I'm going to make you go by the book on this one," the big cop continued. "You want to come back and stir up trouble after ten years of peace and quiet, that's fine. But this time you'll use our rules, like everybody else around here. And those rules say I have a right to question you about this. So, you want to cooperate, or you want us to call Leo and wake him up and see what he thinks we should do?"

Quinn didn't especially want to do that. He didn't want to share his thoughts and plans with Nelson Delaine, either. "What do you want to know?" he asked levelly.

"I want to know who else knows you're back in Stockbridge."

Quinn laughed out loud. "Oh, come on, Delaine," he said. "I'm sure half the town—maybe the *whole* town—knows by now. If you want to know who I've talked to, I've talked to Carrie and Leo. I went to see Steven Solidad, who was busy coaching a Little League game and never got back to me. And I went to see Ted Wright, who had gone to pick up his kids for the weekend and who also never got back to me."

"Is that what they call a full day's work at the FBI?" Delaine's tone was scornful.

Quinn thought about the hours he'd put in agonizing over what he should do about Davey, and how to handle the emotions that had threatened to blow him apart when he'd held Carrie close to him again. It had been as hard a day's work as he remembered ever putting in, but he wasn't about to share that with Nelson Delaine, either.

"Is there anything else you need to know from me?" he asked abruptly.

Delaine had been busy scribbling something down in his notebook. "Just where you're staying," he said.

Quinn told him and excused himself. The worst thing about the policeman's scorn was that Quinn knew he deserved at least some of it. And the curious sideways glances from the other cop and the older man were making him uncomfortable. Besides, there was Carrie . . .

Somewhere in this big barn of a house, there was Carrie, and a nine-year-old boy who must have been frightened half to death by the sound of rocks crashing through the windows underneath his bedroom. Quinn's conflicted feelings were small change compared to that.

The foyer was dark, but he could see a light from the top of the stairs. He crossed the entrance hall quickly, not daring to look at the spot next to the billiard table where he'd held Carrie in his arms yesterday. He'd completely

lost control the moment he'd touched her, and it scared
him.

If her hands hadn't landed on exactly the wrong spot,
the place where the bullet had gone through him a year
ago, Quinn wasn't sure where that unleashing of long pent-
up hungers might have led. He had already been imagining the two of them naked together, frantically seeking the
lost magic they'd shared. He had been very close to taking her right there on the smooth green felt of the billiard
table, and claiming her, body and soul, as his own.

He could hear her soft voice and started up the stairs. He
had always gotten slightly lost in this big house, especially
on the top floors of the main house. The place had an unused feel to it now. As he passed the first of several bedrooms off the main hallway, he could see that the furniture
was either bare or covered with sheets.

He headed for the room that was lighted. There was a
sound like sails flapping in the wind, making it hard to
hear what Carrie was saying. As he stepped into the doorway, Quinn realized that she was unfolding sheets and pil-
lowcases for the twin beds in the room, talking to her son
as she worked.

"They wouldn't have hurt your room, honey," she was
saying. "They were just trying to get attention, not to hurt
anybody. Anyway, there's the sun porch between your
room and the outside. Nobody could throw a rock through
your window."

Her voice was firm and soothing, but Quinn thought he
could hear a thread of anger running through it. Carrie
was far from calm, despite the reassurance she was offering her son.

Their son. It still rocked Quinn to think about it. That
small boy in there, the one who'd been frightened and now
needed comforting, was Quinn's son, too.

And it was Quinn's presence that had caused someone
to lob those rocks through Carrie's windows. He gritted his

teeth, and half turned away from the flurry of activity in the bedroom.

"What about the kids on Monday?" Davey was asking. "Where will they go?"

"We'll get the windows fixed by then," Carrie said. "There are people who'll put in new windows even on Sunday. You just have to pay them a little more. Can you tuck that corner under, honey?"

For a moment there was no sound but the rustling of sheets. And then, in a sudden stillness, Davey's young voice said, "Is this because of the man on the motorcycle?"

Carrie seemed as startled by the question as Quinn was himself. He realized he was holding his breath, waiting to hear what she would say.

"What makes you think that?" Her words were cautious, noncommittal.

"I don't know. I just wondered."

Quinn stepped back from the doorway as silently as he could. He liked kids. He'd worked around them a lot. He knew the sound of a child who'd been thinking deeply about something, puzzling over it.

It was clear that Davey had been puzzling over Quinn.

He supposed it wasn't surprising. The tension in the air on Friday afternoon had been hard to miss, and Davey was obviously a sensitive kid. He wondered if Carrie had been distracted since then, as Quinn was. No doubt Davey had picked up on it, if she had been. And he'd been sharp enough to connect the two strange events happening so close to each other in his otherwise quiet life.

Quinn moved to the top of the big staircase and stopped there. He was going to have to come to terms with these impulses to cut and run, he knew. He either had to get the hell out of Stockbridge, or stay and face all the possibilities that waited for him here, for better or worse.

Worse could be pretty bad.

But better held out a faint, flickering hope for something Quinn had never known and always secretly longed for, some kind of family connection. How could he turn his back on that?

He leaned against the thick newel post on the landing, and wished there was an easy answer for at least one of the questions that were circling around and around in his mind.

Carrie promised one more time to bring Ranger Raccoon from Davey's room, and quietly closed the bedroom door behind her. Davey wouldn't sleep until she was back there with him, she knew. He had been badly scared by the shattered glass, and it had taken a lot to persuade him to settle down in the second floor bedroom while she went and made sure things were locked up tight.

Well, she'd been scared herself. The sound had seemed to go on and on, high-pitched and menacing. She was still feeling shaky inside.

When she saw the big outline of a man on the landing, she jumped. Her heart had started pounding hard before she realized it was Quinn.

He was wearing his old jacket over a black T-shirt. The shirt hung out over the waistband of his worn jeans, as though he'd thrown on his clothes in a hurry. Carrie put a hand over her thudding heart, and glared at him.

"Sorry," he said. "I didn't want to disturb you while you were with Davey."

"It's a bit late to be concerned about disturbing either one of us." Her voice shook as she got the words out, and she leaned against the post opposite Quinn, waiting for her breathing to slow down.

She couldn't tell what he was thinking as he watched her. His face was in shadow, and with his big shoulders and long torso, he was like some lurking monster who had come in out of the night. She wished she could see his eyes, at least. She'd always known with such certainty what Quinn McAllister was feeling when she locked gazes with him.

"What did you tell Davey," he asked, "when he wanted to know if I was connected to the broken windows?"

Carrie felt a flash of the anger that had prompted her to call him in the first place. "I didn't realize you'd been eavesdropping," she said.

"What did you tell him, Carrie?"

"I told him I didn't know, but that the police would find out, if there was a connection."

Her eyes were adjusting to the dimmer light in the hall now. She thought she saw Quinn's eyebrows lower in a frown. "He's obviously a sharp kid," he said slowly. "Do you really think you can slough him off with answers like that?"

Anger was returning full strength now, like a welcome shield against the nearness of Quinn's big body and the familiar rumble of his voice. Carrie stood up straighter, and said, "What do you suggest I do? Tell him you're his father? Set him up to have his heart broken, the way mine was?"

Quinn didn't seem to have an answer. Carrie took advantage of his silence, and stepped past him on the big staircase, heading back to the playroom.

"We have to talk about this," she said, "but I'd rather not do it here. Come on, you can help me pick up broken glass while we figure this out."

Chapter 4

There was something very comforting in the sight of Eugene Prestiss taping plastic up over the shattered playroom windows. It wasn't just that the gaping holes would be covered and the cold night partially kept out. It was the concern on Gene's face that bolstered her spirits, and the knowledge that their longtime neighbor was there to help when she needed it.

Gene was getting older, nearly eighty on his last birthday, but he kept himself looking much younger, as he'd once explained to Carrie, "by just keeping in motion." He had been over here within minutes of the first rock going through the window, and he had been busy finding tape and plastic and scissors while Carrie had dealt with the police and with calming Davey down and getting him settled in a bedroom far away from the damage.

Now Gene was fastening the last piece of tape, pressing it in place with a firm hand. "That should keep the wind out until tomorrow," he said, as Carrie came into the room. "Are you sure you don't want me to stay here, sweetheart?"

Carrie shook her head, and gave the old man a quick hug. "I appreciate the offer, Gene, but I feel pretty sure that whoever did this has made their point, and won't need to come back tonight. Davey and I will be fine up in the main house."

"If you're sure—"

"I'm sure. Besides, you couldn't have gotten here any quicker than you did, even if you *had* been here in the house. I appreciate your help, Gene, and I appreciate knowing you're keeping such a close eye on us."

"Well, it's a good thing somebody is. With that character back in town—"

He cut off his own words, and Carrie turned to see that Quinn had followed her into the playroom. She'd forgotten how silently he could move when he wanted to. It was like having a big panther loose in the place, she thought.

Gene Prestiss seemed to feel the same silent threat in Quinn's presence. He glared at the younger man. "That's who I'm talking about," he said. "What have you got to say for yourself?"

Part of Carrie wanted to tell Gene she could fend for herself, and that he didn't have to leap into his surrogate father role on her behalf. She stayed silent, though, because she was curious to see what Quinn *did* have to say for himself.

She didn't imagine he would remember Gene, except as an occasional crony of her father. But it must be clear that Gene was a valued friend in this house. Quinn's response to the old man's question would tell Carrie whether Quinn still felt himself to be as much of an outsider here as she hoped he did.

He sounded very serious as he said, "I wish I'd been able to do something to keep this from happening, but since I couldn't, I'm glad to see Carrie has friends who are keeping an eye out for her.''

Gene gave a snort that said he wasn't convinced, and picked up the broom that was leaning against the bench that ran along the length of the room. Gently but firmly, Carrie took it away from him.

"We'll take care of it, Gene," she said. "Don't worry, I'll make Quinn do most of the work."

When she got back from seeing her neighbor to the side door, Quinn was still standing among the shards of glass. He seemed to be thinking hard.

"I was serious," Carrie said. "I want a hand cleaning up, and I want an explanation about why this happened. And, while we're at it, I'd appreciate a guarantee that it won't happen again."

"I can't promise that," he said. "But I *am* planning to stay and keep an eye on the place, in case it *does* happen again."

Carrie stared at him. "You've got to be kidding."

"About something this serious? Of course I'm not kidding."

She reached for the broom and began sweeping the broken glass out of her way, clearing a path from the door to the stairway that led to the bedrooms upstairs. Quinn was standing absolutely still, his big hands at his sides. He looked as though he were ready to brace himself against an attack at any moment. Carrie felt much the same way, except that her way of meeting a problem was to do something, to find some kind of activity to put her anxiety into.

She spoke as she worked, raising her voice over the sound of the tinkling pieces of glass piling up against each other. "I seem to be asking more questions than I'm getting answers for, Quinn," she said. "I think you owe me some kind of explanation, don't you?"

"I owe you a lot of things."

She paused, startled once again by the regret she could hear in his voice. She didn't want his regret. She didn't want to be a way for him to work out whatever guilt he may have felt about what had happened ten years ago. She wanted him gone from her life, and quickly.

"I'll settle for a few straight answers," she said, as she started sweeping again. "For starters, who did this, and why?"

He hesitated, but Carrie refused to meet his eyes again. What she had seen there a moment ago had been too unsettling, too compelling. She would do better with Quinn McAllister if she could maintain some kind of distance between them.

Finally he moved to the cleaning supplies she'd pulled out of the closet, and picked up a dustpan and a whisk broom. While Carrie cleared the floor, he swept the piles of glass into the dustpan and dumped them into a big plastic garbage can, talking while he worked.

"I told you I came back here because I've never been satisfied with the official explanation of David's death," he said.

Carrie nodded without speaking. She disapproved of the idea, and she was sure it showed on her face.

"You and I both believed that David wasn't actually involved in whatever drug-running operation was working out of Stockbridge Airport," he went on.

"Really?" She couldn't help speaking this time. "You believed he was innocent? Is that why you took up with him and pumped him for whatever information you could get?"

"I suspected him at first, I admit it. He hung around the airport all the time, so I thought—"

"He loved planes, Quinn. He was fascinated by flying. He was going to be a pilot." She couldn't keep the hurt, the defensiveness, out of her voice. She had been so close to her twin brother, closer to him than to anyone else on the planet. To lose him so suddenly—

"I know that," Quinn said quickly. "Believe me, Carrie..."

She gave an unamused laugh. "We'll do better at this if you stop using the word *believe*," she told him. "Or *trust*, for that matter."

He was bending over, sweeping more glass into the dustpan. She couldn't see his face, but she thought his tawny head nodded slowly in what looked like agreement. "All right," he said. "Let's stick to the facts, then."

"Facts are fine by me."

"A well-known Chicago mob family was using the Stockbridge Airport as a transfer point for big shipments of cocaine from South America. The airport is larger than usual for a town this size, and fairly quiet."

His voice had gotten harder, more businesslike now. She wondered if this was what Special Agent McAllister sounded like when he was working. The change in him was a little chilling, but she told herself she was glad he had switched to a less personal tone.

"We needed witnesses from Stockbridge if we were going to bust up the operation. And we had suspicions— from an increase in the amount of drug use at the local high school—that some of the stuff was finding its way into the community, instead of going to Chicago like it was supposed to."

"I can't believe it was very widespread."

"It wasn't. Somebody was skimming a small amount off the top and making a local profit at it, that was all. But it was enough to give us a potential witness, somebody who might testify against the mob if the alternative was being arrested for trafficking himself.

"I'd been recruited because I could easily pass as a high school senior. I was supposed to see if I could figure out who was buying at the high school, and trace the stuff back to whoever the local dealer was. It stood to reason that that person had some connection with the Chicago family that was running the stuff."

Carrie felt her heart starting to beat faster again as the memories came pushing back. Quinn had made such a convincing eighteen-year-old. She'd been astonished to learn from Leo LaPlante later that his ward had really been twenty-two, and a full-fledged FBI agent.

And his story had been convincing, too. She remembered aching for the loneliness in his blue eyes as he'd told her about his mother in Chicago, who was too sick to look after him now, but who he hoped to get back to someday. She'd believed in that loneliness, damn it. She'd wanted to help him past it. And it had all been a lie.

The memory made her voice tighter as she said, "So, you started with David because he spent so much time at the airport."

"Right." He hesitated, then went on, "I figured out pretty quickly that David wasn't in on the dope deal. But it was also pretty clear that he had some ideas about what was going on, at least among the other guys at school. He was a potential way for me to unravel the case, so I stuck to him like glue."

They both paused then, not meeting each other's eyes. When Quinn spoke again, his voice was deeper, slower, without the cold professional overtones it had had just a moment ago.

"I don't know how to say this without using words like *believe* and *trust,*" he said, "but I *was* fond of David. Too fond, I realize now. If I'd liked him less, if I'd liked *you* less—"

He stopped. Carrie looked over at him, and immediately wished she hadn't. Something in his blue eyes was begging her to understand all the things he couldn't put into words, and it was affecting her just as deeply as it always had. Those eyes were hungry, searching, desperate to have Carrie acknowledge that there was, in spite of everything, some strong connection between them.

The way her pulse started to beat in her throat proved it was still true. And the anxious child upstairs made it very important to insist that there wasn't.

"You're saying you made an error in judgement." She said the words baldly, not offering him any sympathy.

He held her gaze for a moment, then looked away. She thought she saw his broad shoulders settle in a sigh. "I made so many errors in judgement I can't even count them," he said. "Hell, I knew I was supposed to stay objective. But I'd never been in a place where I—where I felt like I belonged. A place where I wanted to stay. You made me feel that way, Carrie. You and David."

They were getting far too close to too many dangerous feelings. Carrie felt all her defenses starting to go up again. "So, now it's our fault," she said. "Our fault, for making you feel welcome here."

"That's not what I meant." He spoke almost angrily. "It was my fault, the whole damn thing. We both know that." He shook his head, and stood up, emptying one more panful of glass into the garbage can. Carrie saw him catch himself as he stood, hesitating as he straightened his spine.

"Why do you keep moving as though you hurt?" The question was out before she could stop it.

He waved it away. "Let's finish with the facts, all right?" His voice was rougher now. "The bottom line is, I had three guys at the high school who I knew were buying cocaine, and I was working on them to let me into the secret when David was killed."

He didn't go into detail about David's death. He didn't have to. Carrie's mind was overrun with memories of the night she would never forget.

David had been out at the airport one warm June evening, as he often was. The airport manager had gone home, and witnesses who lived on Airport Road had reported seeing a long black car driving toward the office, then driving away again. No one had heard the shots. A couple of kids riding their bikes had discovered David's body about an hour later.

Carrie could feel herself trembling in every muscle, catapulted back into everything she'd thought and felt on the most horrific evening in her life.

It took a moment to get the words out past the sudden lump in her throat. "Damn you, Quinn McAllister," she said fiercely. "I hate you for making me remember all of this."

He closed his eyes, briefly. When they met hers again, she thought she saw a sudden shine blurring their blue surface. Before she'd had time to do anything more than wonder about it, it was gone.

"If it makes you feel any better, I'm not too happy with myself either, just about now." Quinn's voice was thick with the unspoken feelings she could see in his eyes. "Can we finish this?"

"Please."

"I came back here because I never did feel right about the way I left. I hated having to walk away without knowing who fired the bullet that killed David. And the more I thought about it, the more convinced I was that this murder didn't fit the known patterns of the mob family who was supposedly behind it. I've gone over and over this case, Carrie, and I'd bet my life that David's killer is still here, in Stockbridge, walking around free."

The idea shook her, but not for the same reasons that it seemed to have been bothering Quinn. "So, you're saying you want to dredge it all up again?" She knew she sounded incredulous.

"Don't you want to know what really happened? How can you stand the thought that whoever killed David has never been punished for it?"

"I don't care about revenge, after all this time."

"It's not called revenge, Carrie. It's called justice."

She shook her head in amazement, and propped the broom against the wall. "The only thing I care about, Quinn, is getting on with my life, and providing a safe and happy environment for my son. This—" She held out an open palm to the destruction that had intruded into her brightly painted playroom. "This isn't particularly safe *or* happy."

His jaw had set in that long, stubborn line she remembered, oh, so well. "Maybe not," he said, "but it does seem to prove that somebody's on the defensive about David's death. It didn't take very long to get a reaction."

"Am I supposed to be pleased about that?"

"I thought you might understand that this could be a way to... set some things at rest."

She shook her head. "I'm sorry if you're suffering from an uneasy conscience, Quinn, although I'd say you have every reason to. What you don't understand is that my life *was* at rest until you showed up. *You're* the danger here, almost as much as whoever threw those rocks. Can't you see that?"

She looked around the playroom, suddenly shaken by the violence of the smashed windows and the invasion of the most innocently cheerful room in the house. It was still pitch-dark outside the window covering Gene had taped up. Somehow the thick plastic was even more unnerving than clear glass would have been. The thought of some unknown watcher lurking out there, threatening her well-being and Davey's, touched a nerve she'd been able to defend until this moment. She started to shake before she knew what was happening, and once she'd started, she couldn't seem to stop.

"Oh, God," she said, her voice breaking over the words. "Can't you just leave us alone?"

She didn't want to cry, not in front of Quinn, not when she had to go back upstairs to Davey and convince him everything was going to be all right. But her feelings had been so deeply stirred up since Quinn had shown up on Friday afternoon. And when she thought about tonight's vandalism being the start of a new nightmare, instead of just a reminder of the old one...

She put her hands over her face, fighting against the sob that threatened. She didn't want any of this—the memories, the damage, the threat to her house and her peace of mind.

Most of all she didn't want the rush of longing she could feel as Quinn took three long steps and pulled her into his arms. His big hands slid around her shoulders, cushioning the sobs she was trying so hard to stifle.

"Shh..."

She could feel him shaking, too, as he smoothed her hair back and gently—so gently—kissed her forehead. When he spoke, his lips grazed her temple. The rough sound of his voice was erotic and familiar, comforting and disturbing all at the same time. It seemed to find its way inside her, kindling something that was almost too tantalizing to ignore.

"I'm sorry, Carrie," he was murmuring. "Sorrier than I can tell you."

She had wanted so desperately to hear him say those words, in the dark days after he'd left Stockbridge. She had been so alone, so confused. She had needed to know that the man she'd loved, the man who had betrayed her and her family, had at least felt some regret for what he'd done. She would have given almost anything, ten years ago, to hear Quinn McAllister tell her he was sorry.

The warm strength of his body surrounded her like a fortress now. She wanted to move closer to him, to accept the comfort he was offering. Her whole frame was still wracked by tears she couldn't hide, and it was getting harder to remember that they were far beyond the point where a mere apology could change or mend anything. It was tempting to linger in the strength of Quinn's embrace, letting the sound of his words resonate in the quiet room, letting her fears out against that hard, powerful chest.

"It isn't...that simple." Her voice was thick with tears.

"I know it isn't." He held her a little closer. "Damn it, Carrie, I know that."

She could feel his frustration in the way he tightened his arms around her quivering body. She turned her head, nestling into him, and felt the steady thumping of his heart against her ear. Was there anything really wrong with accepting, just for the moment, the comfort she had done without all these years?

His next words brought her back to her senses. She had started to relax slightly in Quinn's grasp, and she could feel her body beginning to respond to far more than just the solace he was offering. From the very first time she'd ever seen him, she'd been aroused by his long, lean body and the intensity of his gaze, of his presence. She felt that magnetism acting on her again now, making her tremble with pleasure when she felt his lips moving against the beating pulse in her temple.

All of that changed abruptly when she understood what he was telling her.

"If it was just a question of you and me, and wanting to know what happened to David, it *would* be simple," he was saying. "I'm not so obsessed with justice that I would stick around making your life miserable just to satisfy my own curiosity. But Carrie..."

His words had almost lulled her into thinking that he might be seeing things from her viewpoint after all, that he might actually care enough about her to understand how she felt about him being back here. And then he dropped his bombshell.

"Finding out about Davey changes everything."

She pulled her head back slightly. She wasn't sure exactly what he meant, but she didn't like the new edge she heard in his voice.

"How?" she demanded.

He sighed but didn't loosen his grip. Carrie was fighting two invisible enemies now, her fear about Quinn's intentions and her own instinctive response to his closeness. It was almost impossible to think clearly about anything when he had her in his arms like this, when she could feel the erotic outline of his unmistakable arousal where their bodies met. Knowing that Quinn shared her response only added to its uneasy power.

"I can't walk away from here now that I know we have a child," he said. "Maybe if Davey didn't exist, and you managed to convince me you really wanted me to leave you alone, I would go. But that boy is part of me, too, and I can't leave until I've decided what I want to do about that."

Carrie's heart was still beating at the same quickened rate, but it was fueled by fear instead of desire now. "There's nothing you *can* do about it," she said quickly.

"Of course there is."

His voice was gruff but emphatic. Carrie knew exactly how he had set his long, angular jaw. She saw the same expression every time she argued with Davey about something. Seeing it now when she tilted her head back and looked into Quinn's face was very disconcerting.

"Please don't start thinking you can have a place in Davey's life," she said. "I won't let you."

For the first time since she'd found him lurking in the upstairs hallway, she saw a flash of the anger that had alarmed her on Friday afternoon. Until now, he had been surprisingly warm, willing to give rather than take, to listen instead of demand.

But the look in his blue eyes told her that she had just touched on something he would fight for, something he had decided he wanted.

That something was her son.

Carrie backed away suddenly, out of Quinn's loosened embrace. She'd held on to her anger at Quinn all these years by telling herself he was cold and unfeeling. How else could he have pretended to love her, pretended to care about her brother, and then betrayed them both so cruelly?

Deep down, though, she'd always known there was more to it than that. Quinn was far from heartless. One look into his blue eyes was enough to convince her all over again that he was a man who felt too much, rather than too little.

That almost made things worse. Once Quinn McAllister had made up his mind to do something, he had the inner strength to overcome anything that stood in his way, including his own feelings—or anyone else's.

And now he was turning that implacable strength toward Davey. She took another step away, her feet crunching in the broken glass, her mind searching desperately for an answer that could combat his strength and her own treacherous responses to him just moments ago.

Before she could find one, a faint voice came out of the dark front hallway, calling to her.

"Mom?"

"Oh, God." She knew there were still signs of tears on her face, and maybe of a lot of other things, as well. She grabbed a tissue from a box on the shelf that ran around the edge of the room, and tried to sound as reassuring as she could. "I'm here, honey. We were just cleaning up a little bit."

She could hear Davey's bare feet padding across the polished wood of the foyer floor. There wasn't time to urge Quinn to make himself scarce, or even to glare at him, before her small son appeared at the playroom door, looking rumpled and anxious.

"I didn't like being up there by myself," he said.

"I don't blame you." Carrie was across the room almost immediately, guiding Davey up away from the glass shards. "I'm sorry I took longer than I thought, Davey. Let's go up to bed now, okay?"

Davey nodded, but he was looking at Quinn, not at his mother. Quinn could feel the assessing weight of those big brown eyes. The boy didn't ask what Quinn was doing there, but he was obviously wondering about it.

"It's a big house to be alone in at night, isn't it?" With an effort that tugged at every sinew in his body, Quinn managed to keep his voice level.

Davey nodded solemnly. "Usually my bedroom is up those stairs," he said, cocking his tousled tawny head at the door to the rear of the playroom.

"So I heard." Quinn ignored the look Carrie was shooting at him. His second sight of Davey was affecting him even more powerfully than he'd expected, and he'd be damned if he was going to pretend he was invisible just because Carrie wanted it that way.

"You're probably trying to figure out what I'm doing here, right?" he said, as matter-of-factly as he could.

Davey nodded again.

Quinn wanted to cross the room and be closer to that serious, thoughtful young face, to put his arms around the boy and reassure him as Carrie was doing now. But the look in her eyes told him to stay right where he was. Getting closer could mean setting off more sparks between himself and Carrie, and Quinn didn't want to do anything that would be too confusing for Davey to handle right now. *One step at a time,* he told himself. The first step was to start acting as though he had a right to be conversing with his son this way.

"One of the rocks that came through the window had a note tied around it, and my name was mentioned in the note," he said. He saw Carrie's frown deepen, but he went on anyway. "The police were wondering if I knew anything about what happened."

"Do you?"

One of the things Quinn found most refreshing about kids was that they didn't mind asking questions. It was also one of the things he found most difficult about them. He tried to come up with the right answer for Davey, something that would be the truth but wouldn't alarm the boy.

While he was thinking, Carrie jumped in ahead of him. "The police think maybe Quinn made somebody mad, but they didn't know how to find him, so they threw rocks through our windows instead. They figured we would give him the message."

She was giving Quinn a very different message as she spoke. He could feel the force of her brown-eyed glare.

He refused to give in to it. His hard won self-control was letting him look and sound fairly calm as he watched the woman he had loved and the son he had fathered. But the truth was that everything inside Quinn was in turmoil, still reacting to the soft warmth of Carrie nestled in his arms and the sight of Davey's young face, blending Carrie's features and his own so perfectly, so hauntingly.

He'd come back here because, on the point of death, he'd wanted more than anything to see Carrie again, to recapture if he could some of the sense of belonging he'd felt so briefly in Stockbridge. Now that he was here, he was feeling more alive than he had in ten years. It wasn't something he was prepared to walk away from, no matter what Carrie's expression was ordering him to do.

"If you tell me which bedroom is Davey's," he said to her, "I'll get his raccoon and bring it upstairs to you."

"It's the middle one." Davey spoke before his mother could. Quinn was heading for the staircase almost immediately, certain that Carrie wouldn't try to stop him. Like Quinn, she wouldn't want to argue in front of the boy.

Ranger Raccoon was easy to spot. The stuffed animal lay among Davey's rumpled covers. Quinn picked up the toy, cursing whoever had thrown those rocks, and feeling more determined than ever to clear this whole mystery up.

He closed Davey's door carefully, and made sure all the doors were locked as he made his way back to the main part of the house. It was a useless precaution, he knew—anyone wanting to get in would just have to push past the plastic sheeting taped over the playroom windows. But something in him made him do it anyway. The sight of Davey holding tight to Carrie's neck had made him even more intensely protective of this child, this place.

He saw the same protective instincts in Carrie's face when he handed her Davey's toy. The boy was tucked into bed now, still looking speculatively at Quinn.

Carrie stepped pointedly between them, and said, "Thanks, Quinn, but I think we're all set now."

"I still think I should stay."

She shook her glossy head. "No," she said firmly. "We'll be all right."

He could tell what she was doing. She had taken a determined position next to Davey's bed, and she wasn't moving an inch. She didn't want to be alone with Quinn again, he thought. And she didn't want their son to be alone with him, either.

The two of us are a unit, her stance said. *Davey and I belong together. We live here, and you don't.* She was making him feel like an outsider, an intruder.

Quinn had spent most of his life feeling that way. But the one and only time he'd ever let himself be brought into the circle of someone's love, it had been Carrie St. John who'd extended the invitation. Together, in that moment of belonging to each other, they'd created a child.

Now she was trying to push him away, and Quinn was refusing to go, refusing to take up his old outsider's role. Carrie might not want him in her life, but that heavy-lidded boy in the bed gave him a right to be here. Quinn was still rocked by Davey's resemblance to him, by the McAllister family jawbone and the thick, tawny hair that proclaimed the connection between them.

He met Carrie's gaze and sent her a message of his own: *This boy is my family. And there's nothing you or anybody can do to change that.* For the first time in his thirty-two years, Quinn McAllister knew with absolute certainty that he wasn't all alone in the world.

He said good-night to Davey, and nodded to Carrie. "I'll let you know if I find out anything that sheds some light on what happened tonight," he added, before he turned and headed back downstairs.

The sky was beginning to lighten as he stepped outside. He felt unexpectedly light-headed, almost giddy with the strength of what he had felt when he'd looked into his son's face, and when he'd held Carrie close to him. He wanted to sprint down the front walk, maybe click his heels, grinning like a fool. He wanted to leap onto his motorcycle and go roaring off into the sunrise.

He didn't do any of those things. He made himself take a careful look around the yard, and then he circled the block on his bike, parking quietly on the nearest side street until he'd satisfied himself that the police were cruising by at least once every half hour.

By that time the day had begun, and Quinn was getting funny looks from early morning commuters heading off to their jobs. He rubbed a hand across the stubble on his jaw, started his engine, and finally left the St. John house behind as he headed for his hotel room and whatever sleep he could still manage to grab.

Chapter 5

"Frankly, McAllister, the consensus is that we'd all be just as happy if you got back on that beat-up motorcycle and rode out of Stockbridge for good."

Theodore Wright III was standing next to his fireplace, leaning on the mantel. He seemed to be posing for a Christmas card photo, or maybe for a publicity shot in whatever trade magazines lawyers subscribed to. Quinn wasn't finding Ted Wright any more likable now than he had when both of them were in the senior class at Stockbridge High.

"You speaking for the whole town?" Quinn asked. "Or just yourself?"

"I'm speaking for those of us you seem to have singled out for harassment." Ted moved away from the mantelpiece and involved himself in the complicated business of getting his pipe started. A pipe, for God's sake, Quinn thought. Why not just wear a sign that said *I am a self-important small-town attorney?*

He reined in his annoyance. He had always found Wright's mannerisms annoying, but the fact was that the man *was* a big fish in the small pond of Stockbridge, Illinois. And he was also a suspect in David St. John's murder, at least in Quinn's mind. He knew it was important to pick up what he could from Wright's words.

"Steve Solidad tells me you went to see him earlier this afternoon," Wright was saying. Quinn nodded without replying. "And apparently you've already locked horns with Nelson Delaine. Not to mention the fact that you've been hanging around Carrie's place without being invited."

Solidad, Delaine and Wright himself had been the three young men Quinn's suspicion had fastened on in his investigation at Stockbridge High School. He was still able to look at them in a professional light, as suspects and little more. But Carrie—

Ted Wright lived next door to the St. John house, and he had already made a couple of remarks that made Quinn wonder what the attorney's feelings for Carrie were. Wright was divorced, attractive in a slick, buttoned-down way, and very securely established in the town. Carrie had never had anything good to say about him in high school, but that was mostly because she was worried about the effect of Wright's high living style on her susceptible twin brother.

But ten years had passed since then. The idea that Wright might actually be speaking on Carrie's behalf shook Quinn's composure, at least on the inside. He tightened his jaw, and said, "Did Carrie tell you I was back?"

The lawyer's brown eyes glittered with what looked like triumph. Had Quinn's feelings been obvious, in spite of his efforts to keep his jealousy to himself?

"Actually, I heard it from Nelson," Ted said. "But I'm concerned about Carrie, of course. We've been neighbors—and friends—for years now. I'm upset about her house being vandalized, and even more upset that you've come back to disrupt her life."

He puffed vigorously on the pipe, and finally got it going to his satisfaction. Everything about him looked sleek, from his carefully groomed blond hair to the expensive gold cashmere sweater he was wearing. Across the living room, in his battered old blue jacket and jeans, Quinn felt like a street mongrel next to a purebred golden retriever.

It was hard to admit it, but the golden retriever might be making a good point. Ted Wright was frowning at Quinn now, and he said, "Carrie has worked hard to get over what you did to her, McAllister. What kind of a man comes back to stir up things that can only cause everyone more pain?"

"The kind of a man who doesn't like the feeling he's been duped, I guess." Quinn hooked his thumbs in his jeans pockets and met Wright's stare levelly. "I can't help thinking it was very convenient for somebody that I got yanked out of Stockbridge right after David St. John was killed. It made it easy for everybody to be angry at me, as if I were the one responsible for what happened."

"You certainly had something to do with it."

Quinn had himself back under control now, and he acknowledged Wright's accusation with the merest tilt of his head. "I made mistakes on that investigation," he admitted. "That's partly why I came back—to atone for those mistakes if I can. But I didn't pull the trigger of the gun that killed David. And before I leave again, I'm going to find out who did."

Ted Wright laughed. "And you think it might be me," he said.

"You were a good regular customer for that cocaine back in high school," Quinn replied. "You and your buddies Steve Solidad and Nelson Delaine."

Wright's smile went away in a hurry. "If you've got any proof of that, I suggest you put it on the table right now," he said. "Otherwise, if I hear so much as a rumor about it circulating in this town, you'll find yourself on the receiving end of a slander lawsuit so fast you'll wish you'd stayed in Chicago playing shoot-'em-up with fourteen-year-olds."

Quinn's words had obviously hit a nerve, and he was congratulating himself about that when the last part of Wright's sentence hit him. "So you've been checking me out," he said slowly.

"Of course I have. Look, McAllister, I've got a life and a reputation to protect in this town. Sure, I may have experimented a bit when I was a teenager—who didn't? But don't think I'm going to let some gunslinger with a chip on his shoulder wander into Stockbridge and blow away what I've worked so hard to build up. And Quinn—"

The name sounded anything but friendly. Quinn frowned.

"If you do anything—anything at all—to hurt Carrie or that boy of hers, I promise you I will make your life very difficult. I may have stayed in little old Stockbridge, but I'm a highly competent attorney. I've sued the federal government before, and come out on top."

Quinn didn't want to get into the details of exactly where the FBI stood on this case. Off the record, he had the blessing of his boss and the unofficial cooperation of the agency to dig up whatever he could find about David's death. He knew he could count on his colleagues to help him wrap things up if he managed to solve the ten-year-old case successfully.

But at this point, officially, he was working on his own. If anything went wrong this time, there was nobody to take the heat but Quinn himself.

He didn't really want to share that information with Theodore Wright III. "You got any idea about who might have thrown those rocks through Carrie's window at four o'clock this morning?" he asked.

Wright lifted his cashmere-clad shoulders. "I have no way of knowing how many other people you've annoyed besides me," he said.

"Since you're so concerned about Carrie, I'm a little surprised you didn't come to see what happened. Eugene Prestiss was there almost immediately."

"Gene is a kind of family watchdog for Carrie and Davey. And he doesn't sleep very well these days, whereas I was chasing my two kids around all day and was sleeping like a log. And all those trees between my place and Carrie's tend to muffle sound. You'd be surprised how little I can hear from over there."

Did Ted Wright's sudden burst of explanation mean anything? Quinn wondered. The lawyer seemed suddenly eager to justify his absence on the scene at Carrie's early this morning.

He hadn't had a chance to follow up on it before a skinny teenager with long dark hair came into the living room. Quinn recognized him as the kid who'd been raking leaves on Ted's front lawn on Friday afternoon. In spite of the lawyer's smooth good looks and the boy's sullen expression, there was some family resemblance between them.

"My stepbrother, Jamie." Wright had noticed Quinn watching the two of them. "He's living with me this year. What is it, Jamie?"

"I finished." The boy didn't look at Quinn or his stepbrother as he spoke. Not a happy kid, Quinn thought. He recognized the symptoms. "I'm gonna go rent a movie."

"Make sure it's one the kids can watch," Ted said. "Not one of those horror ones, okay?"

"Come on, man—"

"Jamie." It was amazing, Quinn thought, how different Wright's don't-argue tone sounded from Carrie's.

Carrie's voice was always gentle when she was speaking to her son, even when she was being firm with him. Ted sounded as though he was only being this civil with his young stepbrother because Quinn was watching.

Ted Wright hadn't changed, Quinn thought. It was going to be well worth his while to check up on what Wright had been doing at the time of David's murder.

"The lady next door's comin' up the walk." Jamie Wright gestured toward the front door. "You want me to let her in?"

"Her name's Carrie." Quinn caught the quick glance Ted Wright had shot him. "You know that. And yes, I would like you to let her in."

The teenager turned to leave the room, then looked at his stepbrother. "I'm only livin' here 'cause it's better'n being at home, all right?" he said. "I'm not interested in gettin' all friendly with your neighbors."

The doorbell rang then, and Jamie went to answer it. Interesting, Quinn thought. The boy hadn't been sure of Carrie's name. Even taking teenaged hostility into account, that would seem to indicate that she wasn't exactly a frequent visitor here. Yet Ted had been talking and behaving as though he and Carrie were very close, as though he had a right to speak for her.

The sight of Carrie still made Quinn's blood move faster in his veins. She was wearing jeans today, and a cream-colored sweater with colorful patterns embroidered over the front of it. Her hair was pulled back at the sides, and the style made her look younger than her twenty-eight years. His hands quivered at the thought of undoing the small gold clasps that held the gleaming brown strands. He could almost feel the satiny smoothness under his fingers, just looking at her.

He was absorbed enough in the physical sensations of being near her that it took a moment to realize she was spitting mad about something. She was hiding it, speaking in a civil but cool tone that told Quinn everything he needed to know about her feelings for Ted Wright. But under that calm veneer, something had upset her badly.

"I saw Quinn's bike out front," she was saying, "and I wondered if I could come over and corral him."

"Of course, if you want to." Ted was making his surprise a little too obvious, Quinn thought. "Are you sure—"

"Quinn and I have some business to discuss." She smiled brilliantly at her neighbor. "Whenever you're done—"

"We're done." Quinn moved to her side. He didn't ask why she had come looking for him. He didn't want to do it in front of Wright, for one thing, and for another, something in the way Carrie's dark brown eyes were snapping at him told him he wasn't going to like the reason very much.

Once they had said their rather strained goodbyes to Ted and were outside on his lawn, though, he didn't waste any time. "What's this all about?" he demanded.

He had easily eight inches on her five-foot-five-inch frame, but he was having to hustle to keep up with her. She was upset about something, and he wanted to know what it was.

She shook her head. "We'll talk about it at my place," she said. "I've had about enough of people eavesdropping and gossiping for one afternoon."

That didn't sound good. Quinn lengthened his stride, and followed her down the front walk and toward her own house. Ted Wright's sullen stepbrother was riding away from the curb on a bicycle as they reached the sidewalk.

"You still don't like Ted much, do you?" Quinn spoke to cover his own growing unease, as much as anything else.

Her glossy head shook firmly back and forth. "I never have," she said. "You should remember that."

"I did remember it. But Ted seems to have forgotten. He was talking as though the two of you were good friends."

"That's wishful thinking." They had reached the front walk of Carrie's house now. Quinn took the steps two at a time, and still barely kept pace with Carrie's quick march. "He asks me out occasionally. He thinks it might be fun to start something up with the girl next door. But he treats me as though I should be pathetically grateful for the opportunity. And I refuse to let anybody pity me like that."

She swept up the walk and through the front door before Quinn could sort out which of his feelings had come out on top—relief at the idea that she didn't care anything about her handsome neighbor, admiration for her spirit, or alarm about what it was that she wanted to say to him.

She didn't keep him in suspense for long. They both paused in the big foyer, studiously staying away from the billiard table where they had let things get out of hand once this weekend. Halfway across the open space Carrie turned and said, "It's about Davey."

"Is he all right?" Quinn couldn't stop the sudden clutch of fear in his gut. That boy was a part of his life already. If anything happened to him—

"No. He's not all right." The fear in him intensified, then wavered. If something was physically wrong with Davey, Carrie wouldn't be standing here arguing with Quinn. Then what—

"He's on his way home from my friend Susannah's house. He's been playing there this afternoon with a bunch of kids from her block. And guess what choice piece of information one of them chose to pass along to Davey?"

"Oh, God." Quinn saw it coming.

"Yes. I agree."

She moved again, as though it was impossible for her to stand still when everything was in turmoil inside her. Quinn remembered that about her, remembered being amazed by her energy, her willingness to go out and meet her problems rather than let them run her over.

She was doing it now, talking quickly, trying to get her thoughts and feelings in order. "Apparently Davey came in to Susannah asking if it was true that you were his father. She didn't know what to tell him, so she called me. She's driving him home now, because he was upset enough that she didn't want to let him walk on his own. We've got about four minutes, Quinn, to figure out how to handle this."

In spite of everything—his concern for Davey, the angry barrage from Carrie's brown eyes, his own inner confusion—Quinn was aware of a quiet sense of triumph at the fact that she was inviting him to face this moment with her. They were in this together, and if Carrie thought he was going to try to run away from that, she was going to be surprised.

"All right," he said, keeping his voice as calm as he could. "My inclination is to be as honest as we can without doing anything that might scare him."

She nodded. And she *did* look surprised. She'd expected less of him than this, he realized.

Her voice didn't carry any particular approval, though, as she said, "Unfortunately, what you're doing here *is* scary. Those rocks through our windows prove it. How are we going to deal with that?"

Quinn had been in a lot of pressure situations in his professional life. He'd had to learn how to think hard under high tension, how to weigh his options with a cool head no matter how hot things were around him.

He couldn't remember ever finding it this hard to do. But for Davey's sake—for all their sakes—he knew he had to get it right this time.

"I knew when I left here this morning that I wasn't going to be able to walk away from Davey, no matter what," he said, speaking quickly, quietly, masking the fact that it was more than just Davey he couldn't imagine walking away from. "Even if he hadn't found out from someone else that I was his father, I wanted to tell him eventually. And damn it, Carrie, that kid is smart. He's picking up on what's going on between us. Keeping him in the dark amounts to lying to him, and I don't want to do that."

"You don't want to lie?" Her disbelief cut into him, but he took it without flinching. It was no more than he deserved, after all.

"I don't want to lie anymore." He moved a little closer to where she had stopped, near the big French doors at the back of the foyer. "I *had* to lie last time, and it cost us all too much. This time I want to tell the truth, especially to Davey."

He saw her wrestling with his words, trying to absorb them quickly, to sort through what she could and couldn't live with in what he'd said. "I don't want you making any promises to him that you might not be able to keep," she said. "Nothing about being a part of his life, or anything like that."

"I won't say anything specific."

"I don't want you to say anything at all. Quinn—"

He moved a little closer, and took her arm. He could feel her vibrating under his grasp, or maybe it was his own tension he was feeling. He wished like hell he could pull her close, proving to her that the bond between them was strong enough to support them through the next few minutes.

He knew it wasn't, not yet. Too much loss and guilt and silence still lay between them. But he was feeling the first stirrings of something he'd thought was lost, and that gave him the courage to face her angry eyes and say bluntly, "Whether you like it or not, Carrie, I already *am* a part of Davey's life. I'm his father. Let's just get that out in the open and see where we can go from there."

He saw Carrie's brown eyes widen as she heard a vehicle pulling up the long driveway. Her body tensed in his grip. She was steeling herself, he thought. She was calling up every ounce of that spirit he'd always admired, so she could face their son without letting on that she was afraid.

Quinn knew exactly what she was afraid of. He'd hurt her badly, ten years ago. He'd let her down more disastrously than he'd had any idea of. And she was scared to death that he would do the same thing to Davey.

Her words confirmed it. "Please, Quinn." It wasn't much more than a whisper. "Don't make him any promises, all right?"

At the moment Quinn would have promised her the moon and the stars if he'd thought it would take away the fear in her eyes when she looked up at him. But she had good reasons to doubt him, and he knew it.

He was just going to have to give her equally good reasons to trust him again, that was all. Quinn squared his shoulders, and reluctantly let go of her arm. He heard the kitchen door bang open, and slow footsteps coming into the house.

"We're in here, honey." Carrie's voice was serious, yet calm. How did she do that? Quinn wondered. Maybe when people had kids, they learned to be strong in ways he had never imagined.

Quinn wasn't sure he was that strong. He had faced down mob killers who would have blown him away if they'd even suspected who he was, and embittered teenaged boys with semiautomatic weapons in their jumpy hands. But he didn't remember ever feeling as exposed and alone as he did when Davey came into the foyer.

The boy's feet were dragging, as if he'd walked miles to get here. At first he wouldn't look at Quinn, but when he did, there were so many questions in his brown eyes that Quinn almost couldn't hold his gaze.

"The kids said you were my father," Davey said.

Quinn nodded. "It's true," he said.

"Why did you leave?"

This was even harder than Quinn had expected it to be. Davey had his mother's habit of going straight to the heart of a question. It didn't leave a lot of room for explaining things gradually.

But maybe that was the best way to do it. Quinn took in a deep breath, lowered himself onto his haunches until he was at Davey's height, and said, "Come here, Davey."

The boy came closer, stopping just out of Quinn's reach. *Fine*, Quinn thought. He didn't blame his son for hanging back.

"I work for the FBI," he said. "That's my job. I investigate things. Sometimes I have to work under cover. Do you know what that means?"

Davey nodded.

"I came to Stockbridge as part of an undercover operation. I looked a lot younger than I was, so they had me posing as a high school senior. That's how I met your mother and your uncle David."

Davey looked at his mother, who nodded. Quinn could almost feel her wanting to move toward her son, to stand next to him, protecting him from this dangerous knowledge as she had protected him early this morning. But she seemed to know that Davey needed to hear and sort this through on his own.

"Undercover agents are supposed to be able to blend in wherever they are, without getting too involved with the people around them," Quinn went on. "You can't investigate people properly if you get attached to them. But this was my first undercover case, and I didn't know how hard it could be to pretend to be somebody's friend when you weren't supposed to be really friendly."

He paused. Davey was frowning, and Quinn wondered if this made any sense at all to the boy. "Can you understand what I mean?" he asked.

"You weren't supposed to be their friend, but you were."

"Yes. Exactly." It had been exactly that simple, Quinn thought. Davey's childish phrases expressed his own almost childlike amazement at how good it felt to be part of a circle—even a very small circle—of people who really cared about him.

"I should have kept my distance, but I didn't." He wasn't about to offer excuses about the lonely childhood that had left him all too vulnerable to the warmth that Carrie and David had offered him. "I got far more involved with your family than I ever should have. Your uncle David got killed because he knew something—I still don't know what—about the situation I was investigating. And when that happened, the FBI took me away from Stockbridge in a hurry. I didn't have time to talk to your mother. I didn't know that you had been born, until I saw you in the kitchen on Friday afternoon."

In spite of all he could do, Quinn's voice wouldn't stay steady anymore. Damn it, he'd missed so much of this child's life. It might already be too late to make up for what both of them had lost. He felt the heat of anger in his belly again, and fought against it. It wasn't Davey he was angry at. It wasn't even Carrie, really. It was himself, and fate, that really made his blood boil.

"Why did you come back?" Davey's voice sounded small in the two-story foyer.

"Nobody knows who really killed your uncle. I thought if I could figure it out, it might make up for some of the things I screwed up when I was here the first time."

He couldn't tell how Davey was reacting to any of this. The boy's face was more guarded than he'd seen it before, as though Davey wanted to think this over before committing himself. Quinn was braced for questions about David's murder, or his own plans for the future, or the damage to the house last night—anything but the thoughtful and devastating question Davey finally asked him.

"If somehow you *did* know about me when I was born," he said, "would you have come back?"

Quinn stood up slowly. When he'd first talked to Carrie, he'd been quick to insist that he would have come back if she'd let him in on the news that he'd fathered a child. Now he wasn't so sure. What could he have done, back then? Quit the job he'd just started, the job he loved, come pelting back to Stockbridge, bulled his way back in where he wasn't wanted?

He didn't have the foggiest idea.

"I really don't know," he said to Davey. "I'm sorry, scout, but that's the best answer I can give you."

"How long are you staying?"

"I don't know that, either."

Ask me an easy one, he wanted to say. *Ask me what's seven times six, or whether Santa Claus is real, or something.*

The kid was making him sweat for it, though. His final question was the hardest one yet. "Did you *want* to be my father?" he asked.

Quinn looked over at Carrie, who was standing next to one of the wing chairs. Her hands overlapped each other on the subdued upholstery, seemingly calm, waiting, watching. Someone with an eye less sharply observant than Quinn's might have missed the fact that she was gripping the chair so tightly that her knuckles were white.

Their eyes met, and Quinn saw some of his own anguish reflected back at him. What the hell could he say to answer Davey's question? Of course he hadn't planned or wanted to be a father, any more than Carrie had planned or wanted to get pregnant at eighteen. Davey's existence was a mistake, if you looked bluntly at it.

But when he turned back to the sturdy, perceptive little boy facing him, he knew there were other ways of looking at it. And he had to find some way to communicate that to Davey.

"Sometimes the things that aren't planned turn out to be better than the things that *are* planned," he said slowly. A bullet through his left side, for example. That close brush with death had, in a strange way, brought him back here to meet his son. "I'm glad you were born, Davey, and I know your mom feels the same way. And I'm glad I'm your father."

That wasn't quite the same thing as having wanted to be a father in the first place, and Davey seemed to know it. And it didn't begin to address the question of whether Quinn wanted to be a father now, and how on earth he might go about doing that.

"Can I go up to my room now?"

"Sure, honey." Carrie shot another quick glance at Quinn. "Are you okay?"

"Yeah. I just want to be by myself."

He trailed through the playroom without looking back or speaking. Carrie must have swept up the rest of the broken glass, Quinn realized. Davey's slow footsteps didn't make much sound on the linoleum floor. In fact, the beating of Quinn's heart drowned out those quiet steps long before the boy reached the staircase and disappeared up it.

He suddenly felt as though he'd just run all the way to Chicago and back. He let himself lean against the closest object, which turned out to be the billiard table, and closed his eyes.

"Do you still think that was the right thing to do?" Carrie asked.

"Yes," Quinn said. "I do."

Her tight sigh coincided with a grinding of gears from outside. Quinn opened his eyes to see a truck coming up the driveway. There were big plates of glass strapped to a rack on the side.

"I have to go and deal with these guys," Carrie said. "And then I've got to think about something for supper."

"If I cook something," Quinn said slowly, "will you let me stay and eat it with you and Davey?"

She seemed surprised by the way he phrased the request. Quinn had chosen the humble words on purpose. He wasn't in any position to demand things, and he wanted to let Carrie know that he realized it.

At the same time, he was more determined than ever not to budge on the one thing that really mattered—being with his son, somehow, in some way he hadn't figured out yet. He was willing to eat as much humble pie as Carrie wanted to dish up, as long as he had his way on that.

"I'm not sure how Davey will feel about it," she was saying, tentatively.

"Hell, Carrie, I'm not sure how *I* feel about it." He dragged a hand through his hair, and felt his left side pulling at him as he moved. "All I know is that I don't want to turn my back on this thing now."

"Not even if it upsets Davey?"

"*Especially* if it upsets Davey."

Once again, his answer seemed to surprise her. She gave a little shrug, and started toward the playroom, where the glaziers were already shouting to each other. "There's not much in the kitchen," she said, "but if you can make a meal out of what there is, I guess you can stay and help us eat it."

Chapter 6

Sunday night supper usually involved a variety of leftovers, or occasionally a couple of TV dinners. It felt odd to Carrie to come into the kitchen and be greeted by the smell of simmering soup and baking bread.

"You had some of that frozen bread dough at the very back of your freezer," Quinn said. "It was about to be swallowed by the glazier in there, so I liberated it."

He had taken off his jacket and rolled up the sleeves of his blue flannel shirt. His hands were big and agile, moving capably around the kitchen implements he'd found in her cupboards. She could see the muscles shifting in his forearms as he briskly chopped up some green onions and added them to the big pot on the stove.

"Susannah went through a phase of trying to convince me that even I could bake bread," Carrie told him. "She kept bringing me that dough and telling me it was foolproof, but somehow I could never get it to rise."

"I think you move around too much to be a good cook."

Carrie took off her jacket and hung it on the peg behind the kitchen door. "What do you mean?" she asked Quinn.

"You're always in motion—which isn't a bad thing. I always liked the way you walk right up to problems. It's just that cooking demands a different kind of concentration, and I don't think you have it."

"You obviously do." The idea that he'd been thinking about her this way, assessing her way of living her life, was disturbing. What else was going on behind those penetrating blue eyes?

He shrugged. "I spend a lot of my time scoping out situations before jumping into them," he said. "I think that overlaps with the kind of thought you need for cooking a meal."

He had jumped far too quickly into the situation here in Stockbridge ten years ago. Carrie was about to point that out to him when he cut her off. He seemed to know what she was going to say, and she could tell he didn't want to hear it.

"How's Davey?" he asked.

"Gloomy." She had just been up to her son's room to check on him.

"I'm sorry. Is he going to eat with us?"

"I told him he had to come down for supper. He seemed to be dragging his heels about it."

Quinn ground some black pepper into the soup pot, stirred it, and wiped off the cutting board he'd been using. Everything he did was fluid and purposeful. In some mysteriously masculine way, he managed to be both down-to-earth and intensely sexy at the same time.

She had never met another man whose smallest motion ignited such a response inside her. And all he was doing was making soup, for heaven's sake.

He was doing more than that. She could see him thinking about Davey's response, lowering his brows, setting that long jaw in the line that meant he'd come to a decision about something. "Would it help if I talked to him?" he said finally.

"I don't know." She had always been so sure what her son was feeling, and why. It was disturbing to have a third person intruding into the close bond she and Davey had shared for so long. "You're the reason he's gloomy. I don't know if talking to him would help or make it worse."

Quinn wiped his broad palms on a tea towel and looked briefly into the oven, where Carrie could see a pan of rolls baking. They were plump and golden, just like the package had promised.

"Don't touch anything, all right? It's all under control." For the first time since he'd shown up here, Carrie caught a glimpse of laughter in those piercing blue eyes. She stiffened, instinctively resisting her impulse to smile back at him. She didn't want to laugh with Quinn McAllister. She didn't want to wait here alone while he went to talk to her son—their son.

But that quick amused glint affected her even more deeply than his earlier serious glare. And she couldn't think of a good enough reason to prevent him from talking to Davey if he wanted to. For the moment, at least, Quinn seemed to have strong-armed his way back in here without Carrie quite realizing how he'd done it.

He and Davey were back in five minutes, walking into the kitchen without speaking. Davey still looked sullen, and Carrie's heart turned over at the sight of him. He was usually such a sunny child, and open about what he was thinking. He wasn't quite meeting anyone's eyes now, and he ate as though he knew it was his duty, but it wasn't one he had much enthusiasm for at the moment.

The meal was quiet, and Davey excused himself as soon as it was over. Quinn stayed at the table, rocking back on his chair legs, looking at Carrie.

"You know, I got shortchanged when I was a kid," he said.

"What do you mean?"

"My parents were away a lot, so they farmed me out to a boarding school as soon as they could. I barely saw them, even on vacations."

"Is this the revised story of your life?"

"This is the *real* story."

Carrie looked closely at him. He had hooked his thumbs into the belt loops of his jeans, and crossed one ankle over the opposite knee. The way he was pushing himself back and forth with one long leg was heartrendingly familiar. She'd watched him do exactly this so many times before. And she'd listened to him talking about his past, too, except that it wasn't the same past he was telling her about now.

"You know, I really bought your sad story about your invalid mother who couldn't support you but wanted you back as soon as she was better," she said. "And it turns out it was just a cover for your investigation. That makes it a little difficult for me to get all sympathetic again now."

She made her words blunt on purpose, to counteract the treacherous ache she was feeling as she looked into his blue eyes. She had always responded too readily to the silent emotions she saw there, and she could feel herself doing it again now. She needed distance, she told herself, and perspective. She needed it for Davey's sake, as well as her own.

Quinn rocked his chair all the way forward, and looked at her from close range. "I'm not asking for your sympathy," he said, although his eyes were telling her he'd been hoping for it. "I just want you to understand something about me."

"Fair enough." She realized, to her surprise, that in spite of how much she'd loved him—in spite of the fact that they'd created a child together—she really didn't know a single thing about Quinn McAllister.

"What I'm trying to tell you is that I know what it feels like not to have a full-time, two-parent family. It doesn't feel good."

Carrie already knew that, from her own childhood experience of an elderly, widowed father who had never really gotten over the grief of his wife's death and was never quite sure what to do with the two children she had left behind.

But she didn't want to get into that with Quinn. The less of herself she exposed to him, the happier she would be. "Who were your parents?" she asked instead. "Why were they away so much?"

"They were writers, and archaeologists. Adventurers, really. They went on expeditions and wrote books about them. It was a great life, unless you happened to be the kid they left behind. They died somewhere off the coast of Africa when I was sixteen. I remember thinking after they died that things weren't really going to change much for me. I was still going to be alone most of the time."

"Why are you telling me this?"

"Because sooner or later Davey is going to feel the lack of a father in his life, if he hasn't already."

"We were doing fine," she said quickly, "until you showed up."

He unhooked his thumbs from his jeans and spread his palms wide. "What's the point arguing about that?" he demanded. "I'm here now. And I don't like knowing that I've contributed to another kid getting shortchanged on the family he deserves."

Carrie got up, and started clearing the table. She didn't like where this conversation was headed. "Lots of kids cope with parents who are divorced or single," she said. "It doesn't have to be unhappy for them. Davey and I have managed fine."

"Wait." Quinn stood, too, looming suddenly in the cozy room. He put a hand on each of her wrists, stopping her, and Carrie felt her pulse start to race at the sudden contact with his skin. "You've done a great job with Davey. Anybody can see that. But he knows who his father is now. You can't go on acting as though I don't exist. And Carrie..."

She'd been avoiding his eyes. Now, when she met them, she had that disorienting feeling of being shaken loose in time. It was like falling in love with Quinn all over again, seduced by his rugged good looks and the buried hunger in his eyes.

"You, David and I talked enough about how it hurt to be missing one parent," he said, quietly but intensely. He seemed to remember everything about the brief past they'd shared. "Don't try to tell me now you don't remember how that felt."

He let go of her wrists as suddenly as he had taken hold of them, leaving Carrie shaken and unsure of herself. There were too many things coursing through her, and one of the most disturbing was the realization that she'd *wanted* him to touch her, that she'd felt disappointed when he'd stepped away.

He left the kitchen without saying anything else, and she busied herself cleaning up after the meal he'd made. By the time she felt calm enough to face him again, it was nearly Davey's bedtime, and she headed for the middle bedroom above the playroom, fairly certain she would find Quinn already there.

She did, and she was surprised to see Davey already in his pajamas and sitting up in bed, listening to Quinn reading out loud. Davey still looked as uncertain as Carrie felt, but the book Quinn was reading was his favorite, so the boy must have loosened up enough to share that information with his father.

His father... It still sounded foreign to Carrie. She had gotten so used to thinking of Davey as a child without a father. Was Quinn right that she'd been shortchanging the boy? She'd thought about marriage, the couple of times she'd had steady boyfriends. But somehow she'd always missed the kind of unmistakable sizzle that had attracted her to Quinn. She'd decided marriage just wasn't for her, and that she was happier with the kind of easy partnership she had with Davey, anyway.

The sight of Quinn sitting in the chair beside Davey's bed, reading Davey's favorite book, threatened the very foundations of that partnership. What else would he rock in her world if she let him back into it? In spite of the familiar phrases of the children's story he was reading from, he seemed more threatening than ever, more dangerous.

Maybe I'm just protecting my own feelings too much, she told herself, as she went quietly back downstairs without disturbing the reading pair. *Maybe I'm being too hardline.*

She got almost immediate proof that she wasn't. She had gone back into the kitchen, inspired by Quinn's researches into her freezer and wondering what other goodies might be lurking back there for tomorrow's dinner. She had just started rummaging when she heard something in the backyard.

At first she thought it might be Jamie Wright. Ted's young stepbrother sometimes sneaked out of the house in the evenings to smoke cigarettes in peace, away from Ted's disapproving presence. Carrie had always found Ted Wright overbearing and self-righteous, and she didn't blame Jamie for wanting a break from him.

But this noise sounded different. It was closer to the house than Jamie usually came, for one thing. Carrie closed the freezer door and went quickly into the foyer, walking as silently as she could. Her mind was echoing with the high-pitched sound of the breaking glass in the playroom before dawn this morning, and her heart was beating fast at the thought of how vulnerable this big house was to anyone lurking outside.

Whoever it was, they didn't lurk for long. Carrie saw the dark outline of a person standing just outside the big French windows at the back of the house, and heard the quick scrape of a match. The sound she'd been dreading—the sudden shattering of glass—stopped her in her tracks. Seconds later, the room seemed to explode in flame.

At first the only things burning were the heavy velvet curtains that lined the back foyer wall. But they went up quickly, with a hungry roar. The sudden blaze of light made everything in the room look alien, threatening.

"Quinn!" She shouted his name at top volume, not sure whether she was accusing him or calling for his help.

The flames had leapt from one set of curtains to the next, and the weird glow in the room was getting brighter. For a few awful seconds Carrie felt rooted to the spot, unable to do anything but watch the disaster growing around her. The light from the fire was making huge shadows on the foyer walls, and the way they moved and flickered made Carrie feel as if she were surrounded by menacing specters who had come here to turn her life into chaos.

It was the thought of Davey that snapped her out of her state of shock. She spun around and dashed for the playroom door, calling Davey's name, and Quinn's. At the foot of the staircase, she nearly collided with Quinn's big frame, heading fast in the other direction.

"Call the fire department," he said tightly, pausing just long enough to grab her shoulders briefly. "And get Davey out of here."

She heard Davey's frightened wail from upstairs, and fought against an answering wave of panic in her chest. "I'm coming, sweetheart," she called. "Just a minute, okay?"

There was a phone by her bed. She ran for it, and punched out the number for the fire department. By the time she'd finished gasping out her address to the dispatcher, Davey had joined her, huddling against her in his pajamas, wide-eyed with fear.

"Is it a bomb?"

Carrie kept a hand firmly on his shoulders as she hurried him out of the room and down the stairs. "I don't know, honey." She heard doors slamming and realized that Quinn had had the presence of mind to seal off the foyer, to keep the fire contained. "The fire truck's coming. We just have to get out of the house and wait for them to get here."

Part of her was clamoring to go back inside, to help Quinn with whatever he was doing to fight the blazing fire in the front hallway. But that would mean leaving Davey alone, or taking him with her.

She couldn't imagine doing either one. What if the attacker came back, and Davey was alone on the lawn? The thought of leaving her little boy unprotected made her cringe inside. She couldn't leave him, no matter what.

And she couldn't stand the thought of having him see part of his house in flames. She remembered her own childhood nightmares, the ones where she'd been alone in this house and threatened by fire or monsters or worse.

Since her father's death, Carrie had turned the small annex into a cozy home within the big house, to combat the sense that she and Davey were rattling around here all by themselves. She didn't want to undo that by exposing her son to the horrific sight of the foyer burning, with hungry flames casting those otherworldly shadows on the walls and ceiling.

So she held tight to him, and willed the fire department to hurry up, and prayed that Quinn would be all right until help arrived. She heard the sirens in the distance within minutes, and by the time the driveway was filled with chugging vehicles and flashing lights, her neighbors were on the scene as well.

One of the first to arrive was Eugene Prestiss. She heard him calling to her as he hurried across the lawn, sounding anxious and determined. *Thank God,* she thought. Gene could take care of Davey, while she went to make sure Quinn was okay.

It wasn't until afterward that she realized how focused her mind was on Quinn's safety. It should have been the house she was most worried about, but all she could think of was the way Quinn had raced into the heart of that growing inferno all by himself.

He wasn't by himself now. When Carrie had turned Davey over to her neighbor and hurried around the back of the house, she saw that the firefighters had already hooked up their hose and were spraying the burning French doors with a fierce stream of water. Several people were carrying pieces of furniture out onto the lawn, but she couldn't see Quinn among them.

When she tried to move closer to the house, a man in a yellow rubber firefighter's suit stopped her. "Stay back, Ms. St. John," he said. "Fire's not out yet."

"Have you seen a tall man with dark hair and blue eyes?" Carrie couldn't help asking. "He was in the foyer when you all arrived."

The firefighter grinned. "You mean that crazy guy who was trying to beat out the flames all by himself with a Persian carpet?"

The Persian carpet had been one of old Dr. St. John's greatest treasures. At the moment, Carrie couldn't have cared less. "That's the crazy guy," she said. "Have you seen him anywhere?"

"Last I saw, he was out behind those trees trying to get his breath back." The man nodded toward the kitchen annex. "I'm going to have to get you to move, ma'am. That stream of water's starting to head this way."

There was something nightmarish about the whole scene, Carrie thought. Smoke and spraying water roiled through the foyer, and through the open front door there were flashes of orange and yellow from the lights on the firefighters' trucks. Shapes moved through the clouded atmosphere like dark ghosts, and Carrie's mind was filled with the image of another dark shape—Quinn's—doubled over and gasping for breath somewhere behind the house.

When she went looking for him, though, he wasn't there where the firefighter had seen him. And before she could look elsewhere, she found herself surrounded by people asking questions, wanting to know what had happened, insisting that she examine the damage with them.

It wasn't nearly as bad as she'd feared. The French doors at the back of the foyer were ruined, and the water hadn't done the wooden parquet floor any good. But there was no structural damage, and Quinn's fast thinking in closing the other doors into the foyer meant that surprisingly little smoke had found its way into the rest of the house.

But where was Quinn now? Carrie had seen Chief Leo LaPlante arrive along with one of his men, but they seemed to have gone again. Had Quinn left with them? Would he really just leave like that, without telling her?

She'd spent ten years convincing herself that Quinn McAllister was a man capable of the cruelest kind of betrayal. And now, to her amazement, she found that she couldn't believe he would go across town without letting her know first.

You're letting yourself trust him again, she warned herself as she went in search of her son and Eugene Prestiss. She shook her head, willing the treacherous thoughts of Quinn away.

She found Davey sobered by what had happened, but insistent that he wanted to stay in the house now that the fire department had decided it was safe. And Eugene Prestiss was just as insistent that he stick around "to keep an eye on the place." Carrie accepted the offer gratefully, and made sure that both Davey and Gene were settled comfortably in the annex over the playroom. When she'd satisfied herself that there were no more firefighters or concerned neighbors on the property, she could finally turn her attention back to her search for Quinn.

She'd glimpsed a light from somewhere in the second floor hall. It was from the bathroom that she and Davey had used after last night's attack. Carrie marveled at how innocent the window-breaking seemed now, compared with the sodden, blackened mess in the foyer.

"Quinn?" She called his name softly. "Are you up here?"

"Yeah." The single syllable was rough, and heavy.

"Are you okay?"

"I'm fine." She heard the gentle sound of water trickling into the sink basin, contrasting with the roughness of Quinn's voice. He sounded as weary as she felt, or maybe wearier. And something in his tone made her think he was hoping she wouldn't come any closer.

That only made her more determined to see if he was all right. She stepped into the doorway, and caught her breath.

Quinn had stripped off his blue flannel shirt, and was standing next to the sink. He had obviously been washing away the traces of soot she could see on his face and arms. He held a washcloth in his hand, and his hair looked damp, as though he'd run his hands through it not long ago.

None of that was what stopped Carrie's heart, though. It was the sheer male beauty of him, the power and strength of that bare upper body and the silent eloquence of his aching blue eyes. His shoulders were harder, more heavily muscled than she remembered. But his stomach was as flat as it had been ten years ago, and the point of his collarbone met just as seductively at the base of his neck.

She could see his pulse beating there, quick and strong. She could feel her own pulse rate answering as she started to breathe again.

On the one unforgettable night they had spent discovering each other's bodies, she had placed her open mouth over that pulsing spot. She had tasted the clean warmth of his skin, with passion pounding just beneath it. He had been all hers in that moment, every bone and sinew and muscle in that magnificent body of his.

Her eyes moved downward, drawn by the subtle slant of the hair that feathered across his broad chest. It drew her gaze toward the worn waistband of his jeans, to the way those jeans rode his hipbones, loosely, enticingly. She remembered the way their bodies had felt against each other a couple of days ago. Knowing she had kindled the hunger she had seen in his eyes and felt at his loins had been far more seductive than anything another man might have said or done to excite her. It was exciting her all over again now.

"How's Davey doing?"

The question slowed her racing heart, but not much. "He's okay," she said. "Gene Prestiss offered to stay in the room next to Davey's, and I took him up on it."

"Good." Quinn nodded slowly, not taking his eyes off hers.

At first she thought that intense blue gaze meant he was lost in the same swirling memories and desires that she was struggling with. After a moment, though, she realized there was some other reason for it.

He was trying to keep her from looking at the rest of him.

Carrie frowned. She wasn't sure why she was so certain of that, but something in his expression told her it was

true. There was something he didn't want her to see, and
he was locking his steely blue eyes on hers to keep her from
looking for it.

Taking in a slow breath, Carrie let her eyes rove over his
bare upper body again. She spotted it almost immediately.

There was a long gash starting just behind his right ear
and scraping a trail across his neck. It didn't look deep, but
it had to hurt, she was sure.

"Quinn, what happened?" She moved forward, ignoring the frown that told her not to.

"It's all right, Carrie. You don't have to start sounding
like somebody's mom."

"I *am* somebody's mom—though not yours, fortunately." She'd been afraid of this, when she'd seen him
dashing into the room full of flames a couple of hours ago.
Quinn could be daring to the point of recklessness, as she
knew only too well.

"It's shallow. I'll survive. I was just trying to—get it
cleaned up a little."

He twisted as he spoke, trying to reach the cut with the
hand that held the washcloth.

"How did it happen?"

"I was leaning forward, trying to beat some of the
flames out with the carpet, and one of those damned cur-
tain rods let go right above me. Fortunately, it wasn't the
end that was on fire."

The thought of how much danger he'd been in made
Carrie's heart race even faster. Their closeness now only
added to a driving rhythm inside her that she was finding
it harder and harder to deny.

She had started to reach out for the washcloth, to demand that he let her help him reach the difficult spot, when
something else occurred to her. The back of his neck
shouldn't have been *that* hard for him to reach. But the
way he held his big upper body, twisted at the waist and

straining for the place where he'd been cut, made her think he was in pain from some other cause.

She was standing close to his right side, in front of the sink. It was easy to take a step to one side and get a full view of his broad torso.

He was just as sexy and strong as she remembered him. But his body wasn't as perfect as it had been ten years ago. The scar tissue that criss-crossed his left side just above his waist was harsh and white against the tanned smoothness of the rest of his skin.

This must be the reason for the way he hesitated whenever he stood up suddenly, and for the startled manner in which he'd pulled away from her the day they'd found themselves in each other's arms. She must have pressed against that still-tender wound, she thought, hurting him without meaning to.

She put out a hand, slowly, and felt him quiver when her fingertips met his skin. He was holding himself very still, as if she were hurting him all over again. She knew she wasn't; her exploration was as gentle as she could make it, contrasting the damaged skin with the warm strength of the flesh next to it.

Quinn stayed motionless while she moved her hand over him. She seemed to be asking silent questions, acquainting herself with this part of him that she hadn't known before, and finally resting her palm softly over his scars, looking intently at the place where her small hand touched his damaged body.

He wouldn't have been surprised to discover that the wound had disappeared when she took her hand away. God, he'd dreamed of Carrie doing exactly this, soothing the pain he still felt from the bullet that had nearly killed him, healing the nagging presence that he carried around with him always.

He was already far more aroused than he knew was wise, just standing this close to her in the quiet room. Now there was something more than just physical arousal racing through his body. There was longing, and gratitude, and a crazy wish that this silent moment of peace could go on forever and ever.

It couldn't, of course. He'd known since he'd first decided to come back here that he wasn't going to be able to hide his recent history from her for very long.

She was pushing him to explain it now. "Tell me what happened," she said.

She was starting to move away, and suddenly Quinn couldn't stand the thought of it. He reached up quickly and put his hand over her wrist, anchoring her hand to his side. "I'll tell you," he said hoarsely, "if you'll stay like that just a little while longer."

Her eyes flared open, startled, maybe, by the raw need he couldn't keep out of his voice. He felt her tugging against him very slightly. She seemed to be testing her own willpower, her own ability to pull away if she chose.

And then she chose to stay. Quinn took in a long, relieved breath, and pulled her other arm toward him. She moved against him slowly, not trusting him, he thought, or maybe not trusting herself. He could feel her heart thudding against his bare chest.

He didn't care where this was leading. He only knew he had never felt such peace, such comfort, as he did with Carrie St. John. After the pounding fear of seeing her house on fire just hours ago, surely he could be forgiven for letting himself relax in her warmth for a few minutes.

She nestled against him, and he rested his chin on the top of her head. She smelled smoky, but under that graphic reminder of the fire he caught the faint sweet scent of her skin. It was all he could do not to tighten his grip and swoop down on her seductive mouth with a kiss that would end any possibility of finishing the conversation they'd started.

But there were things he wanted to say, things he needed to get out of his system. Dragging in a shaky breath, he said, "It happened about a year ago. I got shot."

"Who shot you?" In spite of how near they were, she was still holding back slightly. He could feel it in the trembling of her limbs, and in the cautious sound of her voice. She didn't like this stuff, and he didn't blame her. He was beginning to lose the taste for it himself.

"A kid in Chicago."

"A kid? How old?"

"Fourteen."

"I see." She couldn't possibly see, Quinn knew, not without the details of the case he'd been working on, or the reasons why the kid had panicked, or how Quinn had been hoping to get the boy out of the messy situation he'd gotten into through his own youth and bravado. But maybe Carrie didn't need those details. Maybe she *did* see, more than he wanted her to.

"What happened to the boy?"

"He's dead." No point in sugarcoating it, Quinn knew. And somehow, having lied so unforgivably to Carrie ten years ago, he wanted to be absolutely honest with her now.

"Did you kill him?"

"No. One of his so-called buddies shot him, because they found out he'd been talking to the cops."

"Meaning you."

"Yes."

He knew exactly what she was thinking. Her twin brother had died, shot at the age of eighteen, most likely because he had been friends with Quinn. Suddenly Quinn felt like the angel of death, haunting this once-quiet house in small-town Illinois.

The anger and disgust he felt at himself still weren't enough to move him away from Carrie. He needed this, he thought desperately. He needed to be with her. He needed it now more than ever, now that he'd discovered they were drawn together by the bond of their child. If there was any hope of healing his own painful memories, he knew he would find it here, and nowhere else.

"How bad was it?" She was tracing the outline of his scar again, with a feather-light touch that made him quiver all over.

"Pretty bad."

"Damn it, Quinn, will you stop being so cryptic? I want to know, or I wouldn't have asked."

There was a reluctant amusement in her voice, and Quinn was so astonished at the sound of it that he grinned down at her. The quick flash of the smile she was trying to hide made him feel better than he'd felt in a very long time.

"I nearly died," he said. Even the grim words couldn't quite erase his sudden hope that Carrie was beginning to let him back into her life again, at least a little. "I was in the hospital for six weeks, and I'm really only getting back on my feet now."

She shook her head without speaking. Quinn leaned forward—he couldn't stop himself—and kissed the glossy curve of her shoulder-length brown hair. He wondered what would happen if he got any more aroused than this.

"I know what you're thinking," he said. He didn't want to say it out loud. She was thinking about her brother's death, and the threat to her son, and her house, and her quiet life here, and about the danger in Quinn's job, past, present and probably future, too.

Suddenly it all felt like too much to face. Quinn was bone-weary from the effort he'd put into beating back the fire in the hallway, and at the same time, he felt light and gloriously alive because he was holding the woman of his dreams so close to him. The combination made him say things out loud that he ordinarily would have buried deep inside himself.

"Could we...leave all of that for the morning?" he said. "I want to find a way to sort this all out, Carrie. God knows I've been trying. But sometimes—I just get so damn tired. Sometimes I wish I could just be with you and forget that yesterday or tomorrow even existed.''

She didn't answer, but something in her suddenly upturned gaze made him think she shared the same impossible hope. The mere idea of it was enough to sweep everything else aside as Quinn lowered his head to kiss her.

Chapter 7

In saner moments, Carrie could have recited every one of the reasons why she shouldn't be doing this. But right now she wasn't sane. The pleading she'd heard in Quinn's ragged voice—the sound that said *Can't we just pretend none of this ever happened?*—was something she knew only too well.

She knew it was crazy. She knew she would have to come to her senses before long. But just for now, just for this moment, it was too tempting to give in to that plea, too tempting to imagine that nothing stood in the way of the passion that had always flared between them.

She met Quinn's kiss with an intensity she'd never expected to feel again outside her most erotic dreams. She matched his rough hunger with a fierceness that seemed to astonish him as much as it did herself.

She could taste the danger in his kiss. She wasn't quite so far gone that she'd forgotten he was an intruder, a gunslinger come to town with trouble on his mind.

But when his mouth found hers, that danger turned to magic, dark and seductive. And Carrie's blood turned to liquid fire.

She reached her hands into his damp, tousled hair, pulling herself up toward him. His strong arms surrounded her, gliding over her, demanding the surrender of all the secrets of her body.

The faint smoky scent of his hair and skin only deepened the mystery of him. How could he be so rough and so gentle at the same time? He was kissing her as though his whole soul were pouring through him into her body, filling her, leaving no room for anything but the bottomless hunger she could feel in him. And yet he seemed attuned to her smallest response.

She groaned out loud at the sensation of his hands sliding over her thighs, and back up into the small of her back, pressing their bodies together, making his own responses achingly clear. And at the sound of her voice, Quinn lifted his head and let loose something halfway between laughter and erotic satisfaction.

Nothing had pleased him more than her pleasure. She remembered that all of a sudden, and realized how hard she'd worked at forgetting it until now. Quinn had been so stirred by her responses, and so intent on finding out what excited her.

There was a big cedar chest against the bathroom wall, with a long floral print cushion covering it. Quinn wrapped one arm tightly around Carrie now and swept her along with him as he lowered himself onto the seat with Carrie across his thighs.

"I want to see all of you." His voice was throaty and urgent. "I've wanted this for so long, Carrie. . . ."

It had been forever. And it had only been yesterday, she thought, that she'd heard him say those same words. *Let me see all of you.* First his eyes, then his hands, finally his lips, had worshipped her whole body as she'd peeled her layers of clothing off, trembling as though their mutual desire were a strong wind and she was on the point of letting it carry her away.

The remembered ecstasy of that moment had sometimes wakened her from a sound sleep, her heart pounding with the power of her own wanton fantasies. The temptation of it was too much to ignore now. She wanted the fire that Quinn—and only Quinn—could ignite inside her.

She felt his powerful thigh muscles shifting under her as he balanced her body on his lap and took hold of the lower edge of her sweater. She raised her arms, shaken by the hunger that raced through her at the thought of being naked with Quinn again. In one smooth motion he had pulled her sweater and the turtleneck she wore under it clear of her head. The discarded garments joined his own blue shirt in a pile on the bathroom floor.

Carrie moaned again as he kissed her neck, her collarbone, the soft flesh of her earlobe. She could feel the desperation in him, the need for her. But at the same time she sensed him reining himself in, making the moment last. That strength of will that had always frightened her a little was working now to extend the exquisite pleasure of discovering each other's bodies all over again.

She wanted to lose herself in the sensation of his strong arms gliding over hers, gathering her close to him. A shudder ran through her as he ran one big hand over the taut outline of her breast through her lacy brassiere.

Her next shudder rippled through her whole frame. Quinn had slid those knowing fingers around to her spine and found her bra clasp. In one slow and efficient motion, he had snapped it open.

Carrie arched her spine and shed the lacy undergarment. She had a sense of diving into a provocative and pleasurable place where anything might happen. Quinn's hands covered her breasts, and she cried out loud with the eroticism of it. She could feel her nipples hardening even more tightly beneath his broad palms.

"Quinn..."

She gasped out his name, not sure whether she was begging him for more or simply marveling at the way Quinn McAllister seemed to have remembered everything about her body. He was cradling her in his arms now, lifting her against his chest so he could kiss the hollow between her breasts. When he turned his head slightly, she could feel his tawny hair like a caressing touch against her shoulder. His tongue coaxed an even more sultry response from her nipple, luring her a little farther into that erogenous underworld where nothing mattered except pure passion.

She felt his breath warm against her skin, and gasped again as his exploring hand slid over her belly, over the waistband of her jeans, between her legs to the pulsing spot that longed to have him filling her to the point of saturation, satisfying the ache he had created inside her.

She was very close to giving up any attempt at rational thought, and she knew it. She opened her eyes and met Quinn's gaze as he lifted his head from the softness of her breast. She wasn't sure why, but something in her made her raise her hands and cup his face with them, so that she could hold this moment of contact and look deep into those eloquent blue depths.

What she saw there astonished her. Quinn looked impatient, and aroused, and... happy. There was a laughing triumph deep in his eyes that she couldn't remember ever seeing before.

She could hear it in his voice as he murmured, "I don't think there's any other woman on the planet who can make me feel this way, Carrie St. John."

He sounded amazed at his own pleasure. It made Carrie want to push that pleasure to its limits, to ease the loneliness she'd always sensed in him, to reach for the completion she was sure they could bring each other.

But this pause was letting other thoughts back in, too. She leaned back in his grip, keeping hold of his face, smoothing her finger along that long, stubborn jawline and over his full lips. He opened his mouth to caress her fingertip in a purely erotic gesture, and she felt herself starting to turn to liquid inside all over again. And by now, she was starting to wonder if that was such a good idea after all.

"We can't *possibly* do this." It was hard to get the words out when her whole body was urging her on. She made herself think of Davey, sleeping on the other side of the big house, and of the devastation that lay between this room and her son's. That was enough—almost—to calm the fire still burning in her blood.

He went suddenly still, waiting for her to speak again.

"Quinn, where are we going with this?" Carrie said with much difficulty.

He growled out an expletive that was almost too soft to hear. He turned his face away for a moment, and then lowered his lips to her soft skin again. He spoke his next words against her collarbone.

"I thought maybe into the next room," he muttered. "Where the beds are."

"You can't be serious."

"I feel too good to be serious. Carrie—"

His happiness was a sharp knife that could cut two ways, Carrie knew. She had always wanted to soften the lonely passions she could see in his eyes. But the one time she'd tried to do that, he had turned her life upside down. And he could too easily do the same thing again now.

She struggled to get her balance on the hard planes of his thighs. She knew she had to move now, before Quinn's knowing hands and mouth could devastate the self-control she'd come so close to ignoring.

"This can't happen, Quinn," she said. "I can't let myself act like an irresponsible eighteen-year-old who doesn't know the simple facts of life."

The comment stilled him again. For a moment they were both motionless, breathing hard, battling the desires that had propelled them into each other's arms so urgently.

And then Quinn seemed to marshall his own iron will. He shifted his position, easing Carrie gently to her feet. She didn't look at him as she retrieved her sweater and slid it over her head. She didn't bother with her bra. Somehow it seemed more important to counter the dangerous attraction of being half-naked with Quinn as soon as she could.

He hadn't moved from the cedar chest when she finally turned around. He was leaning forward, elbows on his knees, and he had run his big hands through his hair, holding on to his head as if he were trying to contain everything that was running through it. Carrie felt a bolt of pure pity for his loneliness, his strength. And then she took a deep breath that she hoped would summon up some needed strength of her own. It almost worked.

"You're right." Quinn's voice was deep, and rough. "I let things go further than I meant to."

"We both let things go too far." She wasn't about to let him shoulder all the blame, not when she'd been so close to plunging into those erotic depths along with him. "I'm sorry, Quinn. There's obviously still a lot of attraction kicking around between us. But making love, without even thinking about precautions, with Davey in the house, and somebody out there apparently trying to destroy my home—"

All the good reasons for staying aloof from Quinn McAllister were piling up in her mind like weapons now. If only, she thought desperately, she had some weapon she could use against the naked anguish she saw in his eyes when he looked up at her.

"I know I should leave." He seemed to be wrestling with the words, and finding that he couldn't deny how true they were. "I know I'm making things harder for you by being here. But Carrie— "

He raised his hands, as if he was hoping some convenient answer would drop into them. When it didn't, he finished, "I can't leave. I just can't, not now that I know about Davey. And if I'm going to stay, I'm going to have to find out who's responsible for the damage to your house. There isn't any other way to end the danger of it happening again. I wish there was some way around it, but I can't see one."

Neither could Carrie. She sighed, and picked up her bra from the floor. She crumpled it into a ball, as if that could counteract the way her breasts still felt, taut and tingling with the sensation of Quinn's fingers and lips teasing them into arousal.

"But you're right about all the reasons why it would be a mistake to make love right now." His brows were lowered, his face serious again, almost grim. "I won't touch you again, Carrie—unless you want me to."

She almost pointed out to him that he wasn't offering her any comfort at all. She had responded passionately, wildly, to his touch, and there wasn't any point in denying it.

But admitting it only seemed to lead to more unanswerable questions. If she said to him now, *I wanted you as much as you wanted me*, where would that leave them? For everyone's sake, it was best not to leave that dangerous door standing open.

"All right," she said quickly, moving toward the hall. "I should go check on Davey."

Quinn nodded. "After what happened to this house tonight, I'm not going to sleep at all unless I'm here keeping an eye on you," he said slowly. "Can I use one of the rooms on this floor?"

She started to protest. Having him under her roof seemed like a bad idea. But then she thought about staying here alone, or with only her elderly neighbor for support. That didn't seem very appealing, either. Quinn might not be able to prevent someone with a rock or a fire bomb from attacking the house, but if it was going to happen again, his help wouldn't be unwelcome. She didn't like to think about what might have happened tonight if he hadn't been here.

And anyway, the bald truth was that having Quinn McAllister in Stockbridge at all, even across town in a hotel room, had kept her from sleeping very well since the day he'd first turned up. How much more disturbing could it be to have him actually staying in her house?

"You can use the room at the end of the hall," she said. "I'll bring you some sheets and blankets. And Quinn..."

She knew this was crazy, given the fact that it was Quinn's presence that had caused tonight's fire. But she couldn't forget the way he'd dashed headlong into it, or the long scrape that still darkened his powerful neck and shoulder. When she thought about the risks he'd taken—

"Thank you for what you did tonight," she said. "Not everyone would have acted as fast, or done as much."

She left the room before he could put the surprise on his face into words. When she came back with the sheets and blankets a few minutes later, the shower was running in the bathroom and Quinn was nowhere in sight, a fact for which she was decidedly grateful.

Quinn lay in the narrow bed and listened to the twittering of birds in the bushes outside the house.

He'd stayed overnight in this house once before, the night Davey had been created. He hadn't expected to sleep much this time, between thinking of the magic he and Carrie had shared and then lost, and listening for suspicious noises in the building, and battling his own stubborn desires to cross to the other side of the big place and demand that Carrie acknowledge that he had a right to be not only in her house but in her bed, as well.

In spite of all that, he'd slept like a child.

Maybe he was just plain exhausted, he thought when he woke in the early morning to the sound of the birds. God knows, he'd been working himself hard enough in the weeks before his boss had insisted he take some time off. And since he'd been back in Stockbridge, sleep had been almost impossible to come by. And then there had been the adrenalin spike caused by last night's fire, and the emotional tidal wave of its aftermath.

Whatever the reason, Quinn slept all night and woke actually feeling rested for the first time in a long while. He thought about getting up, but decided to wait until he heard sounds from the other part of the house. His body felt drained, and his mind was happy just to wander from idea to idea, half listening to the busy chatter of the birds in the backyard under the window.

He wasn't sure if it was dreams or memories that he drifted into. He had almost forgotten about the hushed emptiness of this enormous house early in the morning and the clear blue sky that looked so different from the sky he saw outside his apartment window in Chicago.

He recalled having the same thoughts the morning he'd wakened with Carrie in his arms and his whole body singing with the joy of having lost himself in her, body and soul. Dr. St. John had driven Carrie's twin, David, to the college he was enrolled in for the next fall. David had been having second thoughts about college, and the doctor was hoping to convince him it was a good idea.

And while they were gone, Quinn and Carrie, caught up in their feelings for each other after an end-of-the-year class party, had given in to their forbidden passions— doubly forbidden, in Quinn's case. He remembered thinking, when he woke up, that he had no right at all to feel so wonderful.

As it turned out, he was right. By that evening, David St. John was dead, and Quinn's superiors had decided it was too risky to let their agent stay in Stockbridge any longer.

Risky! The bitter irony of it still made Quinn want to laugh. After David's murder, he hadn't cared about his own safety. All he'd really cared about was the broken heart of the girl he'd loved and lied to so cruelly.

He'd thought about insisting on staying in Stockbridge and toughing it out, although that would have meant admitting to his boss how far he'd stepped outside the bounds of his job, and how badly he'd let his vulnerable heart interfere in his work.

It hadn't been the thought of the FBI's official reaction that convinced him he had to go, though. It was the look in Carrie's eyes when he'd seen her at the airport the night David had been killed.

He remembered sitting in the passenger seat of Leo LePlante's police cruiser, cursing himself and the world and trying like hell to figure out how he was going to explain this to Carrie. He had already contacted his boss and been told that his cover was now too shaky to maintain. But his job, at that moment, had been the very least of his worries.

Quinn could still recall the scene in hellishly vivid detail: the flashing lights of the ambulance; the clutch of spectators on the other side of the yellow crime-scene tape; the lonely body of the boy who had been Quinn's good friend, sprawled on the pavement at the end of the runway closest to the trees. And then, worst of all—

Carrie had come racing into the airport parking lot in the St. John family car, leaving the door hanging open, obviously terrified beyond words by the report of her twin brother's death.

I have to get to her, Quinn had thought. *I have to tell her.*

But he wasn't sure what he had to tell her, and his own uncertainty had kept him in the car, agonizing over the look on her face. What could he say? *I lied to you. This is probably my fault. I'm sorry. I loved David, too.* She would hate him for half of it, and not believe the other half.

So he'd sat and watched as someone—one of the ambulance attendants, he thought—took Carrie's shoulder and walked with her to her brother's body. The same man pointed a finger toward Quinn a few minutes later, no doubt telling Carrie who Quinn really was, and why he was really here. And Quinn had had to watch the realization that had flooded into her pretty face.

He almost hadn't been sorry that Chief LaPlante had started the engine and driven away before that realization had turned to fury or despair.

Something crashed into his thoughts, and Quinn jumped. He realized he'd drifted back to sleep, into an uneasy dream that had felt all too real. For a moment he was disoriented, and then the chattering of the birds outside reminded him where he was.

Somewhere in the house, there had been a crashing sound that had wakened him. He rolled quickly out of bed and pulled on his jeans and shirt. His gun was in its holster, carefully hidden under the jacket he'd left on a chair. He grabbed the weapon now, and stuck it in the small of his back, under the waistband of his jeans. If Carrie's nighttime visitors had come back to finish what they'd started, they would find themselves facing some more determined opposition than they'd had the last two times.

His bare feet made no sound on the wide carpeted staircase. His heart was pounding, and the dark memories he'd just been reliving were clinging to him, reminding him how high the stakes could be even in this seemingly safe and quiet little backwater. If something was threatening Carrie, or their son—

The moment he heard her voice, he knew she was fine. She sounded annoyed, and to Quinn's anxious ears, that was good news.

"If I didn't know better," she was saying, clearly and irately, "I would say this was a conspiracy to force me into dusting off that darn sewing machine. Whoever did this must have known how much I hate anything even remotely domestic."

"You like cleaning up after the day care kids." That was Davey, his voice echoing in the open space of the foyer. They were surveying the damage, Quinn realized.

"Wrong, honey." The amused tenderness that crept into her voice caught at Quinn. Damn it, she deserved to have her happy, secure life back again. And he was going to see that she got it. "I like having the day care kids around, and that's why I pick up after them. Picking up is a major part of having kids, in case you hadn't noticed."

"You mean you have to pick up after *me?*" There was feigned disbelief in Davey's voice.

Quinn leaned over the bannister in time to see Carrie good-naturedly ruffling the boy's hair. "Once or twice," she said. "Now go get washed, okay? You don't get to miss school just because we had a domestic disaster this weekend."

Somehow she was managing to turn that disaster into one more obstacle to be faced and overcome. And she was doing it with good humor. Quinn wondered how much of that was for Davey's benefit, so that the boy wouldn't be any more alarmed about the attacks on his home. If that was what was happening, Carrie was doing a skillful job of it.

The phone rang while Quinn was debating whether to break into her thoughts. She was looking doubtfully at the ruined windows and the sodden, half-burned masses of velvet that had once covered them. At the very least, the foyer was going to need a lot of cosmetic repair. Carrie seemed almost glad to have to answer the phone as an excuse to stop contemplating the wet, sooty mess.

By the time she was done, Quinn had dashed up to his room and finished dressing. He decided to leave the gun upstairs this time. He had a suspicion Carrie wouldn't be any too happy to know he was carrying it.

The wry look was gone from her face as she came back into the foyer. She watched Quinn coming down the big staircase, and said, "If things go on this way, I'm going to have lots of time on my hands to spend fixing the house."

"What do you mean?"

"That was the third call this morning from parents saying they don't feel comfortable sending their kids to day care here while my house seems to be under attack."

Quinn cursed softly as he joined her on the main floor. He hadn't foreseen this.

Judging from the look on her face, Carrie had. "At least this last caller was honest about it," she said. "The first two had some vague excuses about their kids suddenly not feeling well."

"How can you sound so matter-of-fact about it?"

She lifted a shoulder in a slight shrug. "It doesn't surprise me," she said. "I wouldn't send Davey to a place where there seemed to be even the slightest danger, either. How long do you think it's going to take you to finish what you've started?"

The blunt question startled him, and so did the purposeful hardness in her brown eyes. "It's impossible to say," he told her. "I'm going to push things as hard as I can, but whether I get results depends on how the people involved react."

"Who *are* the people involved?"

"The same as they were ten years ago. Your neighbor Ted Wright, and his pals Steven Solidad and Nelson Delaine. That little clique David wanted so badly to be a part of.''

He thought she was repressing whatever her instinctive response had been. Her level stare wavered slightly, then regained its self-possession.

"As I'm sure you've figured out, I don't need the income from my day care business to make ends meet," she said. "I started it when Davey was little, when I was home with a child anyway. I looked after my friend Susannah's two kids when she moved back here and went back to work, and I've expanded things to the point where I have eight or ten kids here every weekday. My father left enough money that I don't have to work, but I do this because it keeps me connected to the community, especially the parents and children in it.''

He knew why she was telling him this, and he didn't really want to hear any more. But he made himself stand and listen anyway. He thought of the uneasy dream he'd just wakened from, and knew he deserved this, and more.

"There was a time when I felt like a ghost in this town," she said firmly, insisting that he understand her meaning. "The kind of friends I had in school weren't the kind who were used to unwed mothers turning up in their midst. And the other teenaged mothers around here were busy gloating that Dr. St. John's daughter had gotten into such deep trouble. When Davey was born, I felt almost alone in the world.''

"Carrie—"

She lifted her chin, and he saw that the hardness of her eyes was covering something deeper, something that looked all too much like hostility. She'd been rethinking things, he realized, since their encounter last night.

"Let me finish, Quinn. What I'm telling you is that I value the place I've made for myself in Stockbridge. I'm proud of the fact that people trust me to look after their kids. It wasn't exactly easy getting to where I am now, and

I don't intend to give it up. So I'd appreciate it if you would do whatever you can to speed up that investigation of yours. I want my life back, preferably in one piece. Now, do you want some coffee?''

Quinn wasn't sure what to say. *I'm sorry* wasn't nearly enough. And he couldn't—wouldn't—promise anything he wasn't sure he could deliver on. He intended to solve the mystery of David's death, but as far as predicting how or when he might have an answer, or what that answer might be—

He was still in the dark, and he seemed to have lost whatever progress he'd made toward softening Carrie's feelings for him. And when he looked at the damage that someone had done to her home, he wasn't sure he could blame her for wanting to keep her distance again.

So he said yes to coffee, and followed her into the kitchen, trying to ignore the feminine swing of her hips in those tight blue jeans, and to concentrate instead on how he was going to go about finding answers to all the things they both still needed to know.

Chapter 8

"Definitely a homemade bomb of some kind." Leo LaPlante poked at the few blackened scraps of plastic on his desk. "Kids are making them these days in soda bottles. We've had a few mailboxes blown up that way."

"Any chance of tracing what it was made out of?" Quinn knew it was a long shot, but it might be worth checking with the local hardware stores to see if any of his three suspects had been buying the raw materials for a bomb lately.

"I sent it up to the lab, although there wasn't much left of it. I would have saved it for your boys, except you said you were working on your own on this one." Leo raised a bushy red eyebrow at Quinn. "You making any progress?"

"Well, I've obviously got things stirred up. Does that qualify as progress?" Quinn flicked a fingertip at the nearest half-melted plastic scrap, and clenched his jaw at the memory of the panic that had raced through him when he'd heard the dull roar from the foyer on Saturday night.

"Can you pull the file on David St. John's death for me, Leo? I'd like to have a look at it."

"Sure." Leo pulled a pad of forms out of a desk drawer and scribbled something on the top sheet. "I can't let it go out of the station, since you're not here on anybody's official business. But if you want to make copies of anything, you can use our machine, as long as you're discreet about it."

"Thanks."

"Hey." There was determination in Leo's eyes. "I don't like the idea of anybody throwing bombs into Carrie's house any more than you do, Quinn. And since you've started this thing, you might as well finish it as quick as you can." He handed the requisition across the desk. "Give this to Bennie, out front. He'll get the file for you."

Everybody seemed to be trying to hurry him up this morning, Quinn thought, as he waited for the police clerk to find the file on David St. John's murder. He had a strong suspicion that Leo, like Carrie, would be happiest if Quinn did what he'd come for and then cleared out of Stockbridge for good.

He thought about how it had felt to sit next to his son's bed two nights ago, reading Davey's favorite book out loud. And he shuddered slightly at the remembered pleasure of running his palms over Carrie's soft skin, and hearing her moan. He'd been shaken by the need to make her fall apart in his arms, if she would let him take her that far again.

He shook his head slightly, trying to keep his own feelings under some kind of control. Compared with the thought of leaving Stockbridge behind again, solving the mystery of David's murder was starting to seem like the easy part.

Ted Wright hadn't stinted on decorating his office. The place was tastefully painted in dark greens and tans, with expensive-looking framed prints on the wall. The couch where Quinn was sitting looked like a genuine antique, newly reupholstered, and the deep-pile carpet under his feet was as lush as Wright's own neatly manicured front lawn.

The only thing wrong with the place, from Quinn's point of view, was that the lawyer had been letting him sit in the waiting room for nearly an hour.

"I'm sorry, Mr. McAllister," the receptionist said again, noticing Quinn's obvious impatience. She was classy, like the office, and she even managed to sound like she was genuinely sorry to keep him waiting, which Quinn assumed wasn't the case. He suspected Ted had given her instructions to let Quinn cool his heels for as long as possible. "Attorney Wright really can't see people without appointments, unless it's an emergency. He keeps a very busy schedule."

She'd said the same thing three times before. Quinn looked at his watch, and said he'd wait another ten minutes, and would she remind Attorney Wright that this was important, and that it would only take a few minutes of his extremely valuable time.

"I'll try, sir."

While she was in Wright's inner office, Quinn looked through the photocopies he'd made at the police station. He'd copied the whole David St. John file, not knowing what he was going to need, but the part of it that he was paying attention to right now was the alibis of three young men: Steven Solidad, Nelson Delaine and Ted Wright.

Of the three, Wright had always been the ringleader. He'd been the one to decide what was cool and what wasn't, and his friends Delaine and Solidad—and his would-be friend, David St. John—had tended to follow his lead. Quinn had been pretty sure then that experimenting with cocaine had been Wright's idea. And that made him Quinn's prime suspect now.

Quinn had been whisked back to home base in Chicago by the time the grim business of investigating David's death had taken place. But judging by the contents of the file, the Stockbridge Police Department had quickly agreed with the FBI's opinion on the killing.

Quinn's superiors had believed that it had been David who had been getting hold of a small amount of the cocaine that was being shipped through Stockbridge's airport, and had been selling it locally. They reasoned that once the mob had cottoned onto David, his death had been inevitable.

Quinn's protests against the idea weren't taken very seriously. *You got too close to the kid to be objective.* He could still hear his boss's words. *Let us wrap this one up, Quinn. It was your first time out. It's not easy, getting the hang of undercover work.*

So Quinn's own suspicions about Wright, Delaine and Solidad hadn't been acted on, although it appeared from the file that Leo LaPlante had at least had statements taken from the three. Quinn read them over again now, spreading his photocopies out on the glass-topped table in Ted's waiting room.

According to the detective's report, Ted Wright had been at a family birthday party the evening David had been shot. Nelson Delaine had been at a wrestling match. And Steven Solidad had had no concrete alibi, but had said he was home alone watching television.

The alibis hadn't been checked—why would they be, when everyone was convinced the mob was behind the shooting? But Quinn intended to check them now, if he could still follow these ten-year-old clues to any kind of conclusion.

Ten minutes later, Ted was still too busy to answer the simple question Quinn wanted to put to him. The secretary apologized again, and promised to give Attorney Wright the note Quinn said he would leave. He wrote:

Whose birthday party were you at the night David St. John was killed?

He couldn't imagine Ted Wright would be happy to be questioned this way. And that suited Quinn just fine. Carrie had urged him to hustle this investigation along, and Leo had suggested the same thing. And making his prime suspect mad was a proven way of getting things moving, Quinn knew from experience.

As he got back onto his motorcycle, he paused to ask himself whether his suspicions of Ted were colored by the proprietary way the man had talked about Carrie. *Don't let your feelings get in your way again, McAllister,* he told himself grimly. *You've got to keep your head clear this time.*

The problem was that there were so many more feelings to complicate things now. When Quinn thought about Carrie being with another man, maybe marrying someone, about Davey having a stepfather, his vision blurred with something between anger and an aching sense of loss.

You can't lose what you don't even have. He kicked the bike into life and adjusted his chin strap, trying not to think about how his big black helmet had looked surrounding Davey's young face the first day he'd been here. The roar of the motorcycle's engine as he pulled away from the curb was satisfyingly loud, as though some of Quinn's own frustration had found its way into the sound and was proclaiming itself in the cool November air.

"I saw you playing basketball with Jamie Wright." Carrie turned the heat on under the leftover pot of soup, and looked up a muffin recipe that she had made once without major catastrophe. She'd almost forgotten, until Quinn had cooked dinner on Sunday night, how good the house smelled when something was baking.

It was Tuesday, two days after someone had thrown a homemade bomb into her house. Quinn had been working hard since yesterday morning, and she'd hardly seen him except at dinnertime. He had brought home hamburgers and fries for the three of them last night, but tonight Carrie had announced that she would take care of the food. She wanted to make the point that she had managed to feed herself and Davey quite adequately—if not always elegantly—the whole time Quinn had been absent from their lives.

She was worried that Davey was already starting to act as though that absence might be over. Slowly, tentatively, the boy was opening up to his father, asking Quinn's opinion on things, sharing the small details of his day over dinner.

And Quinn was responding in the same manner he'd used the day Davey had demanded to know if Quinn was really his father. Watching the two of them together, conversing seriously, Carrie hadn't had the heart to break in and interrupt. But she was becoming more and more afraid of what would happen when Quinn disappeared—as he inevitably would—from Davey's life.

So she was keeping her own distance as resolutely as she could. It still made her heart flutter to walk past Quinn as he sat tilted back in the old kitchen chair watching her cook, but she refused to let him know that. Instead, she kept the conversation firmly focused on what he'd been doing. And the last thing she'd seen him doing was tossing a basketball with Jamie Wright, her neighbor's young stepbrother.

He was nodding now, looking at her with that blue gaze that always made her think he knew more than he was saying. "Seems like a nice kid," he said. "I gather his parents pretty much booted him out last summer."

Carrie couldn't keep the disapproval out of her voice as she pulled two bowls from the cupboard and started measuring flour and sugar into them. "Jamie *is* a nice kid," she said. "But his parents had some very old-fashioned ideas about raising him—very strict curfews, no pocket money, things like that."

"Sounds like your own father, with David."

She'd been hoping he wouldn't point out the obvious parallels. But since he had, she refused to avoid the subject. "At least with my father there was some genuine love behind all those strict rules. But Jamie's parents—well, they seem to want a model child without going to the trouble of helping him grow up that way."

She stirred her dry ingredients together and moved to the refrigerator to get the eggs. Quinn's long silence was beginning to disturb her when he finally spoke.

"I haven't really told you," he said slowly, "how much I admire the way you've raised Davey."

Carrie stiffened instinctively. He was trespassing onto something that had been hers alone for a long time now. Her father had been a kind but distant grandparent until his death a few years ago. And there had been no one else to interfere with her parenting of her son. "I'm not looking for your approval," she said.

"I know you're not. I just wanted you to know that I'm glad you welcomed his birth the way you did, instead of resenting it the way you probably had a right to."

"There was no point in resenting Davey. None of what happened was his fault. I put my resentment where it belonged, Quinn, right on your doorstep."

Somehow it made it harder to keep on resenting him when he accepted her comment with nothing more than a slow nod. It would have been easier to stay mad at him if he'd argued, or bullied her the way he had that first afternoon in the foyer.

This matter-of-fact acceptance of her anger was difficult to deal with. Carrie turned her attention back to her recipe.

"So why are you making friends with Jamie?" The thought of the kid next door made her feel stronger again. If Quinn was befriending another lonely teenager just to make use of him in an investigation—

It sounded as though he were. "I've been checking out alibis," he said. "I wanted to be able to prove what those three guys were doing when David was killed."

"Jamie was only eight years old at the time. What could he remember about it?"

"Plenty, as it turns out." Quinn rocked his chair forward and stood up. "Do you realize you're about to mix all that together without adding any baking soda?"

"I thought I did."

"You got the box out and then put it away again, but you didn't use it."

"Oh." Carrie checked the recipe. "Well, it only calls for a little bit. I'm sure it won't—"

"The muffins won't rise without it. Trust me."

"I thought it was baking *powder* that made things rise."

"They both do."

"No wonder I get them confused."

His sudden grin caught her by surprise. The smile transformed his face, erasing that somber stare and hinting that somewhere, deep inside the difficult man that Quinn McAllister had become, there was still a boy who could laugh without thinking of tomorrow, who hadn't given up wishing for the love and warmth he'd never really known.

That flashing grin shot straight to Carrie's heart. She found herself breathing faster, drawn into the amusement she could hear in his deep voice.

"You get them confused because you're thinking about something other than cooking," he told her. "You're always thinking about people, not ingredients. It's one of the most endearing things about you. And it also makes you a terrible cook."

She didn't know what it was that made her laugh, his blunt words or the compliment buried inside them or the way his blue eyes changed when he smiled. She couldn't fight her own impulses this time. Quinn's heart-stopping grin was more than she could resist, just as it always had been.

"I figure if I try enough things, *some* of them are bound to come out right," she said.

He didn't smile this time. For some reason her light-hearted comment seemed to sober him again.

They were standing side by side at the counter, looking down into the mixing bowl where Carrie's latest culinary disaster was about to happen. And then, before she could react, Quinn pulled her toward him with an urgency that caught her completely by surprise.

She was still caught in the spell of his sudden laughter, still wishing—as she'd wished so often when she'd known him before—that there was some way to coax more laughter out of the closely guarded depths of Quinn McAllister. He had already gotten past her own safeguards now, and she was reveling in the strength of his arms wrapping themselves around her before she could think of all the good reasons why she shouldn't be letting this happen.

It wasn't an erotic embrace, although Carrie could feel his heart beating hard against his chest, and her own body was quivering into life deep inside as he held her. But he seemed to have reached for her because of something else, and for a confused few seconds she couldn't imagine what it might be.

And then she heard his deep voice at her ear, sounding gruff and strangely reluctant, as if he had fought against putting this into words. "Don't ever change, all right, Carrie?" It was a plea, pure and simple. "Whatever happens, please don't ever change."

She was still confused, unable to force her concentration beyond her body's hungry response to the way

Quinn's hips rode against her, and the unmistakable swell of his own arousal. What did he mean, *don't ever change?* They had been talking about cooking, for God's sake.

And then she remembered Quinn, ten years ago, telling her that her sunny faith in tomorrow, her belief that things could always change for the better, gave him a kind of hope he'd never had before.

He had needed that hope, she thought now. He had told her he loved her for it. And then he had done his damnedest to take it away from her.

There was still no guarantee that he wouldn't do the same thing all over again. If Carrie let herself be drawn into his hunger and his passion a second time, she wasn't sure her heart would be able to stand the pain of losing him again.

She *was* sure that Davey's nine-year-old heart wouldn't be up to the strain. And the thought of her son gave her the will to step away from Quinn and push her disordered hair back off her forehead. Part of her was still longing for him, longing to have him kiss her again, to feel his hands all over her the way they had been on Sunday night, intimate and gentle and sure. But that part of her wasn't the same as the part that had a small son to protect and a life to get on with after Quinn McAllister was gone.

And the phrase he'd used—*whatever happens*—made her uneasy. What *was* going to happen, now that Quinn had forced this old, dark business back into the daylight again?

She kept her voice as level as she could as she said, "If you mean don't ever change as in don't ever stop being a terrible cook, I don't think you have to worry. Did you notice any other ticking bombs, Quinn, or will these muffins work once I've added the baking soda?"

'Ticking bomb' was all too accurate a description of what Quinn was in her world, and by the way his serious expression settled back over his features, he seemed to know it, too. He didn't go back to his chair, but took up a stand on the other side of the table, arms crossed, brows lowered, a brooding presence in the comfortable room.

"Ted Wright's alibi for the night David was killed was that he was at a family birthday party." He plunged back into the grim business of her twin brother's death without a preface. "Wright himself keeps finding reasons to stall me off, but I happened to find out from Jamie—who's got a list of family grievances longer than he is tall—that it was Jamie's eighth birthday party Ted was supposedly at that night. And big brother Ted, it turns out, was a no-show. Jamie was hurt by it at the time, and hasn't forgotten it."

Carrie paused as she mixed the muffin batter together. Quinn was moving to one of the cupboards now, pulling out the muffin pan she'd forgotten to set out. She watched him greasing it, but her mind was on what he had just said.

"So Ted *doesn't* have an alibi for that night," she mused.

"No. And furthermore, he must have lied to the police about it."

"It's possible his father might even have covered for him, if Ted had a good enough excuse," Carrie said. "Mr. Wright has always thought Ted could do no wrong."

And Jamie could do no right. It was, as Quinn had pointed out, an eerie reminder of the very different ways her own father had treated his two children.

"What about the other alibis?" she asked, becoming interested in spite of herself.

"Nelson Delaine's checks out. I interviewed the wrestling coach, and looked up the account of the match in the paper. Nelson was there, all right, and won a trophy to prove it."

"You're being very thorough."

He looked pointedly at her as he handed over the neatly greased muffin pan. "I intend to get it right this time," he said shortly.

So far Carrie's house had been vandalized twice, her son's life had been turned upside down, and she was fighting off her own near-constant fantasies about the one man she knew she could never have. If this was what he called getting it right, she hoped to heaven he could keep things from going wrong.

Her worry made her voice a little shaper again. "You're not involving Jamie in this in any way, are you?" she asked. "The two of you looked pretty friendly when I saw you this afternoon."

"He's a troubled kid. I was listening to him beef. I don't see anything wrong in that."

Quinn held the oven door open, and Carrie slid the muffin pan into it. When she stood to face him, she was starting to feel angry again.

"You were letting him beef about Ted, weren't you?" she demanded. "You were hoping to find out things Ted won't tell you himself."

"Of course I was. For one thing, I wanted to know whether Jamie might have heard anything on Sunday evening when that bomb got thrown in here."

"I can't imagine Ted Wright had anything to do—"

His face hardened. "I have to imagine all the possibilities," he said. "And so far I know that Wright lied to the police about his whereabouts the night David was killed. That puts him into a special category. It makes sense to check out his movements on Sunday evening."

"Could Jamie tell you anything?"

"Just that Wright was apparently driving his two kids back to their mother's about then. He was gone all evening, according to Jamie."

Carrie sighed. She didn't know Jamie Wright very well, but something about him reminded her powerfully of her twin brother at Jamie's age, angry and uncertain and not sure where he wanted his life to go next. Quinn had seemed like such a good friend to David back then, drawing him out, offering him friendship. And then—

"I don't like this, Quinn," she said.

"My talking to Jamie? There's no danger to the boy, Carrie. I wouldn't—"

"Wouldn't what? Involve him? You've already done that, by pumping him about his stepbrother."

"I wouldn't endanger him."

"Like you didn't endanger David? Or the boy who shot you? You said his buddies killed him because they knew he was talking to you."

She watched him building his defenses back up again, stoically, painstakingly. He clearly didn't like what she was saying, and she didn't like watching him retreat into his tough loner's shell again, but neither of them could deny the truth in her words.

"The kid who shot me was in over his head long before I arrived on the scene." He sounded as if he hated to have to justify what he'd done, but he felt he had to try. "I was trying to help him, not get him killed."

"You were trying to help David, too. And now you want to be Jamie Wright's buddy, because you feel bad for him. Did it ever occur to you, Quinn, that there might be better ways of helping people than the ones you've chosen?"

She saw him flinch, and his eyes hardened until they were as unyielding as granite. "Yes," he said, slowly and very distinctly. "It has occurred to me. I just haven't figured out yet what that better way is."

He headed for the kitchen door with long, determined strides, and Carrie realized that she had hit him in a place that was far more vulnerable than she'd known. Before she could say anything, he had reached the doorway and turned to say roughly, "If you set the oven timer for about twelve minutes, you'll stand a chance of getting those muffins out before they turn to charcoal. And if you're looking for me, I'll be working on that mess in the foyer."

* * *

"There's a fax for you down here," Leo LaPlante said over the phone, "but I think somebody must be pulling your leg. It looks like a couple of pages out of the television guide, and some old baseball scores."

"It's not a joke, Leo. I'll pick it up later this morning, all right?"

The FBI researcher he'd contacted on Monday hadn't found anything strange in Quinn's asking to see a ten-year-old television listing. In the unpredictable work of investigation, there was no such thing as an odd request.

It was Wednesday, and he still hadn't managed to corner Ted Wright. He had contacted all the witnesses who'd seen the mysterious car on Airport Road the night David was killed, and had grilled them about their memories of that evening. He had checked the ballistics reports in David's file, although he already knew that the murder weapon had in all probability been a .22 caliber rifle. It was one of the things that had made him question the official conclusion on David's death: the mob family that was involved had been known to favor handguns, not rifles.

"Don't make too much out of that," had been his boss's advice. "Could be they sent the B team down here, since it was such an easy job. Maybe they've got a new shooter we don't know about. And anyway, once your cover's blown, you have to start all over again somewhere else. Let's just get on with it, all right?"

And so the bureau *had* started all over again somewhere else, and had eventually managed to shut down that particular conduit for South American cocaine. And David St. John's death had been written off as an unfortunate footnote to the investigation, the result of Quinn's inexperience and the mob's cold-blooded ways of doing business.

Quinn had talked to the manager of the Stockbridge Airport yesterday, without learning anything new. But while he'd been there, he'd forced himself to walk out to the far end of the runway, to the quiet spot where David's body had been found.

David St. John had been one of the few human beings Quinn had ever really shared his feelings with. And David's twin sister was still the only woman he'd ever met who seemed to see straight into his heart. It had been painful and exhilarating to feel himself opening up to those two. It was just as painful and exhilarating to remember it now.

"I'm going to finish this up, David." Quinn made the promise out loud to the empty pavement at the far corner of the municipal airport. The chilly November breeze picked his words up and carried them into the gray sky above him. "And then I don't know what the hell I'm going to do."

Chapter 9

On Wednesday morning, Carrie handed Quinn an opportunity to visit the one suspect he hadn't encountered face-to-face yet. When she told him she had to go to Steven Solidad's sporting goods store to get Davey some hockey equipment, Quinn asked if he could go along for the ride.

"I suppose so."

"Don't you have day care this morning?"

"No. Two more parents called in with excuses not to bring their kids, and two others are already gone for the long weekend."

"What long weekend?" For a moment Quinn couldn't imagine what she meant.

The look she was giving him was one he remembered very well. It was exasperated, and surprisingly fond. She'd always favored him with it when he'd displayed his almost complete lack of familiarity with the simple rituals of family life.

"Thanksgiving weekend, Quinn," she said. "Tomorrow is Thanksgiving. Did you just forget, or do FBI agents not get holidays like everybody else?"

Most FBI agents did, but those tended to be the people with families to spend their holidays with. For Quinn, one day was pretty much like the rest. He had spent most of last Thanksgiving in an airplane seat, handcuffed to the guy next to him. The Thanksgiving before that, he recalled dimly, he'd been on a stakeout in North Dakota. It had been a very cold, very boring day.

"I've gotten out of the habit of holidays," he said now.

"Well, if you're going to stick around here, you'd better try to remember how it goes. Davey celebrates holidays with a vengeance, and Thanksgiving is his favorite."

"Fond of turkey, is he?"

"I think it's actually the four consecutive days off school, plus the start of Saturday morning hockey league the same week. Are you ready to go?"

They made a stop at the police station so Quinn could pick up the fax that had come in from his office in Chicago. When he came out, Nelson Delaine was leaning against Carrie's van, talking to her. He didn't look particularly happy to see Quinn.

"I heard you've been checking me out, Agent McAllister," he said, straightening up.

"I've been checking out lots of people."

"I heard that, too. It isn't adding to your list of admirers in this town."

Quinn opened the passenger door, and said, "Fortunately, I didn't come back here because I wanted to be Mr. Popularity. Can you think of any reason why Ted Wright would have lied about where he was on the night David was killed?"

The burly cop was startled, he could tell. But he covered it quickly with his usual belligerence. "You'd do better asking Ted, not me," he said. "Look, I gotta go. We'll keep those patrols coming by your place, Carrie. Don't worry about that.''

Quinn slid into the front seat of the van as Nelson Delaine pulled away in a patrol car. It was interesting, he thought, that Delaine had barely bothered to stick up for his old buddy. Officer Delaine seemed mostly concerned with covering his own backside, just as Ted Wright had been worried about his reputation as an upstanding young attorney. Quinn suspected that if one of the three was guilty, the others might eventually be willing to trade information for a guarantee that their own name wouldn't suffer.

"What do you think of Steven Solidad?" Quinn asked, as Carrie started the van again.

"I like Steve. He's changed since his macho jock days in high school. He only came back to town a couple of years ago, when his father died. Steve had decided he'd had enough of playing baseball for a living, and he came back to run the family sports store.''

"So, he did go after that baseball career after all." Quinn had already looked up the details of Steve Solidad's life in the past ten years, but he was interested to hear what Carrie would say about the man.

"Well, he spent six years in the minor leagues and one week in the majors, if that's what you mean. He says it was enough for him, and he's just as happy being back in Stockbridge, involved with all the kids' sports.'' She looked sharply over at him. "I'm presuming you aren't coming with me because you care about Davey's Saturday morning hockey.''

Quinn *did* care about Davey's Saturday morning hockey. Davey had already confided to Quinn that he thought it would be the coolest thing to actually go to a Chicago Black Hawks game someday, and Quinn had been trying to figure out ever since whether there was any chance of Carrie letting their son visit him in the city during this year's hockey season.

But Carrie was right, it wasn't hockey equipment he was interested in at the moment. "I have a feeling I might be more welcome at Solidad's place if I'm with you," he said. "Nelson Delaine and Ted Wright haven't exactly been falling all over themselves to answer my questions, and I'm getting tired of being shut out."

He saw her full mouth tighten in what looked like disapproval. "You'll use anybody who's handy, won't you?" she said.

"I don't think of it as using you, believe me."

"How *do* you think of it?"

Quinn ran his hands through his hair. Carrie's driving had always been a little like her cooking—her thoughts tended to wander away from the task at hand—and he wished they weren't tackling this thorny subject while she was trying to negotiate Stockbridge's Main Street.

However the traffic was light, and Carrie's question had demanded an answer. Quinn stuffed his hands into his jacket pockets, and said, "I think of it as enlisting whatever help I need to do a job that's important to more people than just me."

"I didn't ask you to come back and reopen this investigation."

"Carrie." He half turned in the seat, looking over at her as she pulled into a parking space in front of Solidad Sporting Goods. "Somebody out there knows more than they're telling about David's death. That's obvious, from the damage to your house. If someone is hiding the truth about David, how can you not want to know about it?"

She turned off the engine and sat for a long time looking through the windshield. She was worrying her lower lip in a way that made Quinn want to take her in his arms and comfort her, or kiss her, or just hold her close.

"You're right, although I haven't wanted to admit it." She sounded surprised to be admitting it now. "I keep thinking, if you *did* just go away again, and things went back to the way they've always been, would I always wonder, in the back of my mind, who in Stockbridge killed my brother and is now pretending to be my friend."

Quinn felt a sudden surge of triumph, but he waited without speaking, letting Carrie finish her thoughts.

"I hate the idea of dragging this all out again, Quinn." Her eyes were very wide and soft as they met his. "But I can't live the rest of my life wondering which one of my neighbors might have killed my brother, either. You've taken the lid off too many questions to put it back on now. And that's why I let you come along this morning. I can't say I'm wild about being part of your interrogation, but I'm coming to understand why this has been eating at you for so long."

There wasn't time to tell her how much her words meant to him because she was out of the van and walking up to Solidad's store's front entrance before he could say anything.

That didn't mean Quinn was done with it though. He hurried after her and took her arm as she was walking through the entrance. Was it his imagination, or did she tense and then relax every time he touched her? It was almost as though she wanted to fight against him, but couldn't. The thought was heady and distracting.

"Interrogation isn't the name of the game," he said to her. "I hardly ever use my rack and thumbscrews, unless somebody's really jerking me around."

She hadn't pulled her arm away from him, so he stayed close to her as they threaded their way through the colorful racks of sports jerseys and bathing suits. "Place looks more prosperous than I remember," Quinn commented.

"Steve's put a lot of money into it. And he does a lot for the town."

That was obvious from the plaques and commendations and trophies that lined the back wall of the store. There were framed photographs, too, showing handsome, black-haired Steve Solidad with various famous and less-than-famous big-league ballplayers.

Solidad himself was behind the counter, and he didn't hide his surprise at the sight of Quinn and Carrie crossing the store arm in arm. "Heard you were back," he said to Quinn. "Come to pick up that uniform, Carrie?"

"*And* a new stick, *and* some skate guards, *and* a pair of shin pads, and all those other things little hockey players seem to grow out of so fast." Quinn had to admire Carrie's poise. She was smiling at her old schoolmate as though this were an everyday transaction, with no dangerous outsider listening in.

"You can't keep up with them when they're that age," Solidad said. "On the other hand, it keeps me in business, so I'm not complaining. Hold on, and I'll get your order."

Quinn was thinking of all the years and the growth spurts he'd missed in Davey's life. He also wondered whether or not he could be a part of the ones that were coming up.

His own boyhood felt like a hundred years ago, when he thought of the death and despair he'd seen since then. But somehow, standing around the local sports shop waiting for his son's hockey gear to be packaged up, the domestic details of daily life with a small child suddenly seemed much more momentous than the difficulties and rewards of his job.

"If you've heard I'm back, you've probably heard why I'm here." Quinn let go of Carrie's arm, reluctantly, and moved to the doorway of the back room where Steve Solidad was assembling the gear Davey needed. Carrie headed for a rack of sports jerseys, leaving Quinn the chance to talk to Solidad in private.

"I heard you had some idea about reviving the investigation into Carrie's brother's death."

Quinn nodded, prepared for yet another attempt to tell him it was a bad idea.

To his surprise, it didn't happen. "I can't say I agree with you that anyone around here could have been responsible," Solidad said. "But I always thought it was a shame that nobody went to jail for David's murder. He was a good guy."

"You didn't think so at the time."

Solidad looked up with what seemed to be genuine regret on his handsome face. "I was into that peer pressure thing in high school," he said. "Had to be cool at all costs. But a few years out in the real world cured me of that. When I think about David now, I'm sorry I wasn't better friends with him. I know he would have liked to hang around with me and Ted and Nelson, and we weren't exactly gentle about putting him off."

Quinn knew all about the pain of being put off by the rest of the world. It was one of the things that had made it easy for him to get close to David. It was startling to hear Steven Solidad's honest apology now. And it made it harder to view the man as a suspect.

Careful, Quinn, he warned himself. *You're still letting your own feelings get in your way.* He glanced back at Carrie, who was looking through a display of sneakers, and then turned back to Solidad.

"I'm glad to hear you say that," he said. "And since you're sympathetic to the idea of my finding out who killed David, do you mind if I ask you what you remember about the night he was shot?"

"Did you find out anything?"

Carrie lifted the hatch on the back of the minivan, and waited while Quinn stowed the hockey gear in the back. He lifted the heavy load with ease, although she did notice him favoring his left side as he lowered it into the vehicle. She remembered putting her hand over his scars there on Sunday night, and hoped he wouldn't notice her quickened breathing now as she thought about the desire that had poured through her at the intimate contact of their two bodies.

"I found out a couple of things." He stood back while she closed the door. "One of them being that young boys need hockey gear that weighs far more than they do themselves."

"Tell me about it." Carrie shared his quick smile. "And then when spring comes, it's time to get them new baseball gear because they've grown out of last year's things." She looked over at him as they climbed into the front of the van. "Weren't you ever a small boy who needed unending amounts of sports equipment, Quinn?"

"I wasn't into sports much. Too sociable for me. I liked track-and-field, because I could do most of it on my own."

He'd told her that once before, when she'd known him ten years ago. She'd spent years telling herself that everything he'd said then had been a lie, and it was disconcerting now to realize that he'd based at least some of his undercover persona on his real background. That loner's pose, for one thing, had been no lie, but his natural defense against a world he had obviously not felt a part of.

"I remember you and David shooting basketballs at the hoop on our garage for hours at a stretch," she said. She spoke slowly, wondering how close she really wanted to get to the potent memories of Quinn and David and herself. Watching Quinn bouncing a basketball with Jamie Wright in the driveway next door these past couple of evenings had been troubling enough.

But it was getting harder and harder to shut Quinn out, and easier to remember the impulses that had led her to want to draw him in, in the first place. It was still dangerous, she knew, but it was starting to feel almost inevitable that Quinn should be here, sitting in the front seat of her van, talking about old times.

"Shooting hoop is different," he said. "That's not a sport. That's something you do with your best buddy. See, if you're a teenaged guy, you can't just hang around and talk. You have to be *doing* something while you talk, preferably something masculine. Shooting hoop is really just conversation, thinly disguised."

"Speaking of conversation, what did you find out from Steve Solidad?"

"That he admires you a lot."

His voice had changed. He was being deliberately cool now, as though he'd just reverted to the youth they'd just been discussing. "Does that have anything to do with your investigation?" she asked him.

"No. I just thought I'd mention it."

She looked over at him before pulling out of the parking space. "Why?" she asked bluntly.

He hitched his thumbs into the belt loops of his old jeans, and looked fixedly out the windshield. "A lot of people seem to admire you around here," he said. "I keep wondering if there's anybody you particularly admire—or like—in return."

The words sounded so tentative that it took her a moment to figure out what he meant. "Are you asking me if I've got a boyfriend?" she said finally.

"More or less." It wasn't like Quinn to dodge the point, or to avoid her eyes, either. But he was doing both.

"Would it matter if I did?"

"Yes, it would matter." The words came out quickly. But then she sensed him hauling himself back under control again. He sounded almost grim when he added, "I've got a right to know if there's some other father figure in Davey's life, maybe some potential stepfather. You can't deny me that."

So it was Davey he was concerned about, not Carrie. For a moment she felt a wave of disappointment going through her. When he'd asked about boyfriends, she'd immediately wondered if he was jealous, if he didn't like the idea of Carrie being with another man.

She had wanted him to feel jealous. She realized it with startling clarity, the same way she'd realized, that first day, how much she had missed him.

She had wanted him to be interested enough in her that he cared if she had other men in her life.

And he had just made it clear that the only male in her life he was concerned with was her son. Their son. That was the only real connection between them now.

"I've had a couple of boyfriends in the past," she said, coolly now. "Nobody really serious. To tell you the truth, I prefer my life the way it is now, with just Davey and me. It's a lot simpler that way."

His silence might have meant anything at all. He didn't say anything until they were clear of Main Street, and then he reverted to the subject of his investigation as though neither of them had strayed away from it.

"I checked out Steve Solidad's alibi for the time of David's death," he said. That factual, special agent sound was back in his voice again. "According to the police report, he was home by himself watching TV. When I asked him about it just now, he said he had planned on going to watch Nelson Delaine's wrestling match, but he'd stayed home because there had been a spectacular no-hitter earlier in the week in Detroit, and he wanted to catch the footage of it in the weekly baseball roundup."

"That sounds like Steve. He's got an encyclopedic memory for baseball."

"So I gather. Anyway, it checks out. There *was* a baseball roundup on that evening, and there *had* been a no-hitter pitched in Detroit."

She looked over at him. "How on earth do you know that?"

He pulled the folded fax paper out of his jacket pocket. "I looked it up," he said. "Or more accurately, somebody at my office did. Anyway, it looks as if Steve is probably telling the truth."

"It's not absolutely certain, though, is it?" For the first time, she was starting to see this the way Quinn must see it—as a puzzle to be solved, a set of clues to be put in the right order.

"Not absolutely, but in my experience, the person who tries too hard to give you a cast-iron alibi is probably lying. Alibis like Steve's, without corroborating witnesses, are often the most truthful."

"So you still think Ted Wright is the one to look into."

"It sure looks that way to me." He fell silent again until they were almost at Carrie's driveway. Then he said thoughtfully, "Remember the place everybody used to go to make out?"

She shot him a startled glance. "I didn't know you knew about that," she said. "I mean, we never—"

"No, I know we never went there. Believe me, Carrie—" She couldn't tell, from the look on his face, whether he was amused or serious. "I would have remembered. Being with you isn't something I could forget even if I wanted to."

It was a disturbing thought, especially since she'd just managed to convince herself that he was only interested in her because of their son. Carrie turned on her turn signal, and pulled the van into her drive. "Why did you mention Lovers' Point?" she asked, using the local name for the place that still saw a lot of activity on Friday and Saturday nights.

"Because, as the airport manager reminded me when I interviewed him yesterday, it looks down over the airport."

He got out of the van without explaining himself, and didn't speak again until he had helped her carry the hockey equipment into the house. By then, Carrie thought she could see where he was headed.

"You're trying to figure out how someone knew there were drugs being shipped through Stockbridge, right?" she said.

He gave her a look that seemed approving. "Very good," he said. "I always wondered, if it *was* Wright or Delaine or Solidad selling the cocaine locally, how they got in contact with the mob couriers who were running it. But if one of them—let's say Ted Wright, for the sake of argument—happened to look up from his girlfriend's...ah...body structure late one Saturday evening and saw a plane coming in for a landing when the airport wasn't supposed to be open—"

"And if he saw it again on other Saturday nights," Carrie finished, "he might figure something funny was up."

"Right. And if he was an ambitious kid without a whole lot of scruples—which you have to admit describes Ted pretty well—he might have decided to investigate."

"Why would the mob let him in on their deal?" Carrie asked.

"Money talks. And couriers are notorious for trying to make a little extra wherever they can. It's one of the reasons it's such a high risk profession. Ted Wright had enough money of his own that he could have bribed the courier into skimming a little cocaine off the top of every shipment, with Ted selling it locally and the courier making a percentage on the deal."

Carrie looked dubiously at the back of her foyer, where plywood now covered the ruined French doors while they were waiting for repair. She'd never liked Ted Wright. But was it possible he had done this to her house? That he had been a part of the kind of scheme Quinn was suggesting? That he had killed her brother David?

If he *had* done those things, she wanted to know about it. For the first time, she felt herself fired by some of the same fierce need for justice that had obviously brought Quinn and his questions back to Stockbridge.

"Is there any way to check?" she asked him. "About Ted and Lovers' Point, I mean?"

"Do you have any recollection who his girlfriend was at the beginning of senior year?"

"Oh, Lord." Carrie shook her head. "There were so many. We used to joke about Ted Wright's revolving door policy."

"I know. The guys in the locker room had a slightly less elegant way of putting it."

He shot her that grin again, and it occurred to her that he was smiling more easily now than when he'd first arrived. A couple of days ago, his first real grin had nearly knocked her socks off. Now, though, she was catching the quick flash of his teeth and the softening of his blue eyes more often.

It still affected her the same way, and she was finding it easier and easier to smile back at him. She could see traces of his amusement still lingering in his eyes as he said, "Steve Solidad was a lot more forthcoming than I expected him to be. I'm going to call him up and see if he has any recollection of who the woman of the moment was at about the time those drug shipments started coming through here. Maybe, if we can track her down, she could fill in a few of the blanks for us."

Carrie wondered if he even noticed that he'd said "we" and "us" as though they were conducting this investigation together.

She wondered, now that she'd given her approval for what he was doing, if they *were* conducting it together.

She watched him cross the foyer, heading for the telephone, and wondered what had happened to her since that moment, only last week, when she'd faced Quinn McAllister across this same room and told him in no uncertain terms that she wanted to have nothing to do with him, now or ever.

Quinn was catapulted out of a deep sleep the next morning by a sudden explosion of movement at the foot of his bed.

"Wake up, Quinn! It's Thanksgiving."

Quinn *was* awake, instantly. His heart was pounding and his hand had reached instinctively for his gun before he realized that it was only his nine-year-old son, leaping onto the bed from a running start at the door of the room. He lay back down, breathing hard, glad he hadn't gotten all the way to the loaded weapon that was in the drawer of the bedside table.

"Jeez, Davey, is it even dawn yet?"

"It's just cloudy. It's seven-thirty. Don't you want to get up?"

"Yes." He grinned at the boy, now that he was starting to recover from the surprise wake-up call. "I do want to get up. Slowly, gradually, the way grown-ups like to get up." He'd been dreaming hungrily about Davey's mother, about making love to her, slowly, gradually, about climbing into her bed with her and maybe never leaving it again. Davey's sudden entrance was like several buckets full of cold water thrown over the fantasies Quinn had just been indulging.

"When I'm a grown-up, I'm going to get up as early as I like on holidays," Davey announced.

Quinn chuckled. "I'll check back with you when you're a grown-up, and see if you still mean that," he said.

"Are you going to be here for Thanksgiving dinner?"

"Just try to keep me away."

"Susannah and her kids are coming over. And Mr. Prestiss."

"I know." Quinn was getting out of bed now, heading for the bathroom. "How about a game of football in the backyard this afternoon?" he asked. Since he'd decided to do small-town Thanksgiving in the first place, he was letting himself go all the way with it. He was amazed at how good it felt.

"All *right*. Susannah's kids are kind of little to play, though."

So was Davey, but Quinn wasn't about to put a dent in the nine-year-old's pride. "We'll take it easy on them, then," he said.

"Can we get the football out and start practicing?"

"Not yet." Quinn ran a hand over his jaw. "I need to shower, shave and find some coffee, in that order."

"Can I watch you shave?"

Quinn paused at the bathroom door. Now that Davey had warmed up to the idea of having a father, he was plunging headlong into it, eager, it seemed to Quinn, for an adult male in his life. Was it fair for Quinn to encourage that, when he wasn't sure he could ever be anything but a temporary presence for the boy?

But Davey's happy brown eyes made it impossible to refuse him. And Davey wasn't the only one who was eager for this. Quinn himself had never expected to feel a part of anyone's family, much less to have a family of his own. Even a temporary one was far too good to pass up.

"Sure," he said, "as long as you promise not to tell me any more bad jokes while I'm shaving."

Davey had already regaled his father with his full repertoire of jokes. "You mean like the one about the elephant and the ballerina?" he asked.

Quinn groaned. "I definitely need to be clean before I can listen to this," he said. "Hold the fort, all right?"

When he came out of the bathroom a few minutes later, showered and wrapped in a towel, Davey was sitting on the edge of Quinn's bed, intently inspecting the gun Quinn had left in the bedside drawer.

Chapter 10

For a moment Quinn's whole world froze. Every kid he'd ever seen in danger, every life that had ended too soon with a bullet in a young body, rolled itself into the awful sight of his son with that loaded weapon in his hands.

He started to yell a command to drop it, but his sixth sense about danger told him that startling the boy was the worst thing he could do right now. With an effort that made him feel as though his bones were cracking inside him, he brought his nerves under control enough to be able to speak almost normally.

"Davey, I don't want you to move a muscle until I get over there to take that thing away from you. Do you understand me?"

Davey's big brown eyes looked startled enough, and Quinn knew some of his panic was coloring his tone in spite of how hard he was fighting to keep it out. It was just that the thought of Davey—

It was a thought he couldn't even contemplate. On quivering legs, he crossed the bedroom and held out a hand for the gun. When it was safely in Quinn's palm, he lowered himself onto the bed next to his son, unable to speak for a moment.

When he did, he put all the strength he had into getting his meaning across. "You shouldn't ever, *ever* pick up a weapon that way," he said. "You don't know anything about this gun, whether it's loaded or not, how it fires, what it might do. Guns in real life aren't like they are on TV and the movies, Davey. They do a lot more damage than people realize. Unless you have some reason to handle one, and unless you've been trained to use it the right way, you shouldn't have anything to do with them. All right?"

Davey was nodding solemnly, and Quinn hoped to God the boy was as impressed by Quinn's words as he seemed to be by the serious tone Quinn was using to get them across. As Davey looked back down at the gun, his eyes paused, caught by the scars on Quinn's left side.

Quinn would have liked to have kept that sight from his son, but maybe it was just as well he'd seen it, given the situation. Half turning so Davey could have a good look, he said, "That was from one bullet, Davey. And the person who fired it wasn't even really aiming at me. He was just blasting away, crazy and scared. That's what one bullet can do. That's why you have to be so careful around any kind of gun."

Davey nodded again. Was this too heavy for a nine-year-old? Quinn wondered. His side was aching now, and so was his head. The happy Thanksgiving mood of a few minutes ago was gone, frightened away by the grimness of the world Quinn had brought back to Stockbridge with him.

"Why do you have a gun here?" Davey seemed to have been sharing his thoughts.

Quinn sighed, popped the bullets out of his revolver, and put the weapon and bullets back into the bedside drawer.

"It's part of my job to have to defend myself," he said slowly.

"Do you have to shoot people?"

"Only if they're shooting at me, and sometimes not even then."

"Are people shooting at you here?"

Not yet, Quinn almost said. But what message would that send to this child whose world had been so safe and predictable up until now? He didn't want to leave Davey with the idea that people might come blasting their way into the St. John house at any moment.

"I don't think anybody's going to shoot at me here," he said, and hoped he was right. "But once you've done a job one way for a long time, certain things get to be habits. And carrying that gun is a habit of mine."

He reached an arm around Davey's shoulders, feeling suddenly weak as the reaction from the shock set in. He hugged the boy to him, fiercely, briefly. "I don't want to scare you with this stuff, Davey. I just want you to be careful."

Davey nodded again as Quinn let him go, but Quinn noticed that the kid wasn't meeting his eyes now. The camaraderie of earlier this morning, the interest in watching his father shave, all seemed to have disappeared.

"Can I go now?" The sound of Davey's voice confirmed it.

"Sure, sport." Quinn hid his disappointment as he watched the boy heading out into the hallway.

Damn, he thought, getting slowly to his feet and heading back into the bathroom. Investigative work was Quinn's whole life, and had been for what felt like a very long time. He loved the sense of making things happen, of being on the side with the good guys, of walking into a new town like a gunslinger looking for trouble, and walking away again knowing that the trouble was over.

But was any of that worth losing the joy he'd seen in his young son's eyes when Davey had bounced onto his bed this morning? Did any of it really compare with the feeling of holding Carrie close against him, and the welcoming warmth of her kiss, her caress?

He didn't know. He *did* know that it took all his concentration to get a decent shave when he finally got around to it, because his hands were still shaking worse than they had after any gun battle he'd ever been in.

Carrie couldn't figure out why Thanksgiving got off to such a slow start.

She'd heard Davey bounding out of bed early, as he always did on days off, and from the direction of his footsteps, she'd gathered he was headed for Quinn's room. It had felt surprisingly good to let herself relax in bed, stretching her toes under the warm flannel sheets, easing herself out of some astonishingly explicit dreams and letting some other adult bear the brunt of Davey's holiday enthusiasm.

But that enthusiasm was conspicuously absent when Davey came padding into the kitchen half an hour later. He sat in front of the juice and cereal she'd poured for him without speaking, looking all too much like he had the first day he'd found out who Quinn was.

"Is everything okay, honey?" She sat down opposite him, knowing something was wrong but not wanting to push him too hard about it.

"Yeah, fine." Davey looked down at his bowl.

"You don't look the way you usually do on holidays."

Davey mushed the cereal with the back of his spoon. "Does Quinn—does my dad have a dangerous job?" he asked.

She wanted to say *Yes, very dangerous,* and she knew it would have been nothing less than the truth. But in the face of Davey's determined efforts to include Quinn in his life, to acknowledge the man as his father, it was impossible to take a direct shot at Quinn without hurting the boy, too. Things had gone far beyond the stage where she could disparage Quinn in front of their son.

So she said, as calmly as she could, "Sometimes it's dangerous, but he has a lot of people helping him, and they all try to keep each other safe. Are you worried about him, Davey?"

"A little bit."

His silence told her it was more than a little bit. And she knew only too well how he felt.

When Quinn himself showed up in the kitchen a few minutes later, shaved and showered and looking so intensely masculine and sexy and unsure of his welcome all over again, there was nothing Carrie could do to repress the wave of longing that swept through her. She wanted to erase that uncertain frown on Quinn's face. She wanted to see him smile, and to smile with him.

Suddenly, she realized that she would have given anything for them to be a normal, happy family. But Quinn's dangerous job, the one Davey had just been asking her about, meant that that could never happen.

"I smell coffee," he said. He looked almost wary this morning, and Carrie wondered why.

She wasn't about to pour him a mug of coffee and start acting like Mrs. Quinn McAllister. She might have her longings for happy normality, but that didn't mean she was going to act out fantasies she knew couldn't ever come true.

So she nodded at the coffeepot, and got busy looking for jars of spaghetti sauce in the cupboards, hoping she had enough to feed seven people for dinner. She was still hunting through the cupboard over the counter by the time Davey left the kitchen and Quinn got up to get a second cup of coffee.

At least, that's what she assumed he was doing. She wasn't prepared to feel him stepping up directly behind her a moment later, or for the seductive feeling of his big palms sliding around her, pulling her close to him.

He was moving slowly, and she could feel something like weariness in the way he drew her toward his body and lowered his head onto her shoulder. He seemed hesitant this morning, and his usual intensity was muted.

That didn't keep her from responding to him though. He had wrapped his strong right arm around her, clasping her left shoulder, and had hooked his free left hand over his own forearm, making a kind of net around her, powerful and silent and sensual. Carrie raised her hand and laced her fingers over his without realizing she was doing it. Something in his silence seemed to be begging for some human touch, some human comfort, without quite having the words to ask for it out loud.

When he did finally speak, his voice was muffled against her shoulder. "I'd appreciate it," he said, "if you would tell me that I'm not the only one in the world who finds being a parent a very hard thing to do."

There was something appealingly forlorn in his tone, and Carrie smiled in spite of herself. Whatever had been going on between Quinn and Davey this morning seemed to have left both of them uneasily trying to adjust to their discovery of each other.

"Parenting gets easier with practice," she told him. "But it's never exactly easy."

"Thank you." He lifted his head, after kissing her neck very gently just above the collar of her pink sweatshirt. The kiss, and the sudden loss of his surrounding strength when he stepped away a moment later, left Carrie breathing hard, and all too aware of how much she was starting to want these embraces of Quinn's to go on. Every time he touched her, another forbidden desire sprang back into life. By now, just being in the same room with him—even

in the same house with him—was making her body pulse
to a long-denied but insistent rhythm.

If he felt any of the same things, he was hiding them
better than she was. He moved to the stove for his second
cup of coffee, and said almost casually, "I couldn't help
noticing you're getting out spaghetti sauce."

"It's our traditional Thanksgiving meal around here."

"You're not serious."

"*You're* not serious if you imagine I've been whipping
up full-blown turkey dinners on my own all these years."

His wry smile acknowledged that she had a point.
"Well, you've got assistance this year, so why not make
use of it?"

"We don't have a turkey, for one thing."

"Sure we do." He pulled open the refrigerator door. "I
keep telling you, Carrie, you should explore your own refrigerator once in a while. I bought this yesterday, while
you were cleaning up after Davey's bath."

She was astonished to see a sizable turkey nestled at the
back of the lower shelf. Quinn was pulling out drawers
now, displaying cranberries, pie shells, and what seemed
to be enough vegetables to feed an army on the move.

"Is this some kind of campaign to turn me into Betty
Crocker?" she demanded. She was trying to resent the way
he had marched into her kitchen and taken it over, but the
truth was that the traditional spaghetti dinner on Thanksgiving had been a final response to too many turkeys that
had burned, or refused to cook, or refused to thaw in the
first place. The idea of serving a real, disaster-free holiday
dinner had undeniable appeal.

"Who says you're going to be cooking?" Quinn's perceptive blue eyes seemed to see all of that. "And don't
imagine I'm doing this to make some sort of a point, Carrie. The truth is that I haven't really had a chance to cook
in years, and I've missed it. So if you'll put away all those

jars and show me where your mixing bowls are, I can get to work.''

Carrie didn't cook, but she helped. She chopped and stirred and occasionally, without admitting it to Quinn, she started to understand what he meant when he said she didn't stay still long enough to be a good cook. When she found herself savoring the smell of the fresh celery she was adding to the stuffing mix, and then deciding it needed just a little more thyme to go with it, she thought she knew why his methodical way of doing things worked better in the kitchen than her full-steam-ahead approach.

The one thing she couldn't figure out—although she was watching him closely—was how he'd managed to slip whatever magic ingredients he was using into their food. She was sure there had to be some kind of wizardry going on, because by the time they were ready to start cooking things, around noon, she was feeling more relaxed than she had in a long time.

And Davey had come back into the kitchen, drawn, it seemed, by his parents' conversation and their occasional laughter whenever Quinn pointed out something really outrageous that Carrie had done or was about to do.

"What's so funny?" Davey had demanded, suspiciously.

"Your mother was telling me about the time she tried to roast the turkey with the plastic wrapper still on," Quinn said.

"It was pretty gross," Davey confirmed.

"I can believe it. This one's going to be better."

Davey's eyes had widened at the sight of the turkey Carrie was stuffing at the counter. "*Mom* can't cook a turkey," he said.

"Mom has wisely bowed to superior talent," Carrie said. "Quinn's cooking the turkey, and I'm just helping. You want to jump in and give us a hand, honey? Somebody needs to check over those cranberries for leaves and twigs."

"I thought cranberries came in a can."

Carrie laughed again. "I thought so, too, but apparently they have a previous existence out in the wild somewhere."

"They travel in herds," Quinn said. "The fall roundup is quite a sight."

Davey still looked doubtful as he pulled a stool up to the counter. Carrie knew he was trying to reconcile her light-hearted mood, and Quinn's, with the tension that had been buzzing around the big house ever since Quinn had arrived.

At the moment, she was only too happy to let that tension ease. It just felt so good to be laughing with Quinn in this kitchen again, as though the past ten years had never happened and the future was a hopeful place once more. And after his initial uncertainty, Davey let their laughter reach him, too. By the time the turkey went into the oven at noon, the energy level in the kitchen had risen to the point where food fights were starting to seem hilarious and inevitable, and Quinn was suggesting that some outdoor exercise might do them all good.

"Football!" Davey cried, running to get the ball.

Carrie groaned. "I always get wiped out at this," she said.

"Call Susannah." Quinn was grinning at her as he wiped his strong hands on a tea towel. "Tell her to get her kids over here early. Davey and I'll take on the rest of you."

"Why do I still feel like I'm being ganged up on?" Carrie grimaced, but headed for the phone anyway. She actually felt as though she were being handed an unexpected gift—one happy, carefree day out of all the darkness and danger that usually surrounded Quinn McAllister—and she didn't want to waste it.

They forgot their system for keeping score halfway through the game, and agreed that they didn't really need to keep track, anyway. Jamie Wright joined them after about an hour, when the shrieks and laughter from the backyard had penetrated into the quieter property next door. By the time Eugene Prestiss showed up with a couple of bottles of wine at about three, there were enticing smells wafting out of the house, and everyone's appetite was in peak condition.

At five they all sat down to eat at the kitchen table, seven of them squeezed in together, elbow-to-elbow. "We used to call the upstairs dining room the mausoleum," Carrie told Susannah's children, who were too young to remember the days when old Dr. St. John had insisted on eating in the much more formal room. "I always pictured maids and butlers hovering around with silver serving tools."

"But you didn't have maids and butlers, right?" Davey asked.

"Right. Just that old dumbwaiter to carry the dishes up and down. Once, when I was your age, I crammed myself into it and my twin brother tried to crank me upstairs."

"What happened?"

"I got stuck and claustrophobic, and it wasn't any fun at all, if you're considering trying it."

Davey's quick glance at the dumbwaiter had already told her what he was thinking. His grin now—so like Quinn's that it made her heart turn over—said he knew he'd been caught.

"Does anybody want to go see the fireworks at the fairground?" Susannah asked, when they'd all eaten more pie than any of them had thought was possible.

The kids chorused their approval, but Gene Prestiss said the only activity he was up for at the moment was a slow walk back across the street to his own house. Carrie found herself waiting to see what Quinn would say, aware that Susannah's sharp eyes were watching for the same thing.

Was it possible, she wondered, that her friend had picked up on the unexpected harmony between Carrie and Quinn, and was offering them a chance to be alone if they wanted to?

Quinn's blue eyes were moving slowly from Davey's excited face to Carrie's, and she felt something soften inside her when she saw the hunger in his face.

"Well," he said, thoughtfully, "I've done turkey and stuffing and cranberry sauce and pumpkin pie, and touch football and Gene's homemade raspberry wine. I have a feeling that if I do a fireworks display at the fairground, too, my reputation as a tough guy from the city is going to be damaged beyond repair."

He said the words so easily, so naturally, that for a moment it was hard to realize that he really *was* the tough guy from the city, and not one of them. There must have been something magic in the dinner, Carrie thought. She never would have believed Quinn McAllister could seem so at home here again, accepted by her friend, her neighbor, most of all by her son.

"Come on, Quinn," Davey was prompting now. "They have these really awesome Roman candles."

Quinn smiled at the boy, but shook his head. "I'll stick around here and clean up," he said.

Carrie knew the silence after his words probably wasn't really as loud or as long as it felt to her. It would have been easy—in one way—just to accept Susannah's invitation and go along with the fireworks expedition. And in too many other ways—

In too many other ways, she couldn't imagine turning down the silent invitation she was seeing in Quinn's eyes. She couldn't imagine walking out of the house, leaving him alone in it. She couldn't stand the thought of missing what might be their single opportunity for some kind of tenderness together, fostered by the happy day they'd spent, and by too many years of loneliness in both their lives.

So she said quickly that she would stay to help Quinn with the disaster in the kitchen, and when everyone else had gone, leaving the place suddenly empty and echoing with past and present possibilities, she hoped to heaven she had done the right thing.

She went back into the kitchen after waving goodbye from the driveway and found Quinn still sitting in his chair at the table. "Quite a mess," he commented.

Carrie looked at the scattered dishes and silverware, and agreed. "Should we get to work cleaning it up?"

Another silence hung between them, even more laden with unspoken words than the last one. Carrie felt her heart starting to beat faster. Her body was already humming with the same kind of arousal she had been feeling all week, but now it was different, because she wasn't fighting against it. The idea made her feel weak and strong at the same time.

Quinn's eyes seemed to be seeing all that, and maybe more. His full mouth quirked into that grin she couldn't resist, and he said, "Eventually."

She'd almost forgotten that she'd been asking about the dishes. It was clear to both of them that the reason they'd stayed behind had very little to do with washing cutlery.

Quinn was leaning back in his chair, and the sexy sprawl of his long body was making Carrie's mind race with ideas that bordered on indecent. When he reached out a hand for her, she extended hers without a second thought. The feeling of his fingers closing around her wrist seemed to surge through her bloodstream.

He pulled her toward him possessively, a strong man claiming the woman he desired. Carrie let him pull her down into his lap. As he wrapped his arms around her she knew suddenly that the hunger in Quinn's blue eyes was for the kind of feminine strength that only she could offer him.

"Have I ever told you what it does to me to see you laugh?" he asked her softly.

Their faces were tantalizingly close. Carrie's hands, resting on Quinn's broad chest, could feel the hammered rhythm of his escalating desire. But his words were fiercely gentle, and she remembered that promise of tenderness she'd seen in his face just before she'd made her decision to stay alone with him.

"You told me—once." He had, too, on the unforgettable night he'd first kissed her.

"Well, I haven't changed my mind."

She ran a finger over the long line of his jaw, then up to caress the lips that could go from stern to gleeful so quickly. "I like to see you laugh, too, Quinn." Her words sounded soft in the quiet room. "I wish you laughed more than you do."

She almost wished she hadn't said it, when she saw the quick shake of his tawny head. She knew he wasn't protesting against what she'd said. It was just that her words got too close to the vexed question of what he was doing here, and how it might end, and what would happen then, when he had to leave again.

"Not now." His own words underlined what she'd just been thinking. "Not now, all right?"

He lifted his hands to cup her face. She could feel him pleading with her for this one moment of gentleness together, this single chance—because that's what it very likely was—to recapture the passion neither one of them had been able to deny.

She didn't answer him in words. Instead, she leaned forward, feeling his powerful thighs shifting under her to support her body. He was waiting for her kiss, letting her take the next step as he'd taken the first one. Somehow the knowledge of their matched strengths and matched desires made Carrie feel bold and seductive in ways she'd forgotten were possible.

She touched her mouth to his lightly, almost teasingly. They had never had time to explore each other the way she'd fantasized about so often. In the early days of their courtship Quinn had seemed to be keeping himself under such a tight rein, and she knew now that it had been because he'd been trying to convince himself that it shouldn't be turning into a courtship at all.

The moment he'd given up trying, they had fallen into each other's arms with an intensity that had left very little time for subtle exploration. Their one night of lovemaking had been urgent, headlong, surreptitious.

She felt a sudden longing to take things very slowly this time. And so her kisses were feather-light at first, just brushing over Quinn's full lips, only barely tasting him. She heard him groan softly, as though he'd figured out what she was up to. But he matched his response to hers, letting her take the lead. The sensual power that flowed through her at the thought was almost as arousing as the unmistakable masculine swell where her thigh rested against Quinn's old jeans.

"What are we going to do—" he spoke between kisses, sounding husky but contented "—if one of your neighbors decides to drop by to wish you a happy Thanksgiving?"

It wasn't out of the question. People in Stockbridge were given to dropping in on each other, and she didn't want to be found in a state of utter abandon with Quinn McAllister among the remnants of her Thanksgiving dinner. She smiled at him, and kissed his mouth again, and felt his smile widening to meet her own.

"I suppose we could always slip into something more comfortable."

"Like a bed, you mean?"

"That's what I was thinking."

"Your place or mine?"

The lighthearted question made her pause. She'd gotten so used to having this place to herself, with only Davey for company. It shouldn't feel as though Quinn belonged here, but when she looked down into those laughing blue eyes, it was suddenly impossible to imagine the place without him.

"Mine," she said finally, amazed at how simple the decision was. She'd been avoiding running into Quinn anywhere near her bedroom, but now it was hard even to remember why that had been.

They crossed the big foyer hand in hand, like two children exploring a brave new world. When Carrie closed her bedroom door behind them, she felt as though it were momentarily possible to shut out everything that was dark and threatening and difficult in their lives, so that they could share this one moment of uncomplicated passion.

She stopped and turned when she reached her double bed, but Quinn kept on going, closing his arms around her, carrying them both down onto it with a powerfully controlled strength that told her how much he had changed since the days of their first reckless embraces.

"You seem to want to take things slow," he murmured. "Well, I can do that, too."

And he did, with a tightly reined intensity that soon shredded what there was of Carrie's self-control. It was heaven to stop fighting her feelings for Quinn, and to let herself relax into the sensations of his hands and lips caressing her.

She wasn't sure which one of them pulled her pink sweatshirt over her head. She was dimly aware of Quinn's deft fingers unsnapping her bra, as he'd done that night after the fire. Then, she'd still been resisting him. Now, she could let herself smile at his skill, at the certainty of all his movements.

He shed his own flannel shirt and jeans quickly, and leaned back down beside her on the bed. Quinn McAllister was the first man she had ever seen naked and aroused, and being with him again now—letting her hands brush over the dark brown hair of his chest, following the sweep of it downward and touching him with an intimacy that seemed utterly natural—was a kind of homecoming Carrie hadn't expected.

Somehow she felt absolutely sure what his response would be if she lowered her head and swirled her tongue around his taut masculine nipple.

She was right. She felt a shudder ride through him, ending in a groan of pure need. She turned her head, letting her hair blanket his chest. She could read his reaction in the feel of his skin under her spread fingertips.

She kissed the suggestive slope of his flat belly, then the confused welter of scar tissue that covered his left side. There was something about those scars—the proof that Quinn McAllister was vulnerable as well as strong—that only made his long body more beautiful in Carrie's eyes.

He pulled her up to meet his lips again. He was breathing hard, and Carrie realized that she was, too. Her longing for this man was pounding inside her, and suddenly she couldn't stand the barrier of her blue jeans between her body and his.

She started to undo the button at her waistband, but once again Quinn forestalled her. He seemed determined to take turns at this. It was like being the hunter and the quarry at the same moment, and Carrie was already half-lost in the exhilaration of it.

The button and zipper presented no problem to Quinn's searching fingers. He helped her slide out of the jeans a moment later. She barely had time to gasp with the delight of her smooth skin against the rough strength of his, before his fingers found the moist core of her body, the place where she had been longing for him for what suddenly felt like forever.

Maybe it *was* forever. Maybe they had been meant for each other even before they had met. Every time they had ever touched, there had been this same undeniable magic, this sense that they were made to love each other and no one else.

That made Carrie suddenly impatient with the slow dance she had started. "I just changed my mind," she gasped, as Quinn stroked and caressed her into a half-liquid state. "Let's save subtlety for another time, all right?"

He went still for a long moment, and Carrie waited with him. Everything inside her was trembling, crying out for more.

"What if there isn't another time?" he asked slowly.

No. A voice inside her protested at the idea, even while she knew it could very well be true. She'd known, the moment she'd touched him downstairs in the kitchen, that this golden moment might be the only one they would be able to steal from the darkness around them.

That only made it seem more urgent to feel him inside her, filling her to completion. Leisurely exploration was for lovers who had all the time in the world. She and Quinn were chasing impossible dreams, reaching for things they might never be able to hold on to. And that thought drove her hunger for him into high gear, making her even bolder as she touched him and entwined herself with his long, strong frame.

Neither of them spoke again. Words could only threaten the fragile strength of their union. The things they needed to say to each other could be expressed in caresses, in the way Quinn's mouth covered Carrie's breast, in her quick gasp as he probed deep inside her, in the way she lifted herself astride him and drove him nearly over the edge with the silky pressure of her thighs.

For a moment she was confused about the way he flung one strong arm sideways, over the edge of the bed. He seemed to be reaching for something—for his shirt?

Then she heard the crackle of a plastic wrapper, and understood what he was doing. It brought her up short to realize she hadn't even thought about protecting herself.

It was even more startling to realize that Quinn had.

With him safely sheathed, Carrie's last remaining inhibitions vanished instantly. She'd been taking a calculated and crazy risk until now, but as Quinn slid inside her and she felt everything in her body contract to welcome him, she let herself fly, free of all the questions and uncertainties she'd been carrying for so long.

His hands circled her waist, following rather than guiding her. She was almost beyond noticing anything but her own delight, but she couldn't help seeing the astonished pleasure on his face when she moaned in his grip. She had always felt this way with Quinn McAllister—as though the greatest gift she could offer him was the strength of her own response to him. Driving her wild seemed to please him more than anything else.

And then she lost track of who was pleasing whom. They were riding together toward something Carrie had almost given up hoping for. And it was rushing toward them, too—she could feel the world around them spinning as they got closer and closer yet to that impossible goal. Her head felt dizzy, light, wonderfully free.

One of them cried out—she wasn't sure if it was her or Quinn. And then she heard him calling her name. At the same moment his fingers bit deeply into her arms where he held her, and Carrie felt herself falling forward, endlessly down and down and still farther down, falling without any thought of stopping herself, toward the only man she had ever loved.

Chapter 11

It took a long time for the world to come back into focus.

Quinn hadn't really taken in his surroundings before. Desire had overridden his instincts about never stepping into a room until he'd had a good look around it, and Carrie's welcoming smile and the sight of the double bed had been all he'd cared about.

Now, he eased himself over onto his right side, drained and fulfilled and already beginning to be aroused all over again by the unimaginable softness of Carrie's body close against him. And as his vision slowly cleared, he looked around her room.

It was a perfect reflection of Carrie herself—comfortable, straightforward, colorful. The down comforter they'd managed to kick into a tangled pile on the floor was covered in bright blues and yellows, and the soft yellow paint on the walls made the room seem warm and serene.

Outside, through the delicate lace that draped the windows, he could see the sky starting to darken as the early winter night came on. Somehow, that made it even better to be lying here next to Carrie, drinking in her warmth and keeping the cold world outside at bay.

If Carrie was concerned even slightly about the outside world, she wasn't showing it. She lay with her head resting on one bent arm, looking up at Quinn with eyes that were dreamy and still clouded by passion.

Neither of them spoke for a long time. And what was there to say, really? Quinn wondered. They had stolen this magic moment away from the realities of both their lives, and it was impossible to say where they might go from here. Judging by Carrie's silence, she seemed to recognize that as clearly as he did.

So he let himself drift in the sensations of stroking her skin, her hair, letting his hands caress her as they had in his dreams all these years, curving over her hips and the slight roundness of her belly, then up to her full breasts, to the nipples that had hardened all over again at his touch.

He couldn't imagine ever having enough of her.

He couldn't imagine she was going to give him the chance to find out. Already, in spite of the still-satisfied look in her eyes, she was growing more serious again. Her hands were exploring him softly, answering his own leisurely caresses, stirring him to hunger for her again. But she paused when she came to the scars on his left side, and he could almost feel her backing away from him a little, emotionally if not physically.

He wanted to take hold of her before that distance could widen, and make her swear that what had just happened between them was far more than a momentary desire. Surely it proved something, that their need for each other had survived through ten years and a lot of good reasons that it should have faded.

But he made himself stay still, one hand resting on the soft slope of her waist. The scars that she was touching so gently were a kind of warning signal about who Quinn was and the kind of life he led. And Carrie seemed to be listening to that warning again.

"Did you know, when this happened, that you almost died?" she asked quietly.

"Yeah."

"What did you think about?"

"You mean did my life flash before my eyes?" He gave her a faint smile, but her own face stayed serious. "Selected parts of it did."

"Will you tell me about it?"

It seemed strange, in this most blissful moment of the past ten years, to be recalling that horrific chapter in his life. But the gunshot wound was what had brought him back here. So maybe it was only fitting to tell Carrie about it now.

Or about part of it, anyway. "Between shock and anaesthesia, I wasn't exactly lucid for a lot of the time after I was shot," he said. "But whenever I *did* have a clear thought, it was always about some piece of unfinished business. You know, a case I hadn't solved, a person I wished I'd been able to reach better than I did."

"People who were dead, you mean?" Her voice sounded carefully neutral.

"Mostly, yeah. I thought about my parents some. I never really figured them out—or, I guess what I couldn't figure out was, if they were going to spend their lives exploring all over the world, why they ever had a kid in the first place."

"Was it possible you were—a mistake?"

He smiled at her again. "You don't have to protect my feelings, Carrie. It seems pretty likely that I *was* a mistake. That's why I wanted you to know how much I admired you for not making Davey feel as though he was one, too."

She seemed about to say something, and Quinn waited, rubbing his thumb over the velvety skin at her waist. But then she shook her head, and raised her own hand to push her glossy hair back, and said, "What other unfinished business was on your mind in those lucid moments?"

He hesitated, and then wondered what the hell he was waiting for. A promise that she would understand? She didn't owe him any promises—if anything, it was the other way around. So he made himself speak bluntly.

"I kept thinking about David's death." *And our love.* But he couldn't add the second phrase, not yet, not with everything still so unfinished. He had no right yet to demand any kind of answer from Carrie about her feelings for him.

"So you decided you had to come back and solve it."

Quinn sighed, and gave in to his need to pull her closer against him. Carrie reached for the blanket at the foot of the bed as they shifted positions. A moment later they were wrapped in its warmth, and in each other's.

He had wanted to be doing exactly this, in those dark days when his life had hung in the balance. He had dreamed endlessly about losing himself in Carrie's arms, hearing her whisper his name as she was doing now.

The problem was that in his dreams, her whispering voice had been full of love and longing. In real life, it sounded almost exasperated.

Dreams, he was discovering, were hard as hell to wake up from.

"Are you going to spend the rest of your life like this?" she asked.

For a moment he thought she was asking if he was going to spend the rest of his life wrapped up with her, and he started to tell her that nothing would make him happier. He moved his hands to the warm hollow of her back, and wondered how it was possible to be so intimately familiar with her body and still so astonished by every new exploration of it.

But then she added, "You have this white knight complex, Quinn, about riding into a place and solving everybody's problems for them. How long can you keep on doing that, and not taking anything for yourself?"

The question surprised him. "I *do* take something for myself," he said. "I get a lot of satisfaction out of what I do."

"When it works."

Quinn had been speaking with his lips against Carrie's bare shoulder, and the thrill of being entwined with her so closely was distracting him from what they were saying. But something in her tone was challenging him now, pushing at him. He lifted his head, reluctant to lose that sweet sense of union, but needing to make sure she understood what he meant.

"Things don't always work out," he said. "I know that. It goes with the territory."

"But when it *doesn't* work, look at what you do, Quinn." Carrie had raised her head now, too, and he could see the determination in her wide brown eyes. "You climb right back up on that white stallion of yours and go riding off to the next trouble spot. Or, when things get really bad, like they did after you were shot, you come riding back to the scene of something that didn't work before."

He didn't answer. Damn it, everything had seemed so clear that day he'd wakened in a hospital room in Chicago and realized he was going to live, after all. It had made perfect sense then to try to fix his own past mistakes, and chase his own lost dreams.

But Carrie's level stare now was telling him nothing was that simple. And she should know. She was the one who'd been left behind to deal with the complicated consequences of Quinn's mistakes the last time.

"What if you can't fix everything up and tack on a happy ending this time?" she was asking him. "What if there *isn't* a happy ending to be had, because this time you're dealing with a little boy's feelings, and that little boy isn't going to understand the satisfaction that you get out of solving people's troubles and then riding out of town again?''

This was getting too near the bone. Quinn sat up, shrugging off the warmth of the blanket. ''I'm not necessarily going to go riding out of Davey's life again, if that's what's worrying you,'' he said.

''What are you talking about?''

Her voice was level, and low, but something in it vibrated with a hidden warning, as though she were getting ready to defend herself.

It was Davey she was getting ready to defend, Quinn knew. And he loved her for the quick response she had toward anything she thought might hurt the boy. But—

''I'm his father, damn it.'' He tried to stay calm, but his feelings got the better of him. ''You can't sweep that back under the rug, now that he knows about it.''

''Does that mean you intend to come back to Stockbridge for good and *be* a father to him?''

''Of course not.'' He waved the question away. ''My life is in Chicago, where my job is.''

''Your life *is* your job, you mean.''

''To a certain extent, yes. Can you imagine me as a small-town cop, or the manager of a sporting goods store?''

Her eyes told him she'd tried to do just that, and come up blank. Quinn knew he couldn't disguise his gunslinger mentality if he had to, and Carrie clearly knew it, too.

''Then what are we talking about, Quinn? How exactly are you planning to be a part of Davey's life if you aren't here?''

Quinn drew in a deep breath. He wasn't ready to say these things yet. He wanted the mystery of David St. John's death cleared up first, so he could tackle the rest of this one step at a time. He wanted to win Carrie's trust again by finding her brother's killer, and he wanted Davey to have a little more time to get to know his father. Then, and not until then, would he feel ready to talk about how they might work things out.

He knew, even as he slung his legs over the side of the bed and groped for his clothes and some answers at the same time, that the most important part of it was the part he really wasn't ready to say.

It was the part about Carrie, and Quinn, and love.

It was the part where he finally got around to telling her how much he loved her, and how the thought of her love was what had kept him going in those bleak days last year when he had been half dead and half alive.

Sooner or later—he wasn't sure how, or when—he was going to find the courage to tell her how he felt. But he couldn't do that until he had some right to expect that she might feel that way about him in return. The defensive look in her eyes now was making it clear that that happy moment had not arrived yet.

Far from it. She was reaching for her clothes now, too, covering that beautiful body quickly, as though she regretted having opened up to him as much as she had.

Quinn knew he had no right to demand love from her yet. She still hadn't forgiven him for his last betrayal, or begun to believe in him again. It was still too soon for that.

But he *did* have rights where their son was concerned. And suddenly it seemed important to hear her acknowledge that fact.

"I don't know exactly how things might work," he said slowly. "But some kind of occasional visits—"

"Out of the question." The words winged back at him before he'd even finished his sentence in his own mind.

And that made him mad. She couldn't deny that he was Davey's father, whatever else she was trying to veto.

"Why?" he demanded.

She was buttoning the waistband of her jeans now, and even his own anger and confusion wasn't enough to quench the longing that flooded into him at the memory of unsnapping that button with his own fingers, and helping her shed the jeans that covered her.

But the defiance in her eyes now warned him that she wasn't about to tolerate any softer thoughts. Quinn paused in the act of buttoning his shirt, caught between two powerful currents: love, on the one hand, and stubborn determination on the other.

"You can't possibly imagine that I would let you take Davey with you to the city, even occasionally," she said.

"I don't see why not. He'd be safe with me."

"Quinn McAllister!" The exasperation was back in her voice, and there was nothing soft or indulgent about it this time. "He's not even safe in his own house when you're here. All you have to do is show up and people are breaking windows, and throwing bombs, and—and—"

She covered her face suddenly, and Quinn wondered for the first time if her protective mother pose was only that…a pose. Hell, he knew all about strapping on lots of armor to convince yourself that deep inside, you weren't really scared.

"Who are you really protecting, Carrie?" he asked. "Davey, or yourself?"

She didn't look up for a long moment. Something about the rigid set of her shoulders made Quinn want to move closer to her, to tell her she didn't have to carry the whole burden of worrying about this on her own.

But he knew he was partly to blame, if she'd gotten used to handling things by herself. So he waited out her silence, and finished putting his clothes on, and clenched his jaw against whatever she might say to him.

It was worse than he'd expected. "Would you mind telling me what you mean by that?" she asked. The coolness in her voice rocked Quinn.

But he refused to soften what he'd just said. "You've admitted that you and Davey have been a unit for a long time now," he said. "Maybe you've gotten to rely on that. Maybe it's what feels safe to you."

"Damn it, Quinn—"

He cut her off. "But that boy's going to grow up sooner or later," he said. "That tight little two-person world of yours isn't going to last forever. Is *that* why you resent me so much, Carrie? Because my being here is bringing that moment a little closer?"

"Don't be ridiculous." Her eyes were dry, but something in her face made her look as though she had just wiped away tears. And the tight sound in her voice made Quinn think he'd struck a nerve.

He lifted one shoulder in a shrug. "It's just something I wondered about, that's all," he said.

"Well, you can stop wondering about it. And you can stop thinking about having Davey visit you, too. Please don't imagine I could ever let him go off with a man whose life is as dangerous as yours, a man who carries a gun for his living, a man who—"

Once again, she stopped. She didn't cover her face this time, so he could see the way her face had twisted in sudden anguish.

A man who carries a gun for a living . . . And she didn't even know about that heart-stopping moment this morning when Quinn had walked in on Davey with a gun in his hands. She was right; Quinn's life contained the kind of dangers that Carrie didn't even want to think about.

That still didn't change the basic situation. He finished her sentence for her, grimly. "A man who happens to be his natural father," he said. "And that gives me some legal rights to see Davey, whether you approve of it or not."

"Legal rights?" She breathed the words out.

"Fathers do have some legal rights to their children," he said.

"But you wouldn't fight me in court over this." It was a plea, disguised as a statement.

Would he? He wasn't sure. But he did know that he needed to push Carrie to the point where she would consider letting him into Davey's life, if not her own. Having come this far, he wouldn't back down on that now.

"I would never want it to get into a courtroom," he said slowly. "That wouldn't do anyone any good, especially Davey. But if you're determined to fight me on it, I'm prepared to take it that far."

She hadn't anticipated this. He could tell from the slow dawning of realization in the depths of her brown eyes. She really had believed she could just tell him to stay out of Davey's world and he would do it.

The thought made him angry. She had locked him out of his son's life from the very beginning, and she was trying to keep him out now. In spite of the passion that was still pulsing treacherously through his body, it was getting easier to meet her challenging stare with a challenge of his own.

The phone by the bedside rang before either of them could speak again, and for a moment Quinn felt glad of the interruption. They needed breathing space, he thought, after the powerful feelings—sweet and bitter—they'd just shared.

But the breathing space didn't last long. Carrie, handing the phone over to Quinn, said, "It's for you."

It was a man's voice, one Quinn didn't recognize. But something about the guttural sound and muffled words made him think the caller was disguising his voice. And that immediately put him on his guard.

"Nice night for fireworks." It was hard to make out the words at first. "Everybody looking up, who's keeping track of where all the little kids are?"

By now Quinn was getting every word. "Who is this?" he demanded, not because he thought he would get an answer but because it seemed critical to figure out why the voice sounded slightly familiar.

The man's chuckle had a nasty sound to it that made Quinn's hackles rise. "It would be too bad if *another* David St. John died because you couldn't keep your nose out of things that don't concern you," he said, and hung up.

Quinn's expletive was loud in the quiet room. He hurled the phone receiver back into its cradle and vaulted back over the bed, grabbing for his shoes.

"Quinn, what is it?" Carrie's voice was tight with alarm. "Is it Davey? Is he all right?"

Did all mothers have this quick instinct about their children, Quinn wondered fleetingly, or was Carrie exceptional? Or had she somehow been waiting for this ever since he had arrived, dreading the loss of the most important person in her world?

He didn't have time to explain, or to argue. He was sure she would want to come with him, and he didn't want that, either. He couldn't think straight, couldn't be of any use to Davey, if he had to worry about Carrie's safety, too.

His fingers were shaking almost too hard to get the laces on his sneakers tied. It amazed him that his voice worked at all as he shot to his feet and said, "I'll call, as soon as I check this out. It'll be all right, Carrie."

Not only did his voice work, it sounded nearly steady, and surprisingly reassuring. Quinn spared a split second to marvel at the way his battle nerves had kicked in, masking his own churning fears. Rule number one, when things were falling apart around you, was to act as though they weren't. Sometimes that could be enough to turn a bad situation around.

This couldn't be falling apart, not so soon, not this way. *Dear God, not Davey,* he thought. How could he have let himself get so wrapped up in his own pleasure that he'd let the boy go out into danger like this?

He knew he couldn't waste time cursing himself, or explaining things to Carrie. He had to get out of here, as fast as he could.

They were at the bedroom door now, and she was demanding to know where he was going, and why. He pulled her to him with a sudden fierceness, and stopped her words with a kiss that was the very opposite of the gentle caresses they'd been sharing earlier.

"Stay here," he said roughly, as he released her again. "I'll call."

He could almost taste the adrenalin pulsing through him. He was sure Carrie could taste it, too. The wildness in him seemed to be reflected in her eyes, and he wondered if his kiss, meant to be a silent promise, a pledge that he would do all he could, had only added to her fears instead.

He didn't stick around to find out. Before she could say anything else, he was pounding down the stairs to the ground floor, digging in his pockets for the key to his motorcycle, racing to keep up with his own thoughts, which were already halfway to the county fairground in search of his son.

The fairground parking lot was overflowing with cars, but Quinn's bike was easy to spot. He seemed to have ditched it in the first convenient spot, and headed into the crowd on foot. She could picture him, hair tousled, blue eyes wild, long legs propelling him through the night, looking for—what?

She was absolutely certain it had something to do with Davey. She had seen the bolt of pure fear that had crossed his face when he'd listened to the man on the other end of the phone. And although that hardened **professional mask** she hated so much had come down almost immediately to cover his feelings, she had glimpsed enough of them to be sure it was Davey he was frightened for. What else could have caused that naked, momentary panic?

She was furious with him for walking out on her. Did he really imagine that she would sit still waiting for his damned phone call, not knowing if her son was all right? Quinn McAllister had a lot to learn about how parents behaved, she thought, as she pulled her minivan up behind his bike and climbed out.

The fireworks display seemed to be heading into its grand finale. The explosions overhead reverberated in Carrie's chest, along with her savagely beating heart. There was something eerie about the way the fire-bursts lit the upturned faces of the watching crowd. The spectators' innocent pleasure, and the cries of appreciation after every display, were a grotesque contrast to Carrie's fears that somewhere on the long hillside or the flat playing ground there was some danger waiting for her son.

She saw Quinn, moving restlessly at the edge of the crowd, scanning it with keen eyes. She headed in his direction, but before she could reach him, he had stalked toward the slope of the hill, ignoring the cries of "Hey, siddown" that followed him.

Carrie shielded her eyes against the bright lights coming from overhead, and saw Susannah and the three kids huddled together on a blanket, looking up gleefully. Davey was pointing, his face bright with delight.

She let out a long breath, and found that her knees had gotten very weak. Quinn was joining the group, waving off their obvious surprise, and all of Carrie's worry about Davey was suddenly rechanneled into anger at Quinn.

How could she have let her own fantasies take hold of her to the point where she had forgotten what a dark force he had always been in her life? She had immersed herself in the magic of making love with Quinn while somewhere, out in the night, someone had been threatening her son. Quinn's racing trip to the fairground only proved what he had refused to tell her in plain words.

Her fury at him had built to boiling point by the time the crowd had cheered the end of the show and started the cumbersome business of heading home. Quinn's height made him easy to spot in the throng, but she lost track of Davey until the two of them emerged suddenly near Quinn's motorcycle, where Carrie was waiting and fuming.

Davey's first words didn't do anything to cool her down. "Hi, Mom," he said. "Quinn says he's going to let me ride on the back of his motorcycle!"

Quinn hadn't even brought his helmet, Carrie noticed. His shirt was still half-unbuttoned, just as it had been when he'd kissed her at her bedroom door and she'd felt his hard flesh under her hands.

But his face was different now. It wasn't just his obvious astonishment at the sight of Carrie waiting next to his bike. He looked shaken, but relieved. And the way he was keeping a possessive hand on Davey's shoulder confirmed that it had been the boy he'd been worried about.

"I'm sorry, Davey," she said firmly, "but you'll have to ride with me in the van. Quinn should have checked with me before he said you could go on the motorcycle."

"Ah, Mom..."

"Davey." She cut short the ritual protests, and squatted down to look her son directly in the face. "I want you to get in the van, all right? I'll be right there."

She hugged him quickly, then let him go. She hated to see the glee ebbing out of Davey's face, but her own relief at seeing him safe was more than enough to cancel out her maternal pangs. As Davey made his way into the passenger seat of the van, Carrie stood up and faced the man who had been able to make her feel the extremes of passion and rage in the space of a single evening.

"I wanted to keep him with me." He was heading off her protest now. "I wanted to make absolutely sure he was safe."

"So that phone call *was* threatening Davey."

He nodded, slowly. "I had to know," he said. "I had to get here as fast as I could. And that meant getting here on my own."

This wasn't the place to explain to him the thousand things that were wrong with that argument, Carrie knew. People were starting to clog up the fairground road now, and Davey was waiting unhappily in the car. She wanted to get home, not to stage a fight with Quinn here by the side of the road with their son and half the town to watch.

But she couldn't let his explanation go without an answer. She stepped closer to him, so that her quiet voice would carry over the noise all around them, and said very clearly, "Don't *ever* walk out on me like that again, Quinn McAllister. Especially not where my son is concerned."

"Our son, you mean."

She let out a frustrated sigh. She knew that stubborn expression of his so well. The only useful weapon for getting past it was tenderness, and she was feeling anything but tender toward him now. Even the ache in his intent blue eyes wasn't enough to dent her determination at the moment.

"Yes, our son," she agreed. "But that's hardly the way you were acting tonight."

She turned and climbed into her van, leaving Quinn standing there defiantly. She had no real hope that he would take the hint and make himself scarce, and the presence of his single headlight in her rearview mirror a moment later confirmed it. He was following her home, as though there was no question that that was where he belonged.

She tried to keep her mind on Davey's somewhat muted account of the fireworks display, but it was Quinn she kept thinking of. *You don't belong here,* she wanted to say to him. *And Davey doesn't belong with you.*

And then she would remember the warmth of the sweet completion she had felt in his arms only hours ago, and her certainty, when they'd joined each other in that lovers' bond, that there was nowhere else on earth she really wanted to be.

"Damn it," she said softly, as she pulled into her driveway. Why couldn't Quinn have been what he had pretended to be at first—a troubled loner in search of a place to call home? Everything would have been so much simpler then.

Davey gave her a startled look. "What's the matter?" he asked.

"Mostly I'm just tired," she said, and there was an element of truth to the words. Being around Quinn had never been easy, even in the days when she'd been happy about it.

Still, tired or not, she knew her own questions were going to keep her awake far into the night. And the one that was nagging at her most insistently was the possibility that Quinn might, in fact, have a legal right to claim some of Davey's time. Everything inside her cried out in protest at the idea of watching her small son ride off on the back of that old motorcycle with his father, heading toward Quinn's violent and unpredictable world.

As she'd pulled into her driveway she'd had an idea about where she could get a quick answer to that question. She'd glanced toward Ted Wright's house as she passed it, and noticed that his study light was still on.

Ted's study had been built on to the side of the house a couple of years ago. She knew he often worked there in the evenings. This might be a good time to ask her lawyer neighbor the question that was tormenting her. *Did Quinn have any legal rights to their son?*

She and Ted were hardly friends, but they occasionally performed neighborly favors. She'd done some emergency baby-sitting recently when Ted had had his kids one weekend and then had been called in to his office unexpectedly. And he was a divorced father who knew firsthand about visitation rights. She knew she couldn't expect a definitive answer, but surely he would be able to tell her enough to let her think about her situation with some degree of realism.

The roar of Quinn's motorcycle met her as she got out of the van. "I'm going next door for a couple of minutes," she said, when he had shut the noisy engine off. "Would you oversee Davey's bedtime routine until I get back?"

The wind had tangled his hair into a tawny knot, and his attempts to comb it flat with his fingers were only making it worse. Carrie thought of how that thick hair had felt under her own fingers, and took a step backward as though she could physically escape the longings that still filled her when she looked at him.

She didn't give him a chance to ask why she was going next door. Or maybe he had already figured it out. His brows were lowered as he opened the front door for Davey, but he didn't say anything.

That suited Carrie just fine. She hurried across the lawn, her mind so full of her own problems that she didn't notice until she had almost reached it that the private door to Ted's study was ajar. That was odd; the neighborhood was a quiet one, but Ted was fond of saying loudly that he was a great believer in locking his doors. It wasn't like him to leave one standing open. But Carrie could clearly see light coming around the edges of the door.

She wasn't ready to absorb any more shocks this evening. She hadn't come up with even one explanation for the slightly open door by the time she reached it. And she was completely unprepared for what met her eyes when she pushed the door open the rest of the way.

Her neighbor, Ted Wright, was sprawled on his back on the carpeted floor of his home office, with a deadly red circle spreading outward from the bullet hole in the middle of his chest.

Chapter 12

Carrie's panicked phone call to the Stockbridge police just before midnight, made after she'd stumbled and gasped her way back into her house, had unleashed a barrage that seemed to include every police and emergency vehicle in southeast Illinois. Most of them were still parked on the street outside, with their lights flashing in a grim parody of the earlier fireworks display.

She remembered—all too well—how those flashing lights could become hypnotic after a while. She'd felt that way the evening David had been killed, while she'd tried to absorb the double trauma of her brother's death and the news about Quinn's real identity.

Before long, her mind had gone mercifully blank, and she'd found herself watching the alternating orange and red streaks of the ambulance's lights, and listening to the vague crackle of the dispatcher's voice on the radio in one of the police cars as if it were a gentle lullaby.

She could hear that same crackle now, as the Stockbridge police dealt with this new murder. Another link with Special Agent Quinn McAllister of the FBI—it was all far too close to the nightmare Carrie had tried so hard to escape from.

At least the noise was in the distance now. She had answered all the same questions over and over again. Why had she gone to Ted Wright's house? Was she *sure* the door had been ajar? Was she sure she hadn't heard anyone in the house? Did she know where the dead man's stepbrother was? Finally she was able to go home to be with her son.

She was sitting on the side of Davey's bed now, holding on to him while she waited for him to drop off to sleep. The flashes of red and blue from the police cruisers outside were beginning to exert their strange, hypnotic effect. It was tempting just to let her mind wander, to take a rest from the pain of trying to figure out what was going on and how she should deal with it.

"How's he doing?"

The deep voice from the doorway startled her. She hadn't heard footsteps coming upstairs, hadn't heard anything at all except those disturbing echoes of the last time she'd come face to face with a murder victim.

Quinn McAllister. He was the constant in these two nightmarish scenes. She glared at him now, holding Davey a little closer.

"He's upset," she said. "Naturally."

Quinn came into the room, uninvited. Carrie felt herself bristle instinctively, resisting his presence. And then she let herself take a closer look at him.

He looked ragged, weary, as worn down by this as Carrie felt. His shoulders were sagging, as though the effort of holding his big body straight was suddenly too hard.

And his eyes seemed haunted. Without asking, Carrie knew instinctively that Ted Wright's death was conjuring up nightmares for Quinn, too.

She tried to keep hating him for his part in the old nightmare and this new one. But the look in his eyes— bleak and determined at the same time—choked off the anger she wanted to feel.

He moved closer. She sensed a kind of exhausted reluctance in him, as though he knew he was pushing his way in here but he couldn't convince himself to do anything else. He dropped into the chair on the other side of Davey's bed and dragged one big hand over his eyes. Then he leaned forward, elbows on his knees, and looked at his son.

Davey was tucked into the crook of Carrie's arm. She could sense him watching Quinn. Davey had been full of questions about the hubbub next door when she'd first put him to bed, and most of them had had to do with Quinn. Carrie waited, stroking Davey's shoulder, wondering what the two of them would have to say to each other.

Quinn's words were direct, but gentle. "You know I'm here because I want to find out who killed your uncle David," he said, and Davey nodded silently. "Well, sometimes when you start looking into a crime, the person who did it panics and starts doing things to cover his tracks. I think that's what happened with your neighbor."

"Did Ted kill my uncle David?"

"I don't know."

Carrie could see Quinn's frown in the dim light. Ted Wright had been his prime suspect, the focus of his investigation up to now. And Ted had obviously known something, or he wouldn't have been killed to cover up whatever dangerous knowledge he possessed. That meant everything was up in the air again, with far more questions than answers.

Carrie didn't like that uneasy feeling any more than she had when Quinn had first shown up. More sharply than she'd meant to, she said, "But Quinn and the police are going to find who killed your uncle *and* Ted. Now that this has happened, everybody's going to work hard to find out what's going on.''

She was getting ready to level a pointed look at Quinn, to encourage him to back her up on this, but he was already ahead of her. He leaned forward and squeezed Davey's hand.

''Your mom's right,'' he said. ''A lot of times when you're investigating something things seem worst just before they start to clear themselves up. This is bad, Davey, but we'll get it sorted out, and I'm going to do what I can to make sure it happens fast.''

Carrie could still feel tension in Davey's body, in spite of Quinn's comforting words. Quinn's parental instincts seemed to be on the money this time, she thought. He'd seen immediately that Davey needed reassurance, and lots of it.

''Are people going to shoot at you now, Quinn?'' he asked.

So it was his father he was most worried about. Carrie let out a tight sigh and met Quinn's weary blue eyes across the bed.

''I sure hope not, scout.''

That was the best he seemed able to do, as he reached up and smoothed the boy's hair down. Well, at least he wasn't offering empty promises, Carrie thought, although it wasn't much comfort at the moment.

''Do you have your gun with you, in case they do?''

Carrie gasped. ''Quinn doesn't have a gun with him, honey,'' she said quickly.

''Yes, he does. I saw it, in his bedroom.''

This time it was very easy to feel angry in spite of the beaten-down slant of Quinn's shoulders, and the haunted look in his eyes. ''You brought a gun here?'' she demanded, softly but insistently.

Davey seemed to sense that he'd let the wrong cat out of the bag. ''He said I should never touch it,'' he said.

"He was right." She was sending Quinn all kinds of silent messages.

He shifted his position and started to get out of the chair again. Just before he did, he leaned forward one more time and said, "Don't worry about me, Davey. This is all going to be over before you know it."

But how? Everything in Carrie wanted to call the question after him as he left the room. She could see him working at straightening his shoulders, keeping his tough loner's stance intact. *How are you going to finish this without putting yourself—and the rest of us—in even more danger?*

Her unanswered questions swirled around inside her, making it very hard to stay still on Davey's bed. She wanted to run to Quinn, to shake him until he told her what was in his mind, to hold on to him so that she would never be faced with the awful possibility of looking at *his* shattered body, too.

Her growing fears for him made her wonder if she was getting too close to caring for him again, in a way she knew shouldn't be happening. Somehow she managed to keep herself sitting quietly by her son's side until his breathing finally changed and deepened. But the instant she was sure Davey was asleep, she was on her feet, in search of Quinn.

She found him right next door, talking on her bedside phone. He'd pulled the blankets over the tangled sheets, she noticed. And his voice was hard and businesslike, as though he were trying to pull a cover over the emotions that had led them to tangle those sheets up so crazily only a few hours ago.

But the same emotions were still roiling in his eyes, in spite of the harsh note in his voice as he said, "You realize, at this point, that you're obstructing a murder investigation."

There was a pause. Carrie watched his long jaw tense, and took in a trembling breath as she realized how much she wanted to smooth a hand along it, to ease the tight weariness she could sense in his whole body.

"I don't believe you," he said finally. "You were his friend. Don't you want to find out who killed him?"

The pause was shorter this time. Quinn's voice was abrupt as he ended the conversation. "I see," he said. "Well, I'm sure Leo LaPlante will be around to see you with all the same questions bright and early tomorrow morning. I just thought you might want to get a jump on helping us out." He hung up looking much less brisk than he'd sounded.

"Steve Solidad?" Carrie guessed.

"Yeah." Quinn leaned forward, resting his face in his hands. "Yesterday he was perfectly willing to try to remember the name of the girl Ted Wright was dating at the time the first cocaine shipments came through here. And now—"

Carrie had to force her mind back to the details of the case. At the moment she was so tired, so muddled, so worried about Davey and Quinn and all of them together that she couldn't bear to plunge back into the question-and-answer routine that seemed to be second nature to Quinn.

But she knew it was important to get this settled as soon as possible, and that meant more questions and answers. "Don't tell me, let me guess," she said. "He suddenly doesn't want anything to do with you, right?"

"Good guess." He gave her a worn-out version of his heart-stopping grin.

"Quinn, he's probably just scared."

"Maybe, or maybe he's covering up something."

"He wouldn't shoot Ted. They've always been friends."

Quinn got to his feet, slowly. He looked like he'd been sandbagged, and Carrie remembered that while she'd been sitting quietly with Davey, wishing this would all go away, Quinn had been working, making trips back and forth to the police station and the hospital, sitting in on interviews, trying to sort out the new pieces of this puzzle that just kept getting more complex. No wonder he was tired.

"People will do some mighty strange things if they're scared," he said. "I've been looking into Solidad's finances, and I have to wonder where he got the money he's been putting into his sports store. He didn't make much playing baseball."

"I assumed he inherited it from his father."

Quinn shook his head. "The old man didn't leave a lot." So he'd been checking that, too. Carrie wondered what else he'd found out about these people she'd thought she knew. "Makes me wonder if Steve had a nest egg of his own— maybe built up out of that cocaine trade ten years ago, or if Wright was paying him off to keep his mouth shut, or—"

He cut himself off this time, and sat down again suddenly. He wasn't showing any pain, but something about the way he clamped his left elbow to his side made Carrie think he was feeling some.

"Sorry—I'm just thinking out loud," he said. There was a thread of amusement deeply buried in the hoarseness of his voice. "I've got to get some sleep, or I'm not going to do anybody any good tomorrow."

Carrie waited, pointedly, for him to get to his feet again and make the obvious moves in the direction of his room.

He didn't shift. He looked, in fact, as though he thought he belonged on her bed, and as though he intended to climb into it at any moment.

"Quinn," she said.

He looked up at her, and the hungry look in his eyes tore at her heart. She wanted to give this man so much. If only what he was offering in return was less complicated, less frightening.

"We can't both sleep here," she said, as firmly as she could. "Not with Davey in the next room."

"That's *why* I'm sleeping here," he said. "I don't want to be all the way across the house if something happens in the night."

"What are you expecting to happen?" She spoke quickly.

He shook his head. "Nothing specific," he said. "I just want to be within shouting distance."

There was a pause, as Carrie looked at her rumpled bed. "This," she said, "is a lot closer than shouting distance."

He got up finally, but instead of heading for the door, he went as far as the spot where Carrie stood, and then stopped. His body seemed very large, looming next to her.

"I want to be within *whispering* distance." His voice was raggedly seductive at her ear. "I have to know you're safe, you and Davey. Don't shut me out, Carrie. Not again."

Her heartbeat was picking up speed with all the momentum of the Midnight Express roaring through town. He was barely touching her—just one hand at her elbow, but even that was enough to remind her of all the things they could do to each other, all the passions they had unleashed such a short time before.

She grabbed at sanity but was amazed to find that even thoughts of guns and bullets and the horrific sight of her neighbor's body weren't enough to calm the yearning in her blood for this dangerous outsider who was coming to feel like such a fixture in her world.

Then she thought about Davey, finally sleeping in his bed in the next room. Quinn *wasn't* a fixture in this world—he'd said as much himself. She was more willing to take a chance on heartbreak for herself, but not for Davey.

That gave her enough strength to challenge Quinn's words. "Shut you out?" she repeated. "Isn't that what you were doing to me when you went pelting off to the fairground without even telling me why?"

She felt him sigh, and fought her own urge to move closer to him, into his arms. "I'm used to doing things on my own," he said.

"You already—"

He held up a hand, palm toward her. Carrie thought about how his hands had felt gliding over her earlier this evening, searching out every pleasure point in her body. The thought made her quiver all over again.

Quinn didn't seem to be thinking about pleasure. His voice was serious as he said, "I know. I already told you that. What I *didn't* tell you is that you were right. I should have told you where I was going, and why. I just didn't think you would want to hear it."

"That's not a good enough reason to keep me in the dark, Quinn. I'd rather worry about something concrete than not have any idea *what* I'm worrying about."

"I know," he said again. "I'm sorry. If it happened again—"

He glanced at the phone, as though he half expected that it *would* happen again. But at least this time, Davey was safe in the next room, and Quinn was here keeping a watchful eye on both of them. For the first time Carrie began to think she would be happier, after all, if he stayed close to them tonight.

"If it happened again, I would do things differently," he finished.

Carrie swallowed. It was so tempting to move closer to him. He seemed to be letting his arms hang by his sides that way just in case she should want to be in them again. But there were still things she needed to say, and know, before she would let passion take her over again.

"What *did* happen?" she asked softly. "What did that man on the phone say?"

She could see him resisting the idea of telling her. And she could feel herself resisting hearing it. This was hard for both of them.

"He said it would be too bad if another David St. John got killed because I couldn't keep my nose out of things that didn't concern me."

Hearing it was worse than she'd anticipated. She wanted to rush straight into the next room and shield Davey herself from whatever attacker might be waiting for him out in the night.

But she stayed rooted where she was, because she could see that she wasn't alone in her worry. All her own fears were mirrored in Quinn's blue eyes, and his words just confirmed it.

"I was as scared as I've ever been," he said. "It made me a little crazy. That's why I bolted out of here like I did. I felt that if I repeated those words out loud, even to you, it might make them come true."

She was nodding even before he'd finished. She knew that feeling, that irrational protest against even the idea of something happening to her child. But somehow she hadn't expected Quinn to share it.

He was yawning suddenly, moving away from her toward the bed again. "I don't know about you," he said, "but I'm beyond beat. And I've got a dozen things I have to follow up on tomorrow morning. I've got to get some sleep. Are you still intending to kick me out of here?"

Carrie shook her head. "I'm falling asleep on my feet myself," she said. And it was true, although another part of her was crying out that she wanted Quinn in her arms again, not keeping his distance as his posture told her he was intending to do.

She watched him easing himself down on the edge of the bed, and said, "Your side hurts you again, doesn't it?"

He shrugged. "It happens when I get worn out," he said.

"Quinn?"

He looked up, and she felt the shock of meeting those eloquent blue eyes, just as she'd felt it every time she'd ever looked at him. "Yeah?" He rasped the single word out.

"Did you really bring a gun with you?"

He nodded. "Tool of the trade," he said.

"Would you actually . . . use it?"

She was thinking about Ted Wright, and her brother, and how foreign that kind of violence seemed to her quiet little town.

"If I have to." Quinn was pulling off his sneakers now, still looking up at her. When he pulled his shirt free of the waistband of his jeans, she caught her breath, but he was only loosening the shirt, not taking it off. He dragged the comforter over his body a moment later, seeming intent on sleep and nothing else.

But his voice was still very much awake as he said, "You know, you're acting as though I brought these things into Stockbridge with me—the idea of guns and shooting and violence."

"We weren't shooting at each other before you showed up."

"No." He rolled over slightly, and the piercing intelligence in his blue eyes was enough to quiet her protests. "But whoever killed David and whoever killed Ted Wright—that person was here all along. I may be the catalyst for this, Carrie, but I'm not the criminal. It's something you might want to think about."

Thinking about it kept her awake long after she had slipped into pajamas and turned out the bedside lamps, and listened to Quinn's breathing next to her turn into the slow, deep sound of near-exhaustion in search of some kind of rest.

She gave up looking at the clock radio at about two, and resigned herself to a restless night listening to the bare, late autumn branches tapping nervously at the playroom windows downstairs. She wasn't aware of when she finally eased into sleep, but the clock read four-thirty when she was roused again.

It was a small noise, but she knew immediately what it was. It came from Davey's room, and it was the sound he made when he was having a bad dream. From years of experience she also knew that if she got there soon, she might be able to ease him back into real sleep before he wakened himself crying.

She got soundlessly out of the bed, pushing her feet into her slippers. It was only when she reached the door to Davey's room that it dawned on her Quinn hadn't been in bed next to her.

He was sitting by Davey's bedside, smoothing the boy's forehead, exactly as if he'd known, too, what the quiet sound had meant. And he seemed to know how to soothe his son through whatever nightmare was troubling Davey's small head.

How did you know? she asked him silently, as she watched the two of them together. Had Quinn once been a small boy who had wished for someone to comfort him in the night? From what she knew of his real life story, it seemed very likely. And from somewhere inside that loner's soul of his, he'd dredged up those old memories, and was using them to set his son's mind at rest.

She tiptoed back into her room, but she was far from sleepy when Quinn finally came back to her bed. She could sense his intense weariness in the way he eased himself down and dragged the covers over himself, and suddenly the only thing Carrie wanted in the world was to offer him some of the same comfort he had just been soothing Davey with.

She moved closer to him under the sheet, and felt him flinch when her hand touched his injured left side under his shirt. "I'm sorry," she said. "Did I hurt you?"

She couldn't tell what his muffled answer meant. It sounded slightly surprised.

"I saw you with Davey."

He made another inarticulate sound, then turned over onto his back. He was looking up at the darkened ceiling, not at her. "What does he dream about when he sounds like that?" he asked.

"I don't know. He's never told me."

Was Quinn trying to recall his own boyhood nightmares? Something in his face made her think he might be. She reached for him again, running her fingers very gently through the heavy corn silk of his hair.

"He might tell you about it, if you asked," she said softly.

He rolled the rest of the way over, facing her now. In the very faint light from the streetlight outside, he looked even younger than when she'd first met him. His eyes, usually so wary and watchful, were unguarded for once, and his long jaw had relaxed, whether from tiredness or tenderness she couldn't tell.

She *did* know that the open look in his eyes called up a tenderness in her that she couldn't have denied for the world. She moved a little closer to him, pushing the covers out of her way, and eased their two bodies together. Quinn's arms came around her with a weary desperation that made her wonder how hard he'd been working to stay on his own side of the bed up until now.

"Thank you," she murmured, "for being so caring with Davey."

Quinn snorted, feeling amazed. "I never thought I'd have any family of my own to care about," he said. "How could I not care about him?"

"Plenty of fathers wouldn't, under the same circumstances."

She was testing him, he thought. Probing him to see whether she could trust him with their son. He'd been worried about kids before now, and had gone out on some pretty long limbs to try to help young men who'd gotten themselves in trouble they couldn't handle.

But until tonight he'd never known the blind panic of thinking that your own child might be in mortal danger. Now that he knew firsthand what it felt like, he couldn't blame Carrie any longer for the caution she was showing around him.

But he was so damned tired, and it was heaven just to have her holding him like this. He let his head droop down on her shoulder, and drew in a long breath that was spiced with the sweet perfume of her hair and skin. He remembered waking up with her that one morning in this house, and drinking in this same heady scent.

"You smell so good." He was far too tired to come up with a more elegant way to put it.

She laughed softly. Quinn could feel the sound vibrating against his mouth where it rested on the base of her throat. He'd thought he was too sleepy to move another inch, but it was too tempting just to kiss the smooth curve of her neck, as though he could taste her laughter there.

The shiver that ran through her at his kiss started something building deep inside Quinn. He kissed her again, and swirled his tongue sleepily against the spot that had made her shiver. She let her breath out on a sigh, and shifted her embrace so that he could feel the already pointed tips of her breasts where they met the quickening rise and fall of his own chest.

"I thought you were exhausted."

Her voice was rich with that amusement he'd always found so seductive. It took him a moment to figure out what she meant, and when he did, it was his turn to chuckle. His body was already stirred into arousal, long before his mind had processed anything beyond this amazing sense of well-being that always came from being intimately entwined with Carrie St. John.

"I *am* exhausted," he told her huskily. "In fact, I'm asleep right now. So are you. We're both dreaming this."

She gave a soft, delighted sigh as his fingers found and undid the buttons on the front of her pajama top. He lowered his head to her breasts, lost in the silky sensation of caressing them with his lips and tongue, wishing he could do this for approximately forever.

"It wouldn't surprise me if we were dreaming." She sounded breathless and satisfied at the same time. "Real life almost *never* feels this good."

Quinn laughed again, softly, triumphantly. And as if she'd wrapped him in some magic spell, his tiredness vanished, replaced by an arousal so complete and uninhibited that if he hadn't had the physical evidence of Carrie's warm breath and satiny skin to convince him he was awake, he would have stuck by his dream theory. Carrie was right. Nothing on earth came close to the way it felt to make love with her.

"We're going to have to be very, very quiet." He whispered the words against her ear, as he peeled off the rest of her pajamas and got out of his own shirt.

"I know." That throaty laughter hidden in her voice was going to drive him out of his mind. He kissed her collarbone again, and her neck, and the place just behind her ear that had always made her gasp. It worked again now.

"Quieter than that." He was grinning now. He couldn't help himself. He felt so good, so complete, like a king come home to claim his kingdom and his consort. And the urges that were zinging through him—to run his fingertips over Carrie's taut, rosy nipples; to ease his knee between her legs and feel her wrap herself around him; to kiss her chin, her earlobe, her lips—would have been impossible to ignore even if he'd wanted to.

"If you want me to be absolutely quiet, you're going to have to stop—doing that."

"Doing this?" He'd slid one hand down over her belly and dipped it into that bottomless well where he'd longed to lose himself for so many years. He felt her whole body contracting around him, and knew that his smile of satisfaction had spread until he was probably grinning like a fool. And he didn't even care.

"Yes, that. No—"

He'd started to withdraw his hand, when Carrie's sharp protest made him stop. He lingered, not quite caressing her, not quite retreating, luxuriating in the sensation of her whole body quivering next to his.

Finally she made a soft, frustrated sound, and pushed her fingers into his hair in what seemed to start out as a rebuke and ended up as a caress. Quinn closed his eyes at the familiar, gentle feeling of her hands outlining his face, and turned his head to capture the delicate tip of one of her forefingers between his teeth.

"Don't tease me, Quinn." He could hear passion vibrating in her voice now. "I want you too much to play games about it."

And that finally did it to him. The thought that her hunger matched his own had always been more potent than any aphrodisiac the mind of man could have dreamed up. Quinn managed—with difficulty—to get out of the blue jeans that were constricting him, and into the condom he'd conveniently stuck into his back pocket. When he turned back to Carrie, she looked breathless and dark-eyed against the pure white sheets of her bed.

Warmth and laughter. Those were the two things he'd always loved most about her. They were both waiting for him now, as she held her arms out to him and murmured, "Maybe if we do this very slowly, it'll be easier to be absolutely quiet."

"We never did get around to being slow the last time, did we?"

He wished the sentence back the instant he'd said it, but Carrie seemed too intent on welcoming him inside her to comment. There was no guarantee that this was anything but another momentary attempt at recapturing the past, or warding off the future. There was no guarantee of anything between the two of them, and his words came too close to reminding both of them that any time they made love could be the last time.

That made it easier to move slowly. Maybe, after all, it might be possible to make this moment last forever. Quinn slid deep inside Carrie with a deliberation that left both of them shuddering, and stayed there, motionless, feeling her surrounding him, drawing him in.

When he finally began to move again, he somehow managed to rein in the demands that were coursing through his body, and joined in Carrie's achingly languid pace as she rocked him in the cradle of her body.

He could feel her holding herself back, too. The tension of it made his blood move even faster, and the more he resisted it, the more it built.

"Is this—quiet enough, do you think?" He discovered after he'd started to speak that his voice almost didn't work.

Carrie didn't even try hers. She was looking up at him with eyes that shone like the sun rising. The passion in her face was the only answer Quinn really wanted to any question he could imagine asking her.

Every movement they made together left the fire inside him burning a little hotter. And the silence of their loving, the slow building of something that wanted desperately to explode, seemed to wrap them in a kind of conspiracy of desire. He wasn't sure whether the sweet agony of holding himself back was more likely to tear him apart, or to teach him everything he'd always wanted to know.

He lowered his head to kiss Carrie briefly, and discovered that briefly wasn't nearly long enough. Her lips parted for him, and he dove into her warm liquid welcome like a happily drowning man. He felt her arms around his neck, and her fingers, then her fingernails, pressing into his back.

The sensation urged him to move faster, to claim all of her as his own. But the moment he changed his tempo, Carrie's fingertips found their way down to his hips, to the backs of his thighs. He felt their irresistible pressure there, slowing his pace again, keeping him inside the warm enchanted circle of their love.

"Now who's playing games?" he murmured.

She managed a startled half smile. Her grasp shifted slightly, so that she was holding him in an almost unbearably erotic way. Quinn groaned softly, and gave himself up to the magic of the slow rhythm she was persuading him into.

The outside world had long since disappeared. Quinn closed his eyes and imagined Carrie's smile, the dark glow of her eyes, her smooth white skin. He saw colors he didn't think had existed before. He saw the future, and somewhere in it the woman he loved was holding out her arms to him, welcoming him.

He lowered his face to her neck again, wanting to drink her in, to possess her. The heat he'd been feeling in the center of his body was growing now, spreading through him with a slow burn that left him gasping. He tried to open his eyes and couldn't. He was lost in the universe they were creating together, this age-old and still achingly new world where nothing mattered except the fact that they wanted—needed—each other.

That world shattered almost without warning, without sound, without either of them being ready for it. Quinn felt Carrie's body contracting around him, holding him convulsively. Her legs, wrapped around his, tensed suddenly, and Quinn let out a groan.

And then every dream, every waking fantasy, every wish he'd had for this woman exploded right through him, rocking him to the core. He said her name over and over again, muffling the sound in her dark hair, dimly aware that he was holding her as though she were slipping away from him and he couldn't stand to let her go.

It took a long time for Quinn to realize that she was holding him just as hard. Her body was shaken by the same tremors that had ripped through him, and there was something about the way her arms were circling him— something fierce, almost desperate—that made him think she was fighting the same fears of losing each other, of losing the promise of what they might have together.

This wasn't the time to put any of that into words. And Quinn wasn't sure he could have spoken, anyway. He wasn't aware of when their intense embrace eased into something more gentle, or which one of them moved first so that they ended up lying side by side, with Carrie's arms still wrapped close around Quinn.

This was better than dreams, he thought. It might even be better than heaven. He wondered how long he could keep himself awake so he could savor the sweet release of this moment, the unimaginable rightness of being all wrapped up with Carrie St. John.

While he was still wondering about it, he fell asleep.

Chapter 13

Quinn had never been so tired, or so content.

He woke up slowly, aware of Carrie's warm, breathing presence next to him before he was conscious of anything else. Her face was pressed into her pillow, half hidden by the dark sweep of her hair. He could see just enough of her sweet, full lips to realize that she was smiling very slightly in her sleep.

For a moment he couldn't make himself think about why he had come here, or what might be waiting for him today when he got back to working on the double mystery of Stockbridge's old murder and the new one that had led to him crawling into Carrie's bed with her late last night.

He knew all of that was still out there, unsolved. But for the moment it seemed unreal. The only reality was here, in their two bodies filled with the magic reminders of last night's loving. At least, Quinn's body was still humming with it, and just looking at Carrie was enough to make him want to stay here in her bed forever, learning and relearning all the things they could do and feel together.

If that sleeping smile on Carrie's face meant what Quinn thought it did, she was sharing his reaction to that silent explosion they'd experienced in each other's arms. It made Quinn want to kiss her gently awake, and start the agonizingly sweet building of sensual suspense all over again.

Then he heard the faint knocking at the front door of the house and realized what had wakened him up in the first place.

"Oh, hell."

Carrie never stirred. Somehow that only underscored her vulnerability, and Quinn cursed himself for being such a besotted fool that he'd almost forgotten he was supposed to be keeping all of them safe—Carrie, Davey and himself. How could they survive as a family if he couldn't do something about the mystery that still surrounded all of them?

He got into his jeans and laced up his shoes in record time, wishing he'd thought to bring his gun from the other wing of the house. It was true that the bad guys didn't usually come politely knocking at the front door, but he wasn't making any more assumptions in this case. The stakes had gotten too damned high for that.

He was almost to the bottom of the staircase, buttoning his shirt as he moved, when he realized how naturally he'd thought of himself as part of Carrie and Davey's lives now. He was feeling, for the first time, as though he had a right to be here. And he knew the sweet contentment of their loving last night had a lot to do with it.

It also kept wandering into his thoughts in a way that could be dangerous to all of them. Quinn shook his head, wished fervently for coffee, and headed to answer the tentative knocking at the front door.

The morning sunshine almost blinded him when he pulled the door open. He automatically stood out of the immediate line of fire—he wasn't so far gone that he'd forgotten *all* the rules of this game—but once his eyes had adjusted to the glare, he realized he didn't need to be on his guard. It was only Jamie Wright, looking even scruffier than usual.

"I guess I shoulda called first. It's sorta early." He seemed uncertain of his welcome, and Quinn wondered if his own edginess was still showing in his face. He opened the door wider, inviting the boy in.

"Don't worry about it," he said. "Come on in. And don't say another word until I've made some coffee, all right? I'm barely conscious."

Jamie followed him into the kitchen without speaking. Carrie must have made a start at cleaning up sometime last evening, Quinn realized, because the dishes had been put in the dishwasher and the leftover food cleared away.

There was still a lot of post-Thanksgiving cleanup to be done, though, and Quinn had to clear a space at the table so he and Jamie could sit down. It was amazing, he thought, what a day could do. Was it possible that only yesterday he'd been playing touch football and trying to remember how his uncle's housekeeper had made stuffing?

Jamie's young face was drawn and tense. "You look like you got about as much sleep as I did," Quinn commented, wondering if he was going to have to break the news of Ted Wright's death or if Ted's stepbrother had already heard about it. "Listen, maybe you don't know this, but—"

"Yeah, I know." Jamie waved the words away. "I came back in the middle of all that stuff last night, and somebody told me."

"I'm sorry, kid. I know you weren't exactly the best of friends—"

Jamie nodded quickly. He wasn't sure how to handle sympathy, Quinn thought. From his limited conversations with Jamie Wright, the boy wasn't sure how to handle a lot of things in his life.

"Who shot him?" Jamie asked.

"I don't know yet."

"You going to find out?"

"Just as soon as I can." There was something tight and troubled in Jamie's face, something that seemed to go beyond just being distraught about his stepbrother's death. "Why did you come here this morning?" Quinn asked, as casually as he could manage.

Jamie fiddled with the mug of coffee Quinn had poured for him. "Look," he said finally, "you seem like a good guy, even if you're some kind of cop."

Quinn nodded slowly, and waited for Jamie to finish his thought.

"So, that's why I came to see you, because it seemed like you'd believe me if I tell you the truth."

"Which is?"

Jamie finally met Quinn's eyes. Quinn could see the fear behind that defiant stare. It was the same look he'd seen on the face of the kid who'd nearly killed him a year ago. It was hard to keep his gaze level now, when his gut clenched in sympathy for all the reckless volatility that went with being young.

"I didn't kill him."

Jamie Wright was so far down Quinn's list of suspects that he almost laughed. But the look on Jamie's face was deadly serious, and that kept Quinn serious, too, as he said, "Nobody thinks you killed him, Jamie. I certainly don't."

Jamie seemed unconvinced. "But the cops know he was thinking of throwing me out if my grades didn't get better. That's a whatchamacallit—a motive, right?"

"Back up. How do the police know about your grades?"

"Hey, man, don't play games with me." Jamie put his mug down too suddenly on the table, and some of the coffee sloshed out onto the wooden surface. "I heard them talking about me."

"The cops?"

"My brother and the cops. Last night. I heard 'em in his study. My brother was saying he wouldn't support me forever, and I had to get my act in gear, and if I didn't then he wasn't gonna have me in his house. That's when I split."

Something was buzzing in the back of Quinn's mind now, and it wasn't just caffeine. "When exactly was this?" he said.

"I don't know, man, sometime in the evening."

"Jamie." The hard tone of Quinn's voice seemed to get through to the teenager that Quinn meant business. "Try to remember just when it was, okay? This could be important, and *not* because we're trying to pin Ted's murder on you."

Jamie looked startled. "Yeah, all right," he said. "It was just about when the fireworks thing was gettin' over with, because I took off when I heard Ted sayin' those things about me, and figured I'd head over to the fairground, except by then it was nearly over. I missed most of it."

At just about the same time Quinn had been listening to an anonymous voice threatening his son. And he'd taken off for the fairground too, with Carrie right on his heels.

And next door—

The medical examiner's initial estimate of the time of Ted Wright's death coincided with all those things. Which meant—

This can't be right. Quinn's mind was presenting him with the facts now, but he somehow couldn't believe them. "Who were the cops your brother was talking to?" he asked.

"There was just one. That big guy, Delaine. He's always busting my chops about bein' out of school, stuff like that. Why would he come to the house if it wasn't about me?''

To Jamie's worried eighteen-year-old mind, things seemed very clear. He'd run out of the place to avoid what he thought was going to be an official dressing-down from his stepbrother and the policeman he disliked. And when he'd come back later to find the place overrun by police, he had panicked and taken off again, certain he would be a suspect in Ted's death.

For Quinn, though, everything was falling into place in a very different order. ''Did Nelson Delaine know you were in the house?'' he asked.

''Neither of them knew I was there. I just came in to grab something to eat. But I got no way of proving that, man. That's why—''

''Jamie.'' Quinn drained the rest of his coffee, wishing he had time for more. He leaned forward, trying to impress the kid with how important this was. ''I don't think you had anything to do with Ted's death. But you may be the only one who knows who *did* kill him. Do you understand what that means?''

What little color there was in Jamie Wright's face drained out of it. ''Oh, man,'' he said.

''Yeah.'' Quinn rubbed his tired eyes, and thought about Carrie sleeping so sweetly upstairs, and Davey, who would probably wake up soon. And now there was a teenaged boy who'd gotten far too involved in this nightmare without meaning to—a boy who stood to lose his life at the same age as David St. John had lost his, if Quinn didn't do his job right.

They all had to be protected, and Quinn couldn't do it if he was going to confront the person who had suddenly, crazily, become his main suspect.

''You mean Delaine did it?'' Jamie asked now.

That was exactly what Quinn thought, but it wasn't the whole story. And he needed to *get* the whole story before he could be sure what he had to do about it.

So he cut off Jamie's questions, and asked one of his own, bluntly. "You said you came here because you trusted me," he said. "Do you trust me enough to do what I tell you and not ask any more questions until this is all over?"

Jamie started to say something, then caught the look in Quinn's eyes and nodded instead.

"Good." Quinn got to his feet and started for the foyer. Jamie followed. "Listen, it's possible things could turn out differently from the way I'm planning. If they do, and people start asking you questions, I want you to save your story—about Nelson Delaine coming to see your brother—for the FBI, all right? Don't, under any circumstances, tell it to the local cops."

He didn't know yet how far to spread his suspicions, but he didn't want to take a chance on screwing this up—and endangering Jamie Wright—by being too trusting.

"Hey, no problem." There was a quick flash of humor in Jamie's pale face as he caught up with Quinn's longer stride. "The local cops'n I aren't exactly, like, best friends."

The kid had some spirit, Quinn thought. He hoped like hell Jamie came out of this with some chance to grow into his gangly body and the quick independent smile he had just shown.

Jamie had caught up with Quinn now, and was frowning anxiously at him. "What did you mean, things might not work out like you want?" he asked. "What might happen?"

"With luck, nothing."

With luck, Quinn would be back in a couple of hours with the mystery solved and the way clear to start talking about a new life with Carrie and their son. But he'd

learned too much in the past few years to trust things
completely to luck.

He'd been dreading waking up Carrie and Davey with
the news that he wanted them to get dressed and leave the
house as soon as they possibly could. But when he reached
the second floor of the annex he discovered that Carrie was
already awake and dressed, and in the process of picking
out Davey's clothes.

"Quinn, what's happening?" She seemed to have picked
up on his urgency, from halfway across the big house.

"I'm not sure yet. But I have to go check something out,
and I don't want any of you sitting around here unprotected while I'm doing it."

He grabbed his well-worn jacket, which he'd thrown
onto a chair in Carrie's room last night. He shrugged into
it now, and wished he could take Carrie and Davey in his
arms and reassure them that everything was going to be all
right. They were both watching him with those wide dark
eyes that had the power to see straight through him, and it
was cutting deeply into the resolve he needed to finish this
thing, and fast.

"I want you to go to Susannah's," he said tightly,
fighting against the way Carrie's eyes always softened him
up inside. "I'll follow you to make sure you get there. I
want you to park your van inside her garage, and stay inside the house with her until I call you."

He pulled a business card out of his wallet, and scribbled a phone number next to the words *Quinn McAllister,
Special Agent*. "If anything happens, call this number,"
he said. "I'm not working on this case officially, but I've
got friends up in Chicago who know what I'm up to. If you
need help, they can provide it."

He saw Carrie's gaze falter at the phrase *if anything
happens*. He braced himself, waiting for the inevitable
question, but she didn't ask it, and neither did Davey.
Quinn's urgent mood seemed to have reached both of

them, or maybe neither of them wanted to think about what might be about to happen.

He remembered Davey's frightened reaction last night, and the way Carrie's face had always turned pale when she thought or talked about her brother's murder. He didn't blame them for resisting the monster that had wandered into their quiet lives.

That only made it more critical to capture that monster as quickly as he could. He felt literally as though he were strapping on a suit of armor as he sprinted upstairs in the main part of the house and loaded the bullets into the gun that still lay in the drawer of the bedside table. His fingers were shaking slightly as he did it, and he had to stop and take a couple of long, slow breaths, and to remind himself that there was no room for screwups this time.

Carrie and the two boys were heading for the garage when he came back down. He managed to catch up with her at the back door, and to pull her aside for a moment after Jamie and Davey had gone outside.

And once he'd done it, he didn't know what the hell to say to her.

He couldn't promise her that everything was going to be all right, when he didn't know it for certain. He couldn't tell her what was going on until he was sure of it himself. And he couldn't tell her he loved her. How could he when she was looking at him with that combination of longing and fear in her wide brown eyes?

He didn't know what else to do, so he just pulled her close against him, holding her tightly in his arms for one long moment.

He felt her arms go around his waist, and felt her holding him just as tightly, just as she had in the sweet darkness of those early morning hours when they'd reached for and found each other. The realization rocked his whole body, and turned his mind to all the things he needed to say to her, all those things he hadn't had time for yet.

He wanted to tell her that he'd come to bed last night thinking, for the first time in his life, that he might be willing to trade in his Special Agent's badge for some other kind of life. He couldn't imagine what it would be yet. But he was coming to think that even if Carrie *did* grant him some kind of visitation rights to Davey, that wasn't going to be enough now.

He wanted the three of them. Together. Here. All the time.

He wanted the family he hadn't known he had.

He wanted the whole damn thing, and he was willing to give up the job that had been his whole life, now that he realized he had another kind of life in Stockbridge.

This wasn't the time to start talking about all of that. And he still hadn't done the simple thing he'd come here for in the first place—to put their uneasy past to rest so they could begin to contemplate the future.

So he just held on to her, and felt her pulling herself closer to him, nestling herself in the open front of his old blue jacket. She felt so small in his arms, but so strong, and so unbearably soft.

"Are you going to be all right?" Her voice was muffled against his shirtfront.

"I'm going to do my damnedest."

She leaned back then, and he saw traces of tears on her face. He hadn't felt her crying, and the two faint trails across her cheeks astonished him. He reached out and wiped them away with one of his knuckles, then kissed her forehead as gently as he knew how.

"I don't want to lose you again, Quinn. Not like last time." Her voice sounded shaky, but determined.

Her words lifted the roof off Quinn's whole world, and it took almost more effort than he could muster to get it nailed back down again. He had to keep sharp for the confrontation he was headed toward, and he couldn't let his thoughts about Carrie blind him to what he needed to do next. But the thought that she didn't want to lose him—

He hugged her again, briefly, ferociously. "Oh, God," he said, drinking in the sweet smell of her hair against his cheek. "I don't want to lose you, either." He straightened suddenly, before he could give in to the temptation to seal his words with a kiss that he might or might not be able to break away from.

"And I don't intend to," he added, as he let her go. "Now, let's hit the road. With luck, I'll be calling you in an hour to tell you everything's okay."

There were those two short words again—*with luck*. As he climbed onto his bike and got ready to follow Carrie's van across the still-quiet town, Quinn found himself wishing he had something more to rely on than his intuition, his gun and that very shady lady, luck.

At first it seemed that luck was with him. There were no other cars in Leo LaPlante's driveway, and no cars parked along the street. And the porch door was unlocked, which usually meant the chief was home and agreeable to seeing visitors.

Leo wasn't in the kitchen, where Quinn had expected to find him. He felt a little prickle of suspicion travel up the back of his neck. It was a sensation he'd learned to pay attention to over the years, and he decided to take his weapon out of its shoulder holster under his jacket. With the grip fitting securely into his palm in the pocket of his coat, he felt a lot better.

"Leo?" He stepped through the small kitchen and into the living room. It, too, was empty, but something about the familiar overstuffed furniture and piles of half-read newspapers made Quinn's temper start to simmer. The whole time Quinn had been here ten years ago, relaxing into these half-squashed cushions after a day of playacting at the high school, reading the local papers to get a feel for the place, Chief Leo LaPlante had been playing a game of his own.

"Hey, Leo, you home?"

Did Leo suspect anything yet? Quinn adjusted his hold on the gun in his pocket, and moved quietly through the living room, taking care not to stand in front of any of the doors.

But Leo's voice, when it finally answered, sounded as friendly as ever. "I'm just shaving," he said. "Be out in a minute."

When he emerged, with traces of lather still marking his red face, he was waving to Quinn to sit down. "You don't need to stand on ceremony around here, son," he said. "You know that. I was just getting ready to go to work. Hell of a thing, at my age, having to get into my uniform on what was supposed to be a day off, but I can't imagine sitting still while whoever killed Ted Wright is walking around free."

That was what Quinn had wanted to know. Leo was still keeping up his act, which meant Quinn had gotten the drop on him. The arrest was going to be a simple one, provided Leo didn't resist. And somehow Quinn couldn't imagine the older man, unarmed, putting up much of a fight against Quinn's younger, stronger muscles and the gun he held at the ready.

"Can it, Leo," he said brusquely. "You know who killed Ted, and I know you know it. And we both know who was really behind the local cocaine trade ten years ago, so why don't you save everybody some time and effort by just admitting it?"

The chief's face went slack for a moment, but he recovered himself quickly, and gave an amused snort. "Quinn, boy, you're trying to get by on too little sleep," he said. "You've got it by the wrong end."

Quinn shook his head. "I doubt it," he said, "especially since I've got a witness who'll place Nelson Delaine at the scene of the crime last night, just before Ted Wright got shot."

The dismay that crossed Leo LaPlante's ruddy face lasted a little longer this time, but once again the chief managed to laugh off Quinn's words.

"Of course he was there," he said. "I sent him, to see what that kid brother of his was up to. Jamie's been spotted hanging around near some of those mailbox bombings I told you about, Quinn."

"You were investigating mailbox bombings at nine o'clock on Thanksgiving evening?" Quinn tilted his head. "Pretty dedicated department you have, Leo."

"Who's this witness you say saw Nelson?" There was concern showing through the chief's bravado now, and it gave Quinn the impetus he needed to wrap this thing up.

"Forget it, Leo. We're not on the same side anymore. In about two minutes I'm going to arrest you for David St. John's murder, and for conspiracy in the murder of Ted Wright, but first I want you to know just how sure I am that you're the one behind all this."

He moved between Leo and the door to the kitchen, cutting off the only exit from the house. "I interviewed the airport manager earlier this week, and he jogged my memory about how the police always cruise by the airport after he's closed up for the day. Now, you always took your turn on patrol just like the rest of the staff."

"It's a small department. Seems only fair—"

"It's a small town, too, Leo, and there's not a lot of money in the budget to pay the police chief what you think you're worth, is there? I've heard you complaining about it enough times.

"So when you discovered the midnight drug swaps, you saw a way of supplementing your income. It's too bad you had to kill David when you needed a scapegoat, and it's too bad you had to close down your skimming operation after things got blown wide open. But you did it well, Leo. I had no suspicions, back then.''

"You shouldn't have any suspicions now." The chief was blustering, Quinn thought, still trying to bluff his way out of this if he could. "You've got no proof."

"I've got the duty rosters from the Stockbridge PD for a couple of the nights that we know there were mob drop-offs and pickups here. Guess whose name shows up on patrol duty for those nights? Yours."

"You son of a bitch." The bluster was cracking badly. *Good,* Quinn thought savagely. When he thought about Leo LaPlante pulling the trigger on the gun that had killed Carrie's twin brother, his friend—

"I haven't checked the lists of impounded vehicles yet, but I feel pretty sure we're going to find that there was a dark car with tinted windows sitting at the back of a lot somewhere, just waiting for you to borrow it and use it the night you killed David," he went on. "Since you had access to the police lot, you could take it and put it back without anyone being the wiser. There's no end to the things you can get away with when you've got the law on your side."

Leo wasn't looking at him now. The older man seemed to be sagging, and for a brief moment Quinn felt a flash of angry betrayal at the way Leo had fooled him ten years ago, and again now. Was this how Carrie had felt, he wondered, when she'd found out who Quinn really was? Was a part of her angry at herself, as Quinn was angry at himself now, for being so easily taken in?

Then the chief moved to a chair near the bedroom door, and sat down heavily in it. "All right," he said. His voice was surprisingly strong, when Quinn contrasted it to the defeated set of his shoulders. "All right, let's do it."

At first Quinn was exultant. This was it, he thought. It's over. I'm about to arrest the man who made it all happen. And then he realized what Leo had really meant.

He didn't get to draw his gun in time. The bedroom door opened quickly, and he was facing Nelson Delaine's leveled shotgun at a range that would have blown Quinn into a million little pieces if Delaine had pulled the trigger.

Carrie... Her name was the first thing in his mind. He heard himself calling her, silently, hopelessly, desperately.

"Don't tell him to raise his hands yet." Leo LaPlante was sounding almost jovial again. "He's packing a gun in his right-hand pocket." He reached for a brown suit jacket that lay across the back of a chair, and pulled out a weapon of his own. "I told you when he came calling, he'd come ready to do business."

Nelson Delaine chuckled in the same way that had gotten on Quinn's nerves when they'd been seniors together at Stockbridge High. "Well, he's got lots of business to take care of now," he said. The gloating in the big cop's voice made Quinn snarl as he relinquished his own gun to Chief LaPlante's not-so-gentle urging. "Like calling Carrie and telling her it's all over."

No! Quinn wanted to shout, but he kept the word inside, where it echoed with every moment of loss he'd ever known, and then more.

"He's right, Quinn." The barrel of the chief's weapon was prodding Quinn in the back now. "We've got this all worked out, and there's nothing you can do to get out of it. We knew this might happen, so we've been ready for you. And like you said yourself, there's really no end to the things you can get away with if you've got the law on your side."

"Carrie."

The sound of his voice was all wrong. She'd been expecting triumph, finality, something to tell her that he'd been successful at whatever he'd gone to do. He sounded now as though success was the farthest thing from his mind.

"Quinn, what is it? Are you all right?"

"Carrie, listen to me." There was a very long pause, and Carrie gripped the receiver hard, afraid of missing a single word. When he spoke again, though, his voice was all too clear. "I made a mistake."

"A mistake? In your investigation, you mean?"

"No. A mistake about us."

She almost laughed. Not more than three hours ago she'd gone eagerly into Quinn McAllister's arms, feeling more certain than she would have thought possible that this time he really wanted her, that he wanted the passion they shared and the son that passion had created.

And now he was telling her he didn't.

I can't believe it.

"I—thought we could work something out, but I was wrong. I'm not the right father for Davey. You saw that all along, and I didn't."

She didn't know what to say. Her heart was pounding hard all of a sudden. All she could think of was the tenderness he'd shown in the early predawn hours, sitting by Davey's bed and soothing the boy out of a nightmare. *Not the right father?* Why was he saying this now?

"You wouldn't—couldn't disappear again without explaining this to Davey." She heard the incredulity in her voice as she put the impossible idea into words.

It had been her greatest fear all along. But now that it was coming true, she wasn't sure which was worse: Davey's loss, or her own.

Quinn, don't do this to me... to us.

"He'll take it better coming from you."

His words were blunt, callous. Carrie looked down at the phone in astonishment, and tried to make herself believe this was the same man who'd made love to her with such passionate certainty just hours ago.

You knew this could happen. Quinn McAllister hasn't changed. You only wanted him to, because you've never stopped being in love with him. The nightmare isn't over. It's happening all over again.

"Quinn—"

She had started to say the words "I love you, and I thought you loved me," but he cut in ahead of her.

"Carrie, I don't have a lot of time, but I didn't want to go without telling you."

His voice sounded ragged, as if he was fighting against the words. And so he should be, she thought, as a spurt of anger found its way through the confused betrayal she was feeling. Damn it, he'd had her believing in him, believing he meant it when he said he didn't want to lose her again. And now he was doing this.

"Quinn, don't go." She put all the persuasion she could into the words. "We have to talk about this. About Davey—"

"Oh, God." She heard his voice break over the words. When he spoke again, though, he sounded just as hoarse but more determined than before.

"Tell Davey I love him," he was saying. "Tell him I'm proud to be his dad. But I just can't go through with this the way we'd planned."

And then, abruptly, she was listening to the hum of the phone line.

The way we'd planned?

"We didn't plan anything, you bastard." She said the words out loud as she dropped the phone into its cradle. "You were the one who wanted to avoid talking about the future. Now I see why."

She couldn't face Susannah's concerned questions, much less Davey's inquiring face. How could she—now or ever—look at her son's long, stubborn jaw without thinking about the man who'd fathered Davey and then abandoned him a second time, after winning his trust and love?

She stepped out of Susannah's sunroom into the bright midday light. From downstairs she could hear the sound of Davey playing with Susannah's two kids. Somewhere in the house Jamie Wright was parked in front of the television. And inside Carrie, the whole world was falling apart all over again.

She wrapped her arms around herself and fought against the tremors that had been shaking her ever since she'd heard the cold sound in Quinn's voice. *I made a mistake about us.* He hadn't even tried to soften the blow, or to explain what the hell had changed his mind.

What *had* changed it? Carrie tried to come up with an answer and couldn't. Had his tenderness been nothing but an act, after all? She thought of how he'd been with Davey, and the openness in his blue eyes when he'd come back to bed with her early this morning. Why had he worked so hard, and so patiently, to win a place in her heart and Davey's, if he'd been having second thoughts about it all along?

"It doesn't matter." She said the words out loud, in a voice dangerously thick with tears. Nothing mattered except that Quinn was leaving again, and this time she couldn't imagine how she was going to pick up the pieces.

Susannah's yard extended down a little slope toward a spot that was a colorful garden in the summertime. Carrie headed that way now, not wanting to go back yet to explain what had happened. The stiff brown stalks of what had been bright and cheerful flowers seemed to mock her pain. It was as if the whole world had known her love for Quinn could never come to anything, and only Carrie herself had been too stubborn and infatuated to see it.

It wasn't until she was standing next to the now-dead garden that she was aware of the little voice that kept repeating *I don't believe this* in her head.

I don't believe this is happening.

I don't believe Quinn would do this to Davey.

She almost laughed out loud at the craziness of it. *It's time to start believing it, and getting on with your life without him,* she told herself firmly.

But she *didn't* believe he would leave her again. At least, a part of her didn't.

There was a white garden bench a few feet from where Carrie stood with her arms wrapped tightly around herself. She moved toward it now and sat down, forcing herself to think through the haze of pain and confusion that Quinn's phone call had plunged her into.

Was it possible that Quinn had somehow been forced to make the call?

Don't be ridiculous, her common sense told her. *He's leaving, and you're trying to make excuses for him. Face the facts, Carrie.*

But what if the facts were different? She didn't know who Quinn had been going to see. But she knew there was potential danger in the visit, because she'd felt the metal weight of his gun in the hidden shoulder holster when she'd held him close this morning.

What if something had gone wrong?

She dropped her head into her hands, and wished she didn't feel as though the ground were shifting under her feet. She could hear Susannah calling her from the house now. She had to get her thoughts in some kind of order, and fast.

Her first reaction to Quinn's call had been disbelief. But what if it had been something else—the stirring of some intuition deep inside her?

And what about those odd words he had tacked on to the end of their conversation: *I just can't go through with this the way we'd planned.*

Quinn knew better than anyone that they hadn't planned anything. Then why had he said those words?

Carrie...

She stood up suddenly. She didn't know why her thoughts had dredged up the sound of Quinn saying her name, but she *did* know that she was hearing the sound of pleading in it, almost of anguish.

"Something's wrong." She spoke out loud, testing the idea. In spite of the quiver in her own voice, she sounded more certain than she'd expected. "Something's gone wrong, and I've got to figure out what to do about it."

She turned and started back toward the house before she could second-guess herself into even more confusion. She was either going to vindicate every feeling she'd ever had for Quinn McAllister, or prove to the world that where this man was concerned, she was the biggest fool who'd ever set foot on the planet.

She didn't know which one it would be. But she *did* know that when she thought about Quinn's blue eyes and the way he'd looked at their son last night, and the way her fear for him was blotting out everything else now, she couldn't possibly sit still nursing her own wounds until she'd done everything she could to find Quinn and make sure he was all right.

Susannah was calling to her again, demanding to know what was going on. Carrie could see that Davey was with her, and Jamie Wright as well. They all looked anxious and puzzled.

She hurried up the slope, buttoning her bulky cardigan against the early winter chill and reaching into the back pocket of her jeans for the business card Quinn had given her.

"I'll explain in a minute," she said to the waiting three-some. "But first I've got to make a call."

Chapter 14

"The bureau's going to be all over this like ants at a picnic." Quinn spoke tightly, trying to clamp down on the fear in his gut. "You really think you're going to cover all your traces?"

"Hell, yes." Leo LaPlante's face was placid, even pleased. "Ground's hard. We haven't had rain in a while. There won't be any footprints to speak of. And Stockbridge PD'll be at the scene first, anyway. There'll be lots of time to get things in order before your boys show up."

Quinn was in the back of a police van, and had been for more hours than he'd been able to keep track of. His wrists and ankles were handcuffed together, but he hadn't been gagged. He'd tried yelling at first, but Leo had only grinned at him. Wherever they were, there apparently wasn't anyone to hear Quinn calling for help.

The light was starting to fade outside. Late afternoon, Quinn guessed. Four-thirty, maybe five o'clock.

Leo had already explained the scenario to him. "Nothing about this needs to change the FBI's official conclusions about David St. John's murder," he'd said. "We'll just add that you came back to town looking to ease your bad conscience, and stirred up some things that were better left quiet."

According to Leo's plan, Quinn was going to be blamed for Ted Wright's murder. "You visited him, threatened to expose his little cocaine habit of ten years ago, he went for you, you shot him," Leo had said. "The bullet was the same caliber as your gun—we made sure of that. And since we're handling the investigation, we'll manage to match the bullet and the weapon in the official file. We'll say you got to feeling remorseful about killing Ted, and realized that precious career of yours was going to suffer because of this. Badgering an innocent man, shooting him when he was unarmed, handling an unofficial investigation like you were some kind of vigilante cowboy—it's not going to look good on your record. Plus, you'd gotten Carrie's hopes up again, and that boy's. You couldn't take the consequences of what you opened up. So, you shot yourself."

"At the site of David St. John's murder." Quinn could hardly get the words out. "It's a bit heavy-handed, don't you think?"

"Nah." Leo's smile had been wide and friendly. "A little melodramatic, but so's the whole story, when you think about it. I figure this is a fitting way to end it."

The chief's smile had turned nasty then, and Quinn looked away.

He knew the real story now. Leo LaPlante had been the local connection who'd been skimming a little off the cocaine shipments coming through Stockbridge. Ted Wright had been his go-between, taking care of the actual selling of the coke. Ted had been the one who had lured David St. John to the airport on the night of David's death, and Chief LaPlante had kindly covered up that clue by altering the police report to show that Ted had been at a family birthday party instead.

Wright had been killed because the lawyer had been showing signs of wanting to trade his knowledge of Leo's scam in exchange for an immunity that would protect himself, in case Quinn's investigation managed to get the whole thing into court. And Nelson Delaine—who'd been an eager customer for the cocaine ten years ago and now stood to lose just as much as the chief if the story ever got out—had pulled the trigger for this second murder.

It answered all the questions that had been nagging at Quinn. And the hell of it was that he didn't care anymore.

There was only one thought on his mind now, one thing that tore at his heart. And that was that he was going to die and Carrie and Davey were going to believe he had abandoned them.

Again.

"Damn it."

He strained against the handcuffs, knowing it was useless. Leo LaPlante, engrossed in the day's newspaper, didn't even pay attention to Quinn's struggles in the back of the van.

Quinn wasn't struggling against the cuffs at his wrists and ankles, anyway. He was fighting against the soft anguish in Carrie's voice when he'd spoken to her this morning. There had been a revolver muzzle at his temple and a shotgun prodding his ribs, and a hideous threat ringing in his ears: *Do it right, McAllister, or she and the boy get something a lot bigger than a soda bottle bomb dropped into their house the next time.*

And even that—even the obscene idea that Leo LaPlante would somehow include Carrie and Davey among his victims—hadn't been the worst of it. The worst was hearing the sound of Carrie's voice, her protests, her plea that they had to talk about this, for Davey's sake.

For Davey's sake, and Carrie's, Quinn had forced himself to say the words LaPlante and Delaine had insisted on.

I'm not the right father for Davey. I can't go through with this the way we'd planned.

He'd stuck in that last phrase out of some wild, illogical hope that Carrie would hear it as a false note, a signal that this phone call hadn't been his idea. But he didn't hold out much hope that it had worked.

She'd always thought he might disappear again. She'd been very clear about her skepticism where Quinn McAllister was concerned. She was primed and ready for this second betrayal. And when he remembered the soft heartache he'd heard in her voice, he knew this call hadn't really surprised her, deep down. It was what she'd been expecting all along.

Leo LaPlante knew that. So did Nelson Delaine, smirking at the other end of that damned shotgun. Hell, the whole town probably knew it. It was only Quinn himself, working so doggedly to rebuild the trust he'd shattered ten years ago, who'd actually thought there was some kind of chance that he could get back what he and Carrie had lost.

And now he was going to die. He was amazed to discover that the idea of death didn't bother him nearly as much as knowing that he would never be able to say the words *I love you* to Carrie and their son and know that they believed him.

He aimed a savage kick at the back door of the van, and heard Leo chuckle. Then there was the rustle of newsprint being folded up, and the sound of the engine, ominously loud after the silence of wherever they'd been parked for these last few hours.

No, Quinn wanted to roar. *Not yet. Not until I've figured a way out of this.*

But he couldn't see any way around it. Leo seemed to have all the bases effectively covered. Quinn McAllister was about to go to his death knowing that his son and the woman he loved were going to despise him for the rest of their lives.

* * *

"Well, I've got to lock up, Carrie. Looks like your friends didn't make it."

"I guess not." Carrie steadied herself against the despair that rolled through her and managed somehow to keep her voice steady. Chatting casually all afternoon with Bill, the airport manager, had been one of the hardest things she remembered ever having to do.

"Let me give you a lift home." Bill was sorting through his keys now, locking his office and the small waiting room in the building that served as the airport's control tower. Carrie had been sitting there since one o'clock, the earliest she had thought the promised flight from Chicago might get here.

"Thanks, Bill." She had no intention of leaving, but she didn't want Bill to know that. "Susannah said she'd swing by and get me at six if my friends hadn't shown up by then."

"Getting a little cold outside, Carrie."

Nothing compared with what I'm feeling inside, she almost said, but masked her fears with a smile instead. "I'm sure she won't be long. You know it always takes more time when you've got little kids with you."

Bill had five kids of his own, and Carrie had heard stories about them all afternoon, without absorbing a single word. She'd lied to Bill about expecting some friends with a small plane who'd said they would be flying in sometime this afternoon, and she was lying again now about Susannah. In fact, Susannah was anxiously waiting at her house, where Carrie had pleaded with her to look after Davey and Jamie and not to ask too many questions that Carrie still didn't have answers to.

"When this is all over I owe you about a hundred explanations, I know," she'd said, when Susannah had dropped her off at the airport.

"You're right. Such as, why you couldn't drive your own van here."

Carrie wasn't exactly sure why Quinn had been so adamant about wanting her to keep her minivan out of sight in Susannah's garage. But since she was acting on her crazy assumption that he'd been caught up in whatever danger surrounded them, it seemed wise to assume that he'd had a good reason for making sure Carrie didn't advertise her whereabouts.

"I'll tell you everything when this is over," was all she'd said to her friend. Her heart had lurched at her own words. When would it be over? And would Quinn still be safe at the end of it?

Imagining he'd betrayed her was a horrible thought. Imagining him dead was a thousand times worse. In spite of Bill's friendly chatter, the airport waiting room felt like a prison as she paced back and forth and fought against fears she couldn't even put a name to.

Now, just after six o'clock, she buttoned up her bulky cardigan and waved goodbye to Bill as he pulled away down the long driveway. When she'd contacted a woman at the FBI, she'd mentioned that the airport tower closed at six.

"That won't be a problem," the woman had said. "The only delay might come from getting a pilot and an aircraft at such short notice, since this isn't going through official channels. But don't worry—Quinn McAllister has lots of good friends here. We'll get somebody there just as soon as we can."

It had just better be soon enough. Carrie kept thinking as she huddled in the doorway of the airport building and wondered whether the plane would arrive before or after her feet had frozen solid.

Ten minutes later she heard something that made her forget all about her cold feet.

At first she thought it was just traffic noise, but the sound was coming from the wrong direction. It took a moment to pin it down, because the wind kept swirling the sound of the engine away from her. Finally she realized it was across the runway, on the other side of the airport.

She hurried to the other side of the building, wondering eagerly if it was the plane she'd been waiting for. But there were no lights in the sky, and it sounded more like a car engine, anyway.

It *was* a car, or rather, a van. And it was driving across the flat airport property from the direction of the industrial park that bordered the runway. Its headlights weren't on, although the evening was quickly getting dark.

Carrie started to step forward, then hesitated. There was something ominous about this lonely vehicle hurrying along the long strip of pavement where vehicles weren't supposed to go. Her mind flew immediately to Quinn, although she knew there was no good reason why it should. She was frightened for him, that was all. That didn't mean he had anything to do with the strange van.

And then, suddenly, she began to think he might, because the van seemed to be heading for the spot where her brother had been killed.

Her heart had been pounding hard, off and on, the entire day, whenever she let herself wonder just what was going on around her. Now it started thudding against the wall of her chest.

It was getting harder to see in the growing dusk. The van was at the far end of the runway now, blending in with the trees. Carrie looked around, but except for the single flashing light on the tall pole above the manager's office, and the van's faint red taillights, there was no sign of light or life anywhere near the place. Taking in a deep breath to slow down her racing heart, she headed cautiously toward the end of the runway.

She kept close to the hangar buildings that lined one side of the airport, not wanting to advertise her presence. She was close enough to see the van door opening when she heard a new sound, one that stopped her in her tracks.

It was Quinn's motorcycle. She knew that noise as well as she knew the deep rumble of his voice. The sound of it now made her spin around, frowning. Was Quinn trying to spring some kind of trap on whoever was in the van? Why hadn't he left town, as he'd told her he was going to do?

Quinn usually drove like he'd just been shot from a cannon, but the motorcycle was moving almost sedately now. He couldn't be trying to sneak up on anybody, not at that rate. What was he doing, then?

The bike had reached the van before she realized it wasn't Quinn riding it. Instead of his lean, long-legged frame, she saw a stocky outline and a heavy-footed stance. Were her instincts right, after all? Was Quinn in some kind of trouble, or was he simply in league with whoever was riding his bike?

She had her answer almost immediately. The side door of the van slid open, and someone inside pushed Quinn out onto the pavement. There was no mistaking his big shoulders and long back.

Or the way he sprawled sideways when he landed on his left side and tried to recover from the pain it caused him.

Or the fact that his hands and feet seemed to be tied.

Carrie gasped, without making a sound. She wasn't sure she could make a sound, not when she saw the familiar outline of Stockbridge's chief of police stepping out of the van and holding what looked like a gun to Quinn's head.

At the same moment she recognized the other man as Nelson Delaine. One of Ted Wright's old buddies. The man Jamie Wright had told her about this morning, who had visited Ted just before his death.

She didn't understand how this all fit together. But it was very clear that Quinn was in terrible danger. And the help she'd called for hadn't come. She thought about her brother's body hitting this hard pavement ten years ago, and knew she couldn't stand here and watch Quinn meet the same death.

There wasn't time to run to the nearest house. Who would she call, anyway? The local police? If the chief himself was involved in this, what hope did she have of finding someone else on the force she could really trust? Calling the FBI again wouldn't help, either. They were too far away, and the plane they'd said they would send must still be somewhere between here and Chicago.

It was clear that Quinn had left word he might be heading into something dangerous, and that Carrie's call for help hadn't been a big surprise. But by the time the plane got here, Quinn would be dead, judging by the cruel efficiency of the way Leo and Nelson were manhandling him into the position they wanted now. With a sick lurch of her stomach she realized they were maneuvering him until he stood in exactly the place where David's body had been found.

Suicide. Remorse. Guilt. Suddenly she knew what they were planning. And the fury she felt at the idea of it gave her the strength to start moving toward the three men.

Quinn was putting up as much of a fight as he could. She saw his big body twisting in Nelson Delaine's grip, and caught her breath as Leo LaPlante knocked Quinn's feet out from under him and kneed him viciously in the small of his back. Carrie winced in sympathy as LaPlante's knee met the spot she knew hurt Quinn so much.

She was close enough to hear snatches of what they were saying, although the wind made it hard to get all of it, and the two policemen were keeping their voices down.

"... don't want bruises." That was Delaine, struggling to keep his grip on Quinn's thrashing wrists.

"Quinn, you son of a—" Leo's voice sounded as furious as Carrie felt, as Quinn managed to raise his bound feet, using Delaine as leverage, and lashed out at his former friend. Carrie's heartbeat escalated even more, until she could feel it thumping at her, urging her to break into a run and do whatever she could to stop the insanity that was unfolding in front of her eyes.

"Keep it down, Chief." Delaine spoke around a grunt as he tried to get his balance after Quinn's desperate lunge.

And then Quinn's voice, ragged, hoarse. "There's going to be a hole in this somewhere, Leo. There's too much to cover up by now, and by God, you'll have to answer for it."

Leo LaPlante only laughed. Between them, he and Nelson Delaine managed to wrestle Quinn onto his knees.

Carrie moved faster. The only thing she had going for her was surprise, she knew. And she didn't want to spring it until the last possible moment. But if she waited too long—

She covered the rest of the distance between them with her pulse thundering in her veins. She'd thought, early this morning when they'd joined together in her warm bed in silent communion, that she loved Quinn as much as a woman could love a man. But that had been nothing compared with the way she loved him now, seeing him beaten and forced onto his knees by the man who'd pretended to be his friend.

She couldn't stay silent any longer. Chief LaPlante was pulling Quinn's hands—they were handcuffed in front of him, she could see now—and forcing a gun into them. With both his own hands, Leo was trying to get Quinn to hold the gun to his temple.

Suicide. Remorse. Guilt.

She could hear all the words that she herself might have believed, if she hadn't come here herself. And the protest burst out of her as she sprinted the last few yards.

"No!" She shouted the word, and felt the blood pounding in her ears. "Leave him alone! Let him go!"

She could see Leo's startled leer, and Nelson Delaine starting to reach out toward her. And Quinn's wide mouth—the mouth that had kissed her so gently—forming now into a protesting "No!" that echoed her own cry. His face seemed suddenly, starkly, white, so blindingly white that her eyes were dazzled by it.

It took her a long moment to figure out why. She realized that the thudding she was hearing wasn't in her body after all, but coming from something above them, something that was also responsible for the sudden beam of white light. She saw Nelson Delaine raising his shotgun over his head, taking aim, and watched Quinn rise unsteadily to his feet to knock that aim off again. Leo LaPlante was scurrying toward the trees, Quinn was roaring something over his shoulder, and suddenly the whole place was in chaos.

The only thing she really grasped was that the helicopter must be the help she'd called for, peopled by Quinn's FBI colleagues. Their landing lights must have picked up the fight at the end of the runway, she thought. Beyond that, she didn't know exactly what was going on.

Special agents were pouring out of the big chopper the moment it landed, or maybe even before, and she completely lost track of Quinn and the two Stockbridge cops. Someone was hustling her to the sidelines, telling her to keep her head down, forcing her down even when the sharp crack of gunfire had her trying to scramble to her feet to see if Quinn was all right.

She heard sirens in the distance, and the babble of many voices, and the all-too-familiar flashing of lights and crackling of radios. She asked about Quinn and was told he was being taken to the hospital, and that was all they could tell her. But if she didn't mind, there were a few questions they would like to ask...

Carrie nodded tiredly, and said she would tell them as much as she knew, and wondered if this would ever end.

"Would you hold still, please?" The lab technician held Quinn in position in front of the X-ray machine almost as firmly as Leo LaPlante had been holding him at gunpoint last night, and it didn't help a lot to know that she was at least on the right side. "Apparently you're government property," the technician said, not sounding very impressed by it, "and they want to make sure their investment's in good shape."

"I'd be in better shape if you'd all just let me go." Quinn muttered the words through clenched teeth as the woman left him to go fire the X-ray camera.

Let him go. He could still hear Carrie's frightened voice calling those words, in that horrifying moment when he'd seen her running out of the darkness toward two loaded weapons.

Damn it, he had to get to her, and they wouldn't let him. Last night, when his colleagues had hustled him out of harm's way, there had been too much else going on to explain that there was a woman he needed, desperately, to talk to. And then his body had rebelled against the rough handling he'd gotten at LaPlante and Delaine's hands, and he'd found himself doubled over in pain, with the not-quite-healed bullet wound stabbing at him every time he tried to breathe. A painkiller and a sedative had taken care of that, but it had also wiped out any hope he'd had of reaching Carrie before this morning.

And then this morning the questions had started again. He'd interviewed a lot of subjects over the years, and it was amazing to discover how annoying it was to be on the receiving end of the process.

Still, he knew it was important. It was what he'd set out to do, after all—to prove who'd killed David St. John.

So he laid out what proof he had, and offered his suggestions for backing up what he'd discovered so far. He told as much as he knew of Leo LaPlante's private drug ring, and how Ted Wright, Nelson Delaine and Steve Solidad had been his best customers ten years ago.

"Wright got to be a prominent lawyer, scared his old adventures might come back to haunt him," he explained. "He confided in his buddy Delaine that he was considering telling us what he knew, if we would guarantee his name didn't come into it.

"Delaine conferred with Leo, and they figured out a way to kill Ted and blame me for it. Solidad, the third guy, was badly scared by Ted's murder. He was worried about protecting his own good name in town, too. He's a businessman, and works a lot with kids, but I think he's basically a good guy. Now that the threat's out of the way, I wouldn't be surprised if he's willing to talk."

The words flowed out of him automatically, almost mindlessly, because his mind was somewhere else. He had walked up to the big front door of the St. John house in his imagination a hundred times before the FBI finally sprung him that afternoon and he was free to do it in reality.

The place looked solid and serene, the way it had when he'd seen it ten years ago, the way it had when he'd come back in search of the love he'd lost. Quinn remembered the still-damaged French doors that had shattered under Leo LaPlante's homemade bomb, though, and knew that even here, in this seemingly quiet world, danger was still possible.

But so was redemption. At least, that was his hope as he raised the knocker and got ready to announce that he was here.

The door opened with a *whoosh* before he could let the brass handle back down again. He felt himself drawn inside by the sudden rush of air, and realized that had been what the pint-size doorman had been intending.

"All *right*." Davey was grinning widely. "I knew you'd come, Quinn. Mom said you'd be busy. But I thought you would come."

"I *was* busy, or I would have been here a long time before this." Quinn squatted down to his son's eye level. There were so many things he wanted to say to Davey, so many things to explain and ask, but it all depended on Carrie, and he wasn't about to take her response for granted yet.

So what *could* he say to this boy who was such an uncanny combination of Carrie and himself? It felt like a momentous occasion, a kind of homecoming he'd never expected. And he still didn't quite have the right to say what was in his heart, not yet.

So he stuck with everyday reality, and asked, "Did you start your hockey league this morning?"

"Yeah. We won, almost."

Quinn laughed. "What do you mean, almost?" he asked.

"You know, where you get the same score." Davey obviously didn't want to admit to anything less than complete victory.

Quinn put a hand on his son's head and jostled him playfully. "That's called a tie, as you know perfectly well," he said. "Don't worry, the Black Hawks get those sometimes, too."

"Can we still go see a hockey game like you promised?"

Davey's eyes looked eager, and Quinn felt some of his own exuberance fading. He hadn't actually promised anything, although Davey clearly wished he had.

"We'll talk about it," he said. "But first I need to talk to your mom. Is she here?"

"She's cooking."

"Oh, oh."

Davey nodded solemnly. "She said she was going to do something with the leftover turkey."

Quinn started to get to his feet. "Maybe I should go exercise a little damage control," he said, and then paused. He couldn't look at the mix of emotions in Davey's young face without making it clear that he was just as glad to see the boy as Davey obviously was to see him.

So he hugged his son, briefly, loving the feel of those small arms going around his neck, and said, "Tell you what, scout."

"What?"

"I saw Gene Prestiss raking his lawn across the street when I rode up. He looked kind of tired. I think all the adventures over here have been keeping him from getting much sleep."

"That's what he said, too."

"Did he? Well, it might be a nice neighborly gesture if you went over and helped him rake for a while. In fact, don't tell Mr. Prestiss this, but I'm willing to hire you to do it for the next hour. What's the going rate for raking?"

"A dollar."

"Make it two."

"All *right*." Davey disentangled himself from the hug, but didn't move away. He was looking hard at Quinn's face. "And when I get back, can I watch you shave?"

Quinn hadn't even thought about shaving, or anything else except getting back here. He ran his fingers over the stubble on his jaw now, and watched, amused and touched, as his small son imitated the gesture on his own McAllister jawline.

Davey was so sure Quinn would still be here in an hour, getting down to the everyday business of shaving. Quinn felt his throat tighten up with a longing that just seemed to keep getting more insistent the closer he got to his dreams of home and family and love.

"I'll do my best," was all he could think of to say, but that seemed to be enough. Davey was off like a shot, heading across the street.

Quinn watched until Davey had gotten safely to Gene Prestiss's yard. Quinn knew the threat to his family was gone now, but it was going to take a long time before he stopped worrying about it. Then he headed for the kitchen.

Carrie obviously hadn't heard him drive up. At the soft sound of his sneakers on the kitchen floor, she said without turning, "You know, honey, if Quinn was going to cook a whole darn turkey, the least he could have done was leave me some instructions about what to do with the leftovers."

"Maybe he was planning to come back and help you deal with them."

"Quinn!"

He'd been intending to take this one step at a time. There were a lot of things he needed to ask her, and he'd planned to do it slowly, so there could be no more unanswered questions between them.

But the soft light in her warm brown eyes caught him off guard. And there was no way he could resist her welcoming smile as she spun around and said his name. He strode across the kitchen and had captured her in his arms before she could say another word.

Everything he'd felt since he'd come back to Stockbridge seemed to be shooting to the surface now. He didn't know if he was glad or angry or aroused or scared half to death. He only knew he never wanted to let go of Carrie St. John.

He could feel her soft laughter at his ear, like a warm, bubbling spring that could heal everything that had ever gone wrong in his life. It took him a moment to realize there was an amused protest in the sound.

"If you're going to break all my ribs hugging me, then I'm going to stop worrying if you're all right," she was saying. Quinn relaxed his grip, and Carrie leaned back, looking up at him. Her face grew more serious as she reached a hand up to his face. "Quinn, *are* you all right? They wouldn't let me in to see you at the hospital—"

"I'm fine. I've never been better."

He kissed her, briefly, hungrily, and then let her go. She was wearing a loose pink sweater over a pair of black leggings today. The color of the sweater complemented the rose petal softness of her cheeks, and the simple outfit hugged her curves in a way that had Quinn marveling all over again at how Carrie could look like a girl and a woman at the same time.

He was just as crazy about her now as he'd been ten years before. It felt like starting all over again, as if everything were still new and possible.

But still—

"I have to know something," he said bluntly.

"What's that?"

"Why the *hell* did you come to the airport last night? How did you know I was there? And why—" The memory of the phone call he'd been forced to make still choked him. "—Why didn't you believe me when I said I was leaving?"

That was the question that had been tormenting him all day, the one that had nagged at him even during his drugged sleep last night. She'd had every reason to doubt him. Yet why hadn't she?

She was wearing an apron over her sweater. She undid it now, and tossed it onto the counter. She seemed to want time to put her answer into words.

When she finally did, it was very simple, and very clear. "I thought about how you were with Davey, and how you were with *me*." Her cheeks got slightly pinker, and Quinn knew she meant she'd thought of the two of them making love. His own body started to pulse at the memory of it, but he made himself stand still, hearing her out.

"I tried to imagine you walking away after what we'd shared," she said. "And I just couldn't do it. My mind wouldn't believe it. My *heart* wouldn't believe it."

"I'd walked out on you before," he said.

"But everything was so different then. *You* were different. You were young and inexperienced, and so was I. I could see, when you came back, how much you had changed. I kept trying to tell myself you'd gotten harder, and tougher, but I knew it was really just that you'd grown up. The same as I had."

"You did it a lot more gracefully than me."

She smiled, and Quinn's heart lightened at the warm glow in her eyes. "It doesn't matter *how* we did it, Quinn," she said. "The important thing is that we've finally gotten to where we can see past all the things that hurt in the past, to the things that really matter now."

Her face sobered again, as if, for all her lightheartedness, this was something she still couldn't laugh easily about. "I didn't get to that point until after your phone call yesterday," she said. "I was so close to writing you off. I was ready to believe you would just walk away again, the way you had before. But there was just something inside me that wouldn't let me believe it."

"I never thought . . ." He wasn't sure how to phrase it. "I told you I'd come back here to find out who killed David. But the real reason, underneath the one I was admitting to, was that I knew I couldn't live with myself if I didn't win your trust back, somehow. And I still don't know what shook me the most at the airport last night—that you'd turned up at a moment that was likely to get you killed, or that you'd turned up at all."

"I tried to stay away. I just couldn't do it."

She half whispered the words, and Quinn felt everything inside him turn over. He started to move closer to her again, but she held up a hand to stop him.

"Wait, Quinn." She pushed a stray strand of hair behind one ear. "It still isn't that simple."

He waited.

"I couldn't believe you would walk away without saying goodbye to me, or to Davey." She met his eyes, and he saw the same troubled shadow that had greeted him when he'd first come back. "But that doesn't mean I believe you'll stay forever. There are still a lot of things we've never talked about."

Quinn noticed for the first time that there was a big pot of water on the stove. It was slowly starting to boil now. Carrie moved toward it, and turned the burner heat down.

"You said you wanted some kind of access to Davey," she said slowly. "And part of me wants to share him with you. You're right about not being able to pretend you don't exist, now that Davey knows you. He loves you."

She met his eyes steadily, as if watching to see his reaction. Quinn already knew how his son felt. It had been impossible to miss the spontaneous affection in the hug his son had given him a few minutes ago. He didn't think he'd ever get used to the marvel of it.

"But..." He said the word out loud.

And Carrie sighed. "But after last night, Quinn, when I saw you with those guns pointed at you, and we ended up in the middle of all those officials and emergency vehicles and questions and—"

She shook her head, cutting off her own words. "I think you were right when you said there's a part of me that wants to hang on to Davey because I'm so used to the two of us being a unit. And you're right that he's going to grow up, and I'm going to have to let him do it. But he's still a little boy, and I don't want him to be a part of that violent world you live in. And I don't want to be a part of it, either. What happened last night only makes me more certain about that. I don't want to bump into your holster when I put my arms around you, Quinn. I can't stand the thought of people shooting at you, and maybe killing you the next time. And that's no way for Davey to grow up. You know it isn't.''

That was it. She'd said it, and Quinn could tell from the defiant gleam in her eyes that she was challenging him to argue with it if he could.

He couldn't. He didn't even want to. And he could tell that his slow smile startled her as he said, "You're right."

She frowned. "What do you mean, I'm right?"

"It's not a world Davey should be a part of."

"So you *don't* want him to visit you."

"That's not what I said."

"Quinn McAllister, you have about thirty seconds to explain what you mean."

"No." He couldn't stay on the other side of the room any longer. He moved to Carrie's side, putting his hands on her shoulders, drawing her close to him. "I've got a lot longer than that—if you agree with me that we all belong together. You, Davey and me."

"How?" The question was breathless.

"I can't leave here again, Carrie. Not after I've found you again—and found Davey, too. And I can't imagine settling for seeing Davey by himself on odd weekends. That's not what I want."

"What *do* you want?"

"If you mean, what do I want to do about my job, I haven't figured that one out yet. But I do know, and I think I knew it the moment that kid shot me last year, that I'm losing my taste for this cutting edge stuff. I don't want to live in the middle of danger anymore. I want real life— a home, a family. And *you.*"

He still hadn't said the words he'd come here to say to her. He could feel the familiar weight in his chest, telling him he didn't deserve this woman's love. And then, when he caught sight of the hope dawning in her eyes, that weight suddenly disappeared.

"I love you, Carrie St. John," he said. He tried to say it firmly, but the words sounded shaky. He'd never dared to say them out loud before. "Not just because you're the mother of my child . . . although that only makes me love you more. I love you because you're the only woman in the world who ever made me feel I could be at home wherever you are."

"Quinn . . ."

Hope flowered into a smile so brilliant Quinn wanted to lose himself in its glow.

"Are you telling me you want to stay? Here? With us?"

"Just try to get rid of me."

He growled the words out, suddenly afraid to say anything more. He'd been afraid even to let himself dream about this kind of happiness. He didn't want to test it with any more questions or answers until he had proven to Carrie—in the best way he knew how—that she'd been right to believe in the love that had always bound them together even when fortune had forced them apart.

The way she was responding to his hungry kisses told him she was as eager as he was for the sweet satisfaction of making love. "Turn off that burner and let's go upstairs," he murmured at her ear.

"But Davey—"

"Davey's been paid off. He'll be across the street for about another thirty minutes." Quinn glanced at the clock on the stove. "Should be just about long enough, according to my calculations."

Carrie laughed, and reached out to turn off the burner knob. Quinn captured her hand on the way back, and raised it to his lips, kissing the exact center of her palm with reverent eroticism. Then he shifted his hold on her and captured her under his arm, sharing her laughter as he swept her with him out of the room.

''Why were you boiling water, anyway?'' he asked. ''Davey said you were doing something with the leftover turkey.''

She ran a hand over the side of his face, gently caressing the stubble he had no intention of getting rid of until his son was there to watch. ''I was going to make turkey salad,'' she said. ''I had a flashback from high school Home Ec class, about how you have to boil the turkey first.''

''Carrie . . .''

She'd nestled her head against his shoulder now. The feeling of her warm breath at his collarbone was powerfully distracting. She was strong, and feminine, and loving . . . and the worst cook he'd ever met. Quinn wondered why it was that that should make him love her even more.

''What?'' she asked, huskily now.

''You only boil the meat when it isn't already cooked. This turkey was cooked yesterday, remember?''

Her laughter washed over him, and through him. ''It's a good thing you came back, then, isn't it?''

''A *damn* good thing. This place needs a cook.''

They were almost to the top of the stairs now. Quinn paused, looking down at the big empty foyer, and Carrie lifted her head to follow his gaze.

''You know what this place really needs?'' she asked softly.

''What?''

''More kids.''

Quinn was rocked by the simple statement. It was exactly what he'd just been thinking himself.

''Our kids, you mean?'' he said.

''Ours, but not just ours. Quinn—''

He tightened his arms around her. He had a startled feeling she was about to articulate a dream he'd only begun to admit to himself.

"Those kids you keep running into in the city, the ones who end up shooting at you and at each other..."

"Yes—"

"Don't you ever want to do something for them besides put them in jail?"

"Of course I do. Carrie—"

"And we have all this room, and you know I always said I wanted lots of kids around me."

She'd said *we have all this room* as though it was the most obvious thing in the world that it belonged to both of them. Quinn kissed her, and felt her arms lock around his neck, and suddenly saw the future he'd been so afraid to hope for all these years.

"We could make something here. Some kind of escape from all the craziness, for kids who need it." He started to walk again, heading instinctively for the upstairs bedroom where he and Carrie had first made love, where they'd created their son. He didn't want to spoil this moment with a lot of details. Those could come later. But he knew for certain that what Carrie had suggested was exactly what he wanted to do.

"It could be a place to offer somebody a second chance." Carrie smiled as they passed the doors of all the unused rooms in her old home.

"You already *have* offered somebody a second chance." He pushed the bedroom door open with his foot and kissed her again before they eased down onto the bed together. "And I intend to spend the rest of my life showing you exactly how grateful I am for it."

He felt her whole body shiver under his hands as he touched her. "I love you, Quinn. Oh, I love you!" The words seemed to be a part of the ripple of pleasure that ran through her. It spread until Quinn's body, too, was filled to overflowing with the power of the love they shared, the love that had saved his life last night, the love that would build a happy future here in this big old house.

"How long did you say we had before Davey comes home?" Carrie asked, as she reached for the hem of her pink sweater and looked up at Quinn with very wide, very dark eyes.

Quinn checked his watch. He was beginning to get the hang of this parenting business, he thought. A lot of it had to do with seizing opportunities when they were presented to you. "Twenty-five minutes and counting," he said, "and I don't intend to waste a single one of them."

*   *   *   *   *

Get Ready to be Swept Away by
Silhouette's Spring Collection

Abduction
&
Seduction

These passion-filled stories explore both the dangerous
desires of men and the seductive powers of women.
Written by three of our most celebrated authors, they are
sure to capture your hearts.

Diana Palmer
Brings us a spin-off of her Long, Tall Texans series

Joan Johnston
Crafts a beguiling Western romance

Rebecca Brandewyne
New York Times bestselling author
makes a smashing contemporary debut

Available in March at your favorite retail outlet.

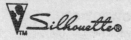

Montana Mavericks

Stories that capture living and loving
beneath the Big Sky, where legends live
on...and mystery lingers.

This March, meet an unlikely couple in

THE LAW IS NO LADY
by Helen R. Myers

Why would an honorable court judge want to marry
a disreputable outlaw? Was it because she loved the
child he sought custody of, or had she simply fallen
for a rugged loner who could give her nothing but
his name?

Don't miss a minute of the loving as the passion
continues with:

FATHER FOUND
by Laurie Paige (April)

BABY WANTED
by Cathie Linz (May)

MAN WITH A PAST
by Celeste Hamilton (June)

COWBOY COP
by Rachel Lee (July)

Only from ❦ *Silhouette*® where passion lives.

HEARTBREAKERS

Hot on the heels of **American Heroes** comes Silhouette Intimate Moments' latest and greatest lineup of men: **Heartbreakers.** They know who they are—and *who* they want. And they're out to steal your heart.

RITA award-winning author Emilie Richards kicks off the series in March 1995 with *Duncan's Lady*, IM #625. Duncan Sinclair believed in hard facts, cold reality and his daughter's love. Then sprightly Mara MacTavish challenged his beliefs—and hardened heart—with her magical allure.

In April *New York Times* bestseller Nora Roberts sends hell-raiser Rafe MacKade home in *The Return of Rafe MacKade*, IM #631. Rafe had always gotten what he wanted—until Regan Bishop came to town. She resisted his rugged charm and seething sensuality, but it was only a matter of time....

Don't miss these first two **Heartbreakers,** from two stellar authors, found only in—

INTIMATE MOMENTS®

Silhouette®

HRTBRK1

Patricia Coughlin

Graces the ROMANTIC TRADITIONS lineup in April 1995 with *Love in the First Degree*, IM #632, her sexy spin on the "wrongly convicted" plot line.

Luke Cabrio needed a lawyer, but high-powered attorney Claire Mackenzie was the last person he wanted representing him. For Claire alone was able to raise his pulse while lowering his defenses…and discovering the truth behind a vicious murder.

ROMANTIC TRADITIONS: *Classic tales, freshly told. Let them touch your heart with the power of love, only in—*

RITA award-winning author Emilie Richards launches her new miniseries, **The Men of Midnight,** in March 1995 with *Duncan's Lady*, IM #625.

Single father Duncan Sinclair believed in hard facts and cold reality, not mist and magic. But sprightly Mara MacTavish challenged his staid beliefs— and hardened heart—with her spellbinding allure, charming both Duncan and his young daughter.

Don't miss **The Men of Midnight,** tracing the friendship of Duncan, Iain and Andrew—*three men born at the stroke of twelve and destined for love beyond their wildest dreams*, only in—

INTIMATE MOMENTS®
™ Silhouette®

WOUNDED WARRIORS

Men and women hungering for passion to soothe their lonely souls. Watch for the new Intimate Moments miniseries by

Beverly Bird

It begins in March 1995 with

A MAN WITHOUT LOVE (Intimate Moments #630)
Catherine Landano was running scared—and straight into the arms of enigmatic Navaho Jericho Bedonie. Would he be her savior...or her destruction?

Continues in May...

A MAN WITHOUT A HAVEN (Intimate Moments #641)
The word *forever* was not in Mac Tshongely's vocabulary. Nevertheless, he found himself drawn to headstrong Shadow Bedonie and the promise of tomorrow that this sultry woman offered. Could home really be where the heart is?

And concludes in July 1995 with

A MAN WITHOUT A WIFE (Intimate Moments #652)
Seven years ago Ellen Lonetree had made a decision that haunted her days and nights. Now she had the chance to be reunited with the child she'd lost—if she could resist the attraction she felt for the little boy's adoptive father...and keep both of them from discovering her secret.

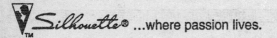

Silhouette® ...where passion lives.

BBWW-1

SILHOUETTE... Where Passion Lives

Don't miss these Silhouette favorites by some of our most distinguished authors! And now, you can receive a discount by ordering two or more titles!

SD#05844	THE HAND OF AN ANGEL by BJ James	$2.99	☐
SD#05873	WHAT ARE FRIENDS FOR?	$2.99 U.S.	☐
	by Naomi Horton	$3.50 CAN.	☐
SD#05880	MEGAN'S MIRACLE	$2.99 U.S.	☐
	by Karen Leabo	$3.50 CAN.	☐
IM#07524	ONCE UPON A WEDDING		
	by Paula Detmer Riggs	$3.50	☐
IM#07542	FINALLY A FATHER by Marilyn Pappano	$3.50	☐
IM#07556	BANISHED by Lee Magner	$3.50	☐
SSE#09805	TRUE BLUE HEARTS		
	by Curtiss Ann Matlock	$3.39	☐
SSE#09825	WORTH WAITING FOR by Bay Matthews	$3.50	☐
SSE#09866	HE'S MY SOLDIER BOY by Lisa Jackson	$3.50	☐
SR#08948	MORE THAN YOU KNOW		
	by Phyllis Halldorson	$2.75	☐
SR#08949	MARRIAGE IN A SUITCASE		
	by Kasey Michaels	$2.75	☐
SR#19003	THE BACHELOR CURE by Pepper Adams	$2.75	☐

(limited quantities available on certain titles)

AMOUNT	$_____
DEDUCT: **10% DISCOUNT FOR 2+ BOOKS**	$_____
POSTAGE & HANDLING	$_____
($1.00 for one book, 50¢ for each additional)	
APPLICABLE TAXES*	$_____
TOTAL PAYABLE	$_____
(check or money order—please do not send cash)	

To order, complete this form and send it, along with a check or money order for the total above, payable to Silhouette Books, to: **In the U.S.:** 3010 Walden Avenue, P.O. Box 9077, Buffalo, NY 14269-9077; **In Canada:** P.O. Box 636, Fort Erie, Ontario, L2A 5X3.

Name:_____

Address: _____ City:_____

State/Prov.:_____ Zip/Postal Code:_____

*New York residents remit applicable sales taxes.
Canadian residents remit applicable GST and provincial taxes.   SBACK-MM

✓ *Silhouette*®
™